THE **XANDER KING** SERIES

KING'S
RANSOM

ALSO BY BRADLEY WRIGHT

Xander King Series

WHISKEY & ROSES
VANQUISH
KING'S RANSOM

KING'S RANSOM
XK3

Copyright © 2017 by **Bradley Wright**

For My Brothers,
You know who you are, and you know that blood isn't the only
thing that makes you family. Thank you for the laughs, the
tears, the dumb decisions, and the shoulders to lean on after
I've made them.

"Hard times don't create heroes. It is during the hard times when the 'hero' within us is revealed."

-Bob Riley

"On wrongs swift vengeance waits."

-Alexander Pope

KING'S
RANSOM

Gone Girl

A relentless ray of bright golden sunshine beamed through the one open slot in the curtains and fixed itself to the forehead of Special Agent Sarah Gilbright. Like a laser beam of "good morning" sent from the heavens themselves, just for her. She would have rather it picked on someone else. Drowning in the fog between dream and reality, Sarah instinctively moved her hand in front of her eyes to shield nature's alarm clock. Beginning to rouse, she moved her hand across the bed next to her. Xander King's bed. Empty. Her hand had meant to find the warmth of Xander's skin; instead, it found only the smooth feel of cold silk. This pulled her clear of her morning fog, and she sat upright, took in the empty bedroom around her, and shot a look of death toward the window that had not so graciously pulled her from slumber. Her long blonde hair fell down along her back, and her aqua-blue eyes peered at the empty stretch of bed beside her.

"Xander?"

Sarah called toward the open bathroom door. Nothing came back to her. She thought for a moment that the smell of bacon tickled her nose. Maybe. She maneuvered a beige ponytail holder off of her wrist and pulled her hair back behind her head. She'd had a bag of her things at one point, but it stayed on the plane with Marv and Mary whom she had left behind in Moscow. It was most likely in Langley, Virginia, right now. A place that she had despised before, but CIA headquarters was going to be a much more pleasant place to go to work now that William Manning was no longer at the helm.

Sarah slinked out of bed, naked as the day she was born. She had the body of a model, but the thing she figured Xander liked most about it was the fact that it could also kick a little ass when necessary. However, she wasn't naive; his lips had spent the better part of a half an hour on her body last night, so it wasn't all about what she could do but also how she looked. The thought of his mouth on her, and the thought of his chiseled body on top of hers, sent a warm ache through her. Thinking about how he wasn't the slightest bit shy about showering her entire body with attention last night made her tingle. She needed some more of that. She walked across the dark hardwood floor toward the bathroom door, poked her head in, and slumped her shoulders in disappointment when she saw that Xander was not inside. She thought maybe he was the source of the wonderful bacon aroma she imagined catching a whiff of a moment ago. With that hope, she opened Xander's chest of drawers in search of something comfortable and appropriate for breakfast. And who knows, maybe she could convince him to have her for dessert.

2

Kyle Hamilton stabbed the edge of the bacon with a fork, turned it, and laid it back down in the skillet. The bacon made that frightful popping sound, and before he could pull his arm away, a spot of scalding hot grease attacked his forearm like a bee protecting its hive.

"Shit!" Kyle leapt back from the frying pan as if his arm were on fire. Sam couldn't help but laugh at seeing the tall, dark, and handsome manly man, which Kyle had turned out to be, hop away from the skillet like a mouse from a cat.

"You okay there, big boy?" Sam chuckled.

Kyle's face was red. Maybe from the heat of the stove, maybe from embarrassment. He would never tell.

"You make fun of me and I won't share my bacon."

"Oh, you'll share that bacon." Sam walked toward Kyle.

The sunlight from the open windows in the room behind Sam wrapped her in a warm yellow glow. Her long black hair hung below her shoulders, and the tight black V-neck T-shirt and grey, second-skin yoga pants hugged every curve on what Kyle found to be quite an outstanding body. If he hadn't already known it, seeing her on this calm and harmonious morning, after the nightmare of the past couple of weeks, he sure as hell could feel it now. He was smitten.

"Or what?" Kyle played back.

Sam shot her hand for the fork, but Kyle managed to pull it away. A half-wrestling-match-half-tickle-fight ensued as they played around the kitchen for a moment. Finally, Sam managed to claim the fork, but Kyle was able to turn the tables, his hands

3

on her arms, wrapped around her from behind. Her hair smelled of lavender. After only a second of struggle, Sam called "Uncle!" and when Kyle let go, she turned into him, taking his eyes in her own. Kyle's stomach dropped. He would've sworn up and down that she desperately wanted to kiss him in that moment. Samantha Harrison, the woman who had merely tolerated him for years just because he was Xander's best friend, now seemed to be, at the very least, entertaining the idea that he could be something more than a playboy. Unfortunately, he wouldn't get to find out just yet, because Zhanna Dragov had just sauntered into the kitchen. It was still odd to Kyle, having her in the house, since she was the daughter of the man that tried to kill all of them. But she had been instrumental in helping them take her father out.

"Am I interrupting?" Her Russian accent was thick, her hair red like fire. It was in that second, seeing the gorgeous Russian walk into the room, that Kyle realized he just might never be anything but a playboy. He should just leave the romantic feelings to Xander.

Sam quickly backed away, and Kyle went back to his bacon. Kyle answered Zhanna over his shoulder as she took a seat at the kitchen table. "Nope, just cooking up a little breakfast. You want fried or scrambled eggs?"

"However you are making yours is good. Any coffee?"

Sam took a seat beside Zhanna at the table.

"Coffee's in the pot, beside the sink."

"Perfect. Would you like?" Zhanna asked Sam.

"I'm already one cup in, but thank you."

"How about you, Kyle?"

"Sure, I'll have some more. Thanks, Zhanna."

Zhanna went to the coffee pot and poured herself a cup.

4

"This place is beautiful," Zhanna announced as she blew on her coffee and peered out the window overlooking the back of Xander's horse farm. Beyond a magnificent lagoon-style pool lay a stunning landscape of plush grass-covered rolling hills. "Why they call this Bluegrass State when grass is so green?"

Kyle laid the last piece of bacon onto a paper-towel-covered plate and turned toward Zhanna with a surprised look on his face. She shrugged her shoulders. "What? You think I am not educated? You think I have not heard of this *bluegrass*? It is one of many things your Kentucky is known for."

Kyle smiled. "I am sure you are educated, Zhanna, but it does surprise me that you have heard about bluegrass."

"So, why it's not blue? Why do they call this green grass *bluegrass*?"

Sam chimed in, "I have always wondered this myself."

With Sam's British accent and Zhanna's Russian accent, Kyle felt like the kitchen had turned into a small version of Disney's Epcot.

"Okay, well, the grass itself isn't blue," Kyle started.

"Obviously." Zhanna sipped her coffee.

"But, in the spring, the seed heads of the grass are blue, and if left uncut, they can grow to two or three feet. If you were to find an unmowed field of grass anywhere around here, it would look unmistakably blue."

Sam gave a laugh. "Look at you, Professor Hamilton."

Sarah Gilbright walked into the room. "Professor Hamilton? What does he teach? STD awareness?"

Zhanna and Sam laughed. Kyle didn't.

"Ha-ha. Good morning to you too, Sarah."

"Anybody seen Xander this morning?" Sarah didn't waste any time.

Sam gave a wry smile. "We figured he was upstairs shagging you again."

Sarah blushed. "Wha—what? We didn't—"

"Don't waste your breath, Sarah. The walls are impossibly thin, young lady." Sam didn't let her off the hook. Zhanna and Kyle oohed and aahed in jest.

Sarah's face turned from blushed to maroon.

"Okay, okay. All right, you guys. Yuk it up." Sarah waved them away as she walked toward the coffee. "Seriously, though, none of you have seen Xander?"

Everyone shook their head.

"I've been up since seven and I haven't seen him. Just figured he was exhausted like the rest of us." Kyle turned and looked out the window. "I think he mentioned something about King's Ransom leaving for Belmont this morning. I'm sure he's just out at the stables seeing him off. That horse is like his kid. He wouldn't want them to take Ransom without seeing him first."

"That's true," Sam agreed.

"I'll leave him some coffee. Hey, anything on the news about Dragov and Moscow?" Sarah asked.

Xander and company had been put through the wringer in Moscow. Kyle wondered how Xander was feeling about everything this morning. He hadn't checked the news, but he was sure that the assassination of the world's most notorious crime boss would have overtaken the airwaves. Unless, of course, Kim Kardashian had taken another half-naked selfie and posted it overnight. Far more of Kyle's concern for Xander was about his father, however, not Dragov. The thought of Xander having to go through the terror of killing his own father sent a chill down Kyle's spine. He shook it off and answered no to

Sarah's question.

Sam and Zhanna said no as well, so Sam, out of curiosity, turned on the television on the back wall and flipped the channel to the news. A reporter was standing outside of what Kyle and Sam recognized as the Hotel Le Bristol in Paris, France. The same hotel they had stayed at the night after Syria, and the same hotel where Xander's now-famous crush, actress Natalie Rockwell, was still temporarily living.

They all listened in horror to the report on the television. There was no news about a half-naked selfie, and there was no news about Vitalii Dragov. This news was much, much worse.

Thanks, Jeremy. I am standing just outside of the posh Paris hotel, Hotel Le Bristol, where Hollywood sweetheart Natalie Rockwell had been staying while filming her new movie.

The words "had been staying" sent yet another chill down Kyle's spine. He knew what was coming was *not* going to be good news. He just hoped Natalie wasn't dead.

I just spoke with the police chief here in Paris, and he told me that a couple of hours ago, at approximately ten a.m. local time, the maid walked into Ms. Rockwell's suite and began cleaning as she normally would. When she got to the bed, she found a note on the pillow and immediately took it down to the hotel manager. The note contained only one short and frightening sentence:

"It will take a King's Ransom to get her back."

When I asked the chief what he made of it, he said he had no idea what it meant, but no one has seen nor heard from Natalie Rockwell since she wrapped on set last night. The film's director—Samuel Hoderburg—said she didn't make it to the shoot this morning. Something he said she had never done.

Needless to say, the drama surrounding Natalie Rockwell is

7

at an all-time high as it appears she has been kidnapped. I will be here all day and night bringing you the very latest on this scary time in the young starlet's life. Back to you, Jeremy.

Jeremy continued with commentary about the missing Natalie Rockwell, but no one in that kitchen heard a word he had to say.

"You have got to be bloody kidding me," Sam said as she turned to Kyle.

Everyone in that kitchen had to pick their jaws up off the floor.

"Where the hell is Xander? We have to find him before someone else tells him about this!" Kyle sat his piece of bacon back down on the plate as everyone else gathered around him. "I'll check the stables. Sam, you check the garage. Zhanna, you and Sarah check downstairs and see if he's in the workout room or in the shooting range. Hopefully he doesn't have the TV on."

Just as the three of them were about to disperse, the doorbell rang.

They all froze and turned toward Kyle. Kyle didn't say a word; he just shot toward the front door. On his way there, which took a matter of seconds, the doorbell rang several more times.

Urgent.

Kyle swung open the door, hoping to find Xander. Instead, he found Gary Trudeau, King's Ransom's trainer—doubled over at the knees, gasping for air, sweat pouring down his face.

A streak of panic bolted through Kyle.

"Is it Xander?"

Gary took a deep breath. "Is he not here?"

"We can't find him, Gary, what is it? What's wrong?" Kyle braced himself for the worst.

Two minutes, a half-mile sprint, and two near panic attacks later, Kyle, Sam, Sarah, and Zhanna were standing in front of King's Ransom's stall in the stables just behind the main house. Hearts in their throats, fear wrapped around their entire beings. There at their feet lay Xander's pride and joy—and the Kentucky Derby winning Thoroughbred horse—King's Ransom. Split in half. His head separated from his body. A lake of blood beneath him. The words *Natalie Rockwell* were scribbled in blood on the wood planks covering the back wall. It was then that Kyle and the three ladies understood the kidnapper's ironic note left on the pillow in Natalie's hotel room. "It will take a King's Ransom," the reporter had said. Kyle obviously hadn't seen the note, but he knew without a doubt that the words *King's Ransom* were capitalized on it. The kidnapper was taking responsibility for the death of Xander's horse, toying with Xander. Pouring salt in the wound.

Kyle had a hard time focusing. His best friend's problems seemed never ending. Would Xander ever get a break? It didn't seem as though he would, and he knew this was going to be as hard on Xander as anything he had been through yet. He didn't know the next step, didn't have a clue what to do. Xander was the problem solver. The only thing that kept running through Kyle's mind were the problems.

King's Ransom was dead.

Natalie Rockwell was taken.

And Xander King was gone.

What You Don't Know *Can* Hurt You

It will take a King's Ransom to get her back.

Xander read the text from the unknown number for about the thousandth time. When he had first seen Natalie's name written on the wall in his dead horse's blood, he was scared for her. Then he was angry. Now, he couldn't really find a feeling. He'd gone numb. Everything that had happened in the last couple of weeks had finally been too much for him. Something snapped inside him. He had the feeling that he might never be the same. How could he be? Just yesterday he had stabbed his father in the neck. Sure, his father ended up being a murderous, maniacal, money-hungry tyrant, but Xander hadn't even known that until yesterday. Hell, he didn't even know his father was *alive* until yesterday. Everything happened so fast. He had taken no time to assess things. Now, here he was again, on the move. More danger, violence, and, most likely, sadness lay ahead.

He couldn't think about Natalie. He couldn't think about her being held captive, tied up, scared, and God only knew what else. He had to keep his mind clear or he would go insane. It was one thing to seek vengeance for something that had happened over a decade ago. It was another thing entirely to be running off into the unknown while someone's life hung in the balance. Someone whom, no matter how much he tried not to be, he was madly in love with. All the while, someone else held a grudge against Xander, and because of that grudge Natalie was the one paying the price. Unfairly paying the price for his actions. Xander had no idea who could have taken Natalie. No idea who killed King's Ransom. He thought he had just laid all of his enemies to rest a day ago.

Clearly, he was wrong.

The sun was shining through the window of his G6 private jet. He felt tired. Tired of the fight. And then he felt guilty for feeling tired, when he was the only reason Natalie was in danger in the first place. The text from the unknown number gave no other information, and he only had the news reports about the kidnapping to go on. The only thing Xander could think to do was start at the place where Natalie was taken. Paris. Xander doubted she would be held captive in Paris. He couldn't think of anyone there he even knew. He really needed Sam, and Marv, and the rest of the people who had helped him so much lately. But he couldn't bring himself to contact them. Kyle, Sam, and Sarah had all been calling and texting him nonstop for the last couple of hours. He knew they would be worried about him. But he knew if he told them where he was, and what he was doing, that they would come running. And Xander was sick and tired of putting his friends in danger. On one hand, he felt like keeping his friends out of it was the right thing to do. On

11

the other, he worried that he was doing Natalie a disservice by not using all of his resources to find her.

The jet interior felt so empty without Sam and Kyle. He knew they would be in a panic by now. Xander wondered how Sarah would feel about this. As if things weren't complicated enough, the amazing night that he shared with her last night threw a whole new monkey wrench into things. They had connected on another level, which at the time, he thought rivaled where he and Natalie had reached just a couple of weeks ago. But he didn't have time to worry about Sarah. She was a big girl. She would understand why Xander had to go and find Natalie. The question was, what would happen if he could save Natalie? It was then that a feeling came over him that he didn't like at all. But it was a feeling that he understood as a certain truth. He couldn't be with either one of them. If he could somehow manage to save Natalie, the best thing he could do was continue what he had already started trying to do: leave her alone. Same for Sarah. Though Sarah understood his world, and even operated well in it, she still had been nothing but in danger since the day they met. Enough was enough. He couldn't keep dragging them into his mess. He could no longer be selfish. He needed to find Natalie, bring her to safety, then leave her and Sarah the hell alone.

Forever.

The Worst Kind of Trouble

Sarah paced the kitchen like a woman waiting on her spouse's cancer diagnosis. She had checked her iPhone several hundred times over the last hour. Hoping each time that Xander had answered her messages. The television on the wall hadn't stopped reporting on Natalie Rockwell since they had turned it on. No new information had come in. The world was turning to social media in an outpouring of fear and emotion for the safety of their beloved sweetheart. Natalie had played the lead in two of the last three highest-grossing romance movies to open in the United States. America—the world—adored her. Xander adored her. Sarah knew it from the first moment she was in a room with them. Their chemistry was palpable. Magnetic. Sarah thought the same of her and Xander last night. Now, she didn't know what to think.

"Sarah, for God's sake, can you please either take a seat or wear out the floor in the other room? You are absolutely driving me mad," Sam said from her seat at the kitchen table. She had been on the phone calling everyone she knew, gathering all the info she could gather, and the entire time she had been forced to watch Sarah walk a hundred miles in about a ten-foot radius.

"I'm sorry, Sam, but I'm worried. I don't know what else to do."

"We're all worried, Sarah. But driving us bonkers won't help anything," Sam continued, frustrated.

"Would you all cool it?" Kyle spoke up. "Seriously! Jesus H."

Sarah stopped pacing. "Sorry. Does anyone have *anything*?"

Sam took a deep breath to settle her nerves.

"That was Marv I just spoke with. He hasn't heard anything. The only thing I have learned is that Xander left in the G6 this morning, but they wouldn't give me a destination. The man said Xander told him specifically to keep it quiet. Even to me. Xander must have disabled my tracker that he knows I have on all of his toys. That means Xander doesn't want us involved. For our sakes, no doubt."

Sarah's shoulders stiffened. "Well, he doesn't have the final say in that."

"I agree," said Sam. "I will be able to find out where Xander is going, but, it will take a little longer. However, I can already tell you, it's Paris. Unless Xander knows something we don't, he will start there."

"Then what the hell are we waiting for?" Kyle stood up, his arms held out to his sides.

"You have a plane I don't know about, Kyle?" Sam asked.

"No, Sam. I don't have a plane. But we can charter one."

"We may not have to," Sarah told them as she unlocked her

14

phone.

"Mary?" Sam asked.

"Mary who?" Kyle asked.

Sarah set down her phone and looked at both of them. She could hardly contain her enthusiasm.

"Mary Hartsfield. The new director of the CIA. She just texted me back. A plane will be at the Blue Grass Airport in half an hour, ready to take us to Paris."

Zhanna walked into the room when she heard Sarah's update.

"Nice work, Sarah." Sam stood from the table and glanced between Sarah and Zhanna. "I've got some clothes for the two of you. That is, if you even want to go, Zhanna. You have no stake in this."

Zhanna raised an eyebrow and folded her arms across her chest.

"No stake? I will never be able to repay Xander for ridding the world of my evil father. But this will be good start, saving his sweetheart."

All three of them looked at Sarah, knowing that last bit would sting. Sarah dropped her head to her phone and an awkward silence followed.

Zhanna tried to recover, "I am sorry—"

Sarah interrupted Zhanna. "It's fine. I just want to help Xander."

Another awkward silence. Sam finally and mercifully broke it.

"Great. It will mean a lot to Xander that you are willing to help, Zhanna. Kyle, pack a bag. I'll reach out to Jack. Xander had chartered him a plane to return from the Ukraine to the US. Maybe I can get him to divert and fly into Paris instead. I bet he'll want to help as well. We have no idea what or whom we are dealing with, so we will need all the help we can get."

"I agree." Kyle looked at Sarah. "Sarah, if you can get the CIA involved, that will help. Don't you think, Sam?"

"Of course."

Sarah put away her phone. "Mary said we have the full cooperation of the CIA. It doesn't hurt that Xander has taken out just about everyone on their most-wanted list this year. She said it also doesn't hurt that Natalie is such a high profile. This is a big case for the CIA. If they can help bring her home, it will be great PR."

"PR?" Kyle made a face. He didn't like the sound of that.

"After a scandal like former Director Manning left behind, working with a mafia boss and all, the CIA needs all the good press we can get," Sarah explained. "It will be a huge help for the start of Mary's time as director as well. It can only help Xander, Kyle."

"Whatever," Kyle dismissed her. "Is there anything I can be doing?"

Sam answered, "Just keep trying to reach out to Xander. Out of all of us, you're the one he will answer first."

"How bad is this, you all?" Kyle asked. "You have dealt with this sort of thing before, right?"

Zhanna fielded Kyle's question. Her time with the KGB gave her plenty of expertise on kidnappings. "I will not sugarcoat, Kyle, this is bad."

Sam added, "She's right. Unfortunately, I don't think this is about money. If it were, I wouldn't be all that concerned. But going to the extreme of coming to Xander's home here in Lexington and killing King's Ransom—that says to me that it is personal. Someone wants to hurt Xander, and they obviously know that Natalie is the way to do it. She is in trouble. The worst kind of trouble."

If These Walls Could Talk

Pure darkness. All-encompassing black, zero visibility, not an ounce of light—darkness. Natalie had no idea how long she had been in there. Wherever the hell she was. She had no sense of time, no sense of anything. Her mouth was dry, due to whatever they had stuffed in her mouth to gag her. Her wrists were raw from the ropes that tightly bound her arms behind her back. She would scream if she could get a scream out, but she couldn't. She imagined it would make no difference if she could. There wasn't much of a smell to the room she was in. The floor beneath her was hard but not porous, so she figured maybe it was hardwood. When she managed to stand, she counted fifteen footsteps, wall to wall, between all four walls. A perfect square. Her throat was scratchy from her earlier fear-riddled shouts. Her eyes burned from releasing what must have been every teardrop her body could manufacture. Her cheeks felt sticky from the salt trails those tears had left behind. There were no noises. Not even the hum of an air conditioner. And it was hot, which was probably why she couldn't hear an AC unit. Beads of sweat dripped down the small of her back. She had had no warning, so all she had on was what she had worn to bed: pajama shorts, which were light blue with navy blue anchors, and a white athletic tank top. With nothing in the room to stimulate her senses, the horror of the night replayed over and over in her head like a terrifying movie scene.

When it happened, at first she thought she had just heard a knock on her hotel room door. Still half asleep, she shouted at the door, telling whom she thought was the maid to come back later. When she glanced at the clock and it was only four in the morning, the first set of alarm bells went off in her head. No way the maid would be knocking that early in the morning. In that moment, she thought back to the night her and Xander were attacked at his home in Lexington. Also at four a.m. She sat up in bed and in a shaky voice called out, "Hello?" to what she hoped was an empty room. She waited, nerve endings on fire, but didn't hear anything else. Just as soon as she started to relax, she heard a click; the lamp in the sitting area of her suite had been turned on. Three figures, dressed in all black, instantly appeared in front of her. The next three minutes were a blur. She gave it all she had, but they were too strong. She tried to scream, but the first thing they did was stuff something in her mouth and taped over it, muffling her attempts to cry for help. Then, as she scratched, clawed, kicked, and punched— whatever she could do to break free of them—she felt a pop on the top of her head. The next thing she remembered was the darkness.

Natalie's head continued to throb. Whatever they had hit her with must have been hard as a rock. She imagined there was probably blood, but there was no way for her to tell. She may as well have been trapped in a cave. On one hand, she wanted to think that this had nothing to do with Alexander King. On the other, she sort of hoped that it did. That way Xander would be coming for her. Wouldn't he? Surely people knew about her missing set-call this morning. Was that this morning? She was so confused, and scared. At least they had left her alone for the moment. Maybe they were negotiating a ransom. She would pay absolutely anything to end this nightmare right now.

For the first time since she had woken up, she heard a noise. It sounded like the jangling of keys, followed by the shaking of a doorknob. Natalie immediately fell into a ball on the floor. Everything inside of her burned in fear. Her breath was short, her heart was pounding, and her entire body shook like someone had hit her with a taser. The rattling stopped and with the creaking of a door, a piercing light, like a sword plunging into her eyes, filled her vision with a bright white pain. She didn't have a free arm to help her shield the light, so she was forced to close her eyes. If she didn't, she felt as though she might lose her sight entirely.

Shadows moved beyond her closed eyelids, and she tried to look once again. She could only make out black figures until finally, a softer yellow hanging light was turned on in the center of the small room, and when the door was shut, three men, all in ski masks, looked down at her in the corner. She blinked the blur out of them, but it only made them clearer, not go away. This was not a dream. As her eyes adjusted, she could finally see the four-walled, square room that they were holding her in. The men didn't move. As Natalie whimpered in fear, she looked around in horror at the walls. Every wall was covered with eight-by-ten photographs, pinned to the wall with thumbtacks. Dozens of them. Every single one of them was a picture of a different dead body. The fear within her was unlike any feeling she had ever encountered. The three men still weren't moving. They just watched her as she looked around the room, tears running down her face. Her jaw began to ache from biting down on the gag so hard. She wasn't even aware she was doing it. It was just the way she was surviving the moment. Natalie had read that when you are faced with such fear, one of two things happens: fight or flight. She hadn't had the chance to read up on what happens if you are unable to do either of the two. She wished she could melt into the floor. She wished they would just do something. *Anything*. Anything had to be better than having them just stand there staring at her. In that moment of sheer terror, she longed for the feeling of passing out. But it never came.

It wasn't but a moment later that she wished she could take that bit about "anything" back. *Anything* wasn't better.

The door opened and in walked a man dressed in what Natalie recognized as an abaya, almost like a black cotton gown, and a black cotton scarf twirled atop his head. Traditional Middle Eastern attire.

The man walked right up to Natalie and pulled her up to her feet by her hair. She squealed in pain and cried in fear. The other three men surrounded her from behind and held her in place. The man in the black turban, clearly the one in charge, tilted Natalie's head up by nudging her chin. Then he moved her head around the room, making sure she was taking in all of the pictures pinned to the walls.

"You see this?" There was anger in the man's voice. His accent was Middle Eastern; his tone, dead serious.

Natalie made no motion to acknowledge the man's

21

question. It wasn't that she was trying to ignore him; it just didn't register to her that he actually wanted an answer.

He shook her face hard with his hand and screamed, "Answer me!"

Natalie quickly nodded, begging with her eyes for him to let her go.

"This, these pictures, these people. These are my friends. *Were* my friends. They were my family! And they are all dead! Do you know why, Miss Hollywood? Do you?" He shouted.

His voice echoed in that tiny room. It shook Natalie all the way through to her bones. She pleaded with him by shaking her head from side to side; no, she didn't know why. The breaths coming in and out of her nose were frantic. She whimpered as she awaited his answer. An answer that she already knew. This was because of Xander. She remembered seeing the news report on television the day after Xander had left whiskey and roses on her balcony in Paris. The news about the terrorist cell in Syria that had been taken out in the middle of the night. More than fifty of them were killed in total. Then, she flashed to the moment at Xander's house in San Diego when CIA Agent Sarah Gilbright explained that it was Xander and his team who had taken them out. All of them. All because he had been led to believe that the bad guy—something Khatib—had killed his parents. Could this be him? Khatib? She knew that Xander had killed him. She remembered it on the news and from the recount of it in San Diego. So it couldn't be him, could it?

"Of course you know why they are dead! DON'T YOU?" The man continued to scream at her. All she could do was shake her head and hope he would leave her alone.

"All of these men, my people, and most importantly, *him!*" The man pointed to a picture that was larger than all the rest on

22

the back wall. The picture showed a man sprawled out on the sand, clearly dead, dressed in the same sort of attire that the man screaming at her was wearing. "He is dead, and I know you know why. You know!"

Once again, Natalie shook her head. Emphatically.

"You say no, but I know. The reason all of my people on these walls are dead is because of your man. Your man who took you to the races. There were pictures of the two of you in magazines, on television. And I think he would like to see what I have got here with me. Don't you?" This time the anger was gone. His voice was cold, his eyes were black, and she imagined his heart just might be as well.

Before Natalie could answer, he had hold of her chin again. This time, instead of showing her the walls, he tilted her upward until she was looking straight into the yellow light bulb that hung from the middle of the ceiling. Her face was a mess: tears running down her bright-red cheeks, her eyes wild with fright, and her mouth gagged and covered with duct tape. It seemed this was exactly what the man wanted to see. She figured this out when he pulled out his phone, forced her to open her eyes, and then took a picture. He admired the phone's screen for a moment, and then his goatee-covered chin helped his mouth form a crooked-toothed smile.

"Yes. I think Xander King will very much like to see what I have here."

He dropped her chin, put away his phone, and let out a maniacal laugh.

And just like that, all four of the men were gone.

And so too was the light.

Shades of Gray

Xander told his faithful pilot, Bob, to settle in because it might be a while; then he said good-bye, turned on his phone, and pulled up the Uber app. Xander didn't want record of him getting a rental car. Not that Sam wouldn't be able to find him anyway if she really wanted to. He had disabled the tracking device on the plane, and he had shut off his phone until he landed, but that would only minimally delay Sam in finding him. She was the best, and that was the reason they were such an amazing team. Regardless, he thought it might be a safer bet. Plus, he just really didn't feel like driving. He waited for the car to pull up before he walked out of the airport. Better to wait inside than get drenched by the driving rain. It was coming down in sheets. They say Paris is magical in the rain. They also used to say cigarettes weren't bad for you.

It was a particularly cool summer day as well. Even for

Paris. Low sixties. The rain would make it feel more like upper forties. He spotted the Uber car, opened the airport terminal door, opened his umbrella, and made his way to it. His feet sloshed through the standing water on the blacktop, and the raindrops crashed into his umbrella like kamikaze pilots into Pearl Harbor. The sky was the sort of gray that would be enough to depress a man on his happiest day. Xander thought he could remember what a happy day was. But he wasn't sure. He thought the Kentucky Derby was a happy day—the day that King's Ransom had taken it to those other Thoroughbreds. But he also had to kill a man that day. Then that night, nine more when they broke in and stole Natalie's innocent view of him. He had thought he had let her go in time after that. He thought letting her go would save her from more trouble. But here he was in Paris, once again trying to save her from one of his messes.

He opened the door to the Mercedes sedan Uber car, closed his umbrella, and managed to get in with at least a couple of dry spots left on his black hoodie.

"I'm Joe. How are you today, Mr. King?" the Uber driver said with a smile. He had a French accent, but his appearance suggested his parents may have been Arab.

"Fine. The Hotel Le Bristol, please," Xander answered bluntly. He was in no mood to chat.

"Le Bristol, huh? I'm sure you heard what happened there, no?"

This is why Xander was in no mood to talk. "No," he lied, "but it sounds like you're about to tell me."

"You haven't heard? Well, have you heard of Natalie Rockwell?" Joe pulled away from the airport and started driving toward the hotel.

"Sounds familiar."

Hearing Natalie's name was like a knife in the heart.

"Yeah, she's that hot actress. Biggest star in Hollywood. Don't you watch the movies, Mr. King?"

"Is there an end to this story, Joe?"

"Oh, yes. Sorry. Well, seems as though she was kidnapped. They took her right out of her room in the middle of the night. Can you imagine how scared she must be?"

Xander didn't answer. All he had been imagining for the last eight hours was how scared she must be. He turned his attention outside the window. The rain danced on the roof of the car and the gray filled in all around him. Outside and in. Joe got the hint that Mr. King didn't want to talk and went on driving. Xander checked his phone: thirty-two new messages and missed calls. He felt bad for not reaching out to Sam and Sarah, but he felt horrible for not answering Kyle. He opened the texts from him and the last one read:

Look, X, I don't care where you are or what you're doing, but at least let me know you're okay.

Xander tapped on the typing slot of his phone's keyboard:

I am fine. Tell Sam to stop looking for me. I'll call you when it's all over.

After pushing send, Xander powered down his phone, closed his eyes, and sank down into the gray leather backseat. He knew that Kyle would tell Sam. And he knew both of them would ignore his request. They were probably on their way to Paris at that very moment. Tracking the GPS in his phone. He could run, but there was no way he could hide from Sam. Xander tried to relax, then slowly drifted off to sleep.

"Xander just messaged me," Kyle announced to his fellow passengers on the plane. Sam, Sarah, and Zhanna bolted upright in their seats. "Says he's fine, Sam, stop looking for me, and he'll call when it's all over."

"Well, let's just turn this plane around then," Sam said sarcastically.

Sarah stood from her seat.

"What? We can't just leave him alone!"

Sarah clearly misunderstood Sam's sarcasm.

Kyle smiled, "She's being sarcastic, Sarah. We're not turning around."

"Oh." Sarah returned to her seat.

"Sam, were you able to get ahold of Jack?" Kyle asked.

"I left a voice mail and a text message telling him what was going on, but I haven't heard from him."

"Damn it. I was hoping we could get someone there before we landed. Xander will just jump right in. He won't even worry about whether or not he has the numbers to make something happen."

Zhanna leaned back in her seat. "I thought Xander didn't need numbers."

Sam took a drink of her gin. "He doesn't. But it makes us feel better if we are there." She gave Kyle a wink.

Sarah said, "So do we know anything yet? Mary said there is absolutely nothing on the wire."

"Marv said he wasn't going to stop hunting the networks until he found something," Sam answered. "But he hasn't reached out to me yet."

Kyle put away his phone.

"Well, we'll be there in a couple hours. Hopefully he finds something by then."

The three women said in unison, "Hopefully."

Just then Sam's phone chimed. Everyone looked to her.

"It's Marv again. Xander just called for an Uber, in Paris. Says he'll keep tabs." She looked up from her phone to the rest of them. "At least we are on the right track."

The Mercedes hit some sort of pothole, and the rattle of the car woke Xander from his sleep. He never fell asleep in a car; he knew his body must be exhausted. His stomach and leg were still sore from the mostly healed gunshot wounds he'd taken during the past month. But at least his shoulder wasn't bothering him. He sat up just as the car was coming to a stop in a parallel parking space on a side street that Xander didn't recognize. However, he knew the area he was supposed to be in, and they were nowhere near the hotel.

"Where the hell are we, Joe?"

"End of the line."

Joe turned to point a gun straight at Xander's chest. However, Joe's boss must not have fully briefed him on the man he had in his backseat. Xander had detected the motion of Joe's shoulder suggesting he was about to bring his arm upward. Computing for Xander was the fact that Joe had driven

28

him to a strange neighborhood, pulled the car to a stop, and hadn't yet begun to explain why they were there. The last mistake, one that all potential killers out there should always keep in mind, is the fact that you should NEVER say something before you turn to shoot someone—especially someone like Xander.

Xander trapped Joe's gun hand before the gun made it around to him. Then he used the side of Joe's front seat as a lever, pulled the gun hand with frightening strength, and snapped Joe's arm in half at the elbow. The crack from the bone breaking sounded like the snap of a hundred broken celery sticks. Speaking of unsettling sounds, Joe had a real set of pipes on him, and unfortunately, the split second before Xander snapped his neck, he managed to scream loud enough to make Xander's ears ring. Joe's body slumped forward so quickly after Xander twisted his neck like a bottle cap that he fell against the car horn.

The little shit had ratted Xander out, from the afterlife.

Xander yanked Joe's body off the horn, took his cell phone from the console, and grabbed his nine-millimeter pistol from the floor where his now broken, wrong way-dogleg arm had dropped it. The obvious next move would simply be to take Joe's car and drive to the hotel. But Xander knew that wherever they were at the moment, Joe had driven there because his pals were going to be there waiting. He looked upward at the brick building just outside the back window. On the third floor of the building, he saw the tip of a rifle aimed in the direction of his car from an open window.

Rookies.

Xander pulled his hood up over his head. Directly in front of the car was a door leading into the building where the gunman was perched. Probably locked. Could this really be the place they were holding Natalie? He didn't think so, but maybe he could get some information from someone inside. Joe's cell phone began to ring. Joe—The Creative One—had the number stored in his contacts simply as BOSS. Really?

Xander answered the call.

"You have five seconds to tell me you're going to hand Natalie over to me, unharmed, or I come find you and kill you. Don't blow it. You ready? Five . . ."

There was a pause, nothing but silence on the other end. Xander ended the count early.

"Time's up. One of your men in this building is going to tell me where you are, and when they do, you'll be a dead man shortly thereafter."

Xander ended the call before the "BOSS" had a chance to respond. He knew the voice would be disguised, and offer no information. Not letting him speak was a risky play, but Xander was betting on the fact that whoever this was, they wanted to put on a show. Otherwise, they wouldn't have gone through the trouble of killing King's Ransom, and they wouldn't be wasting time kidnapping Natalie. The only reason for these theatrics was to make Xander suffer. And the only way Xander would suffer further was to make him watch Natalie die. Whoever this was didn't just want to stab Xander in the heart; they wanted to stab it, twist it, and break it, all at the same time. This had revenge written all over it. This was evident when Joe's phone chirped, displaying that an MMS picture message was waiting from the "BOSS."

Xander wasn't afraid of a lot of things, but he was scared to death to open that message. He stared at the lock screen for a moment, working up the stomach to open it. When he finally did, the caption read:

You should learn to be a little nicer, Mr. King. Otherwise, maybe I won't be so nice to her.

Then he saw the picture.

Two things happened when he saw the fear in Natalie's tear-drenched eyes and the duct tape over her mouth: 1) His heart broke completely in two; and 2) Everything that he had ever learned as a Navy SEAL and during the years he had been hunting his parents' killer all came together in an adrenaline-fueled focus. His tired muscles suddenly felt like a metal coating; his bones suddenly felt like steel. He typed the words *See you soon* into a text message and pressed send.

Xander put the phone in his pocket, made sure Joe's pistol had a chambered round, and funneled his fury into a virtual hand grenade that was about to blow whatever was inside that brick building into a thousand bloody pieces.

Don't Blink

Xander opened the door of the Mercedes. The rain continued to fall in sheets; the sound as it hit the ground reminded him of a waterfall. The door across the sidewalk was a metal double door. This must be the backdoor entrance. Xander didn't want to imagine what might be waiting on the other side. He knew it would only throw him off. He wanted the ability to go on pure instinct. His thought was that a fast entrance would at least catch someone by surprise. That was all he would need.

At full burst Xander propelled himself out of the Mercedes, and at full speed he put a shoulder to the left side of the double door, which gave way with ease as he tumbled inside. He heard the blast of a rifle from outside. The man in the window wasn't ready for Xander to come out at such a torrid pace. When Xander hit the door, he rolled, skidded to his knees, and came to a halt behind a computer desk inside a cubicle. The quick look at the open warehouse facility revealed row after row of the same type of cubicle. Some sort of pop-up office space. He didn't notice anyone at the cubicles, but his millisecond view could never have scoured the entire floor. There were no sounds of typing, talking, or any other typical office activity, so Xander assumed it was empty. As he listened for any movement, he unzipped his soaking-wet hoodie and tied it around his waist. Restricted movement could get him killed. The formfitting black under-tank he was wearing might not keep off the chill, but it would allow him full range of motion. And as he heard the bing of an elevator at the other end of the hundred-yard room, he knew he was going to need every bit of that range of motion.

"Xander?" a female voice echoed through the large open room.

Was that a Russian accent?

"Xander, I know you are in here. There is nowhere for you to go."

It was definitely Russian. Russian? Did this have something to do with him killing Vitalii Dragov? Could this be someone who worked for his father? The only Russian Xander knew was Zhanna. And she was on his side.

It was then that it hit him, like a two-by-four to the groin. The hand grenade he had thrown out the window of his G6 in Moscow as they were jetting down the runway must not have hit the Jeep as squarely as they all thought it had. Melania had survived. And now what? His assistant-turned-traitor, wanted revenge? For what? He had done nothing to her. Why did she want so much for Xander to suffer?

"Come on, Xander, there is no play here. You are trapped."

Xander crouched behind the cubicle, his gun at the ready.

"Trapped? Come now, Melanie—or Melania—whatever

the fuck your name is. I thought you knew me better than that. Frankly, I'm a little hurt."

"I do know you, Xander. That is why I have positioned snipers in the buildings surrounding this one. There is nowhere you can go."

"Snipers? Thanks for the heads-up, stupid." Mister Mature.

"It is you that is stupid, Xander. You come here alone."

"Actually, I was headed to my hotel. Guess my driver got lost. Uber isn't perfect, you know. Don't you worry, though, I'll leave a bad review."

As Xander was biding time with banter, he raised his head slightly to peer over the cubicle. At the far end of the room, he saw a few heads moving along the tops of the rows of cubicles. They were fanning out in all directions. There were no lights on in the room, but the rows of windows all along the walls let in plenty of gray light. Outside, the rain continued pouring.

"Cut the shit. If you want to see Natalie alive, and I know you do, you will come out now and I will take you to her."

"Sounds intriguing, but I'm going to have to decline. Do you want to tell me where she is now, or do you want to wait until I have Joe's gun in your mouth to give me the information? Your call."

"Xander, Xander, Xander. You have yet to learn that you are not superhero."

"Yeah? Give me five minutes, then I'll let you decide what I am. Oh, and Melanie?"

"What, Xander?"

"Don't blink."

The New World Power

Construction sounds of hammers striking nails, socket wrenches cranking, and welding torches spitting fire echoed throughout the intimate ballroom-style dining room. The dining tables and chairs that normally filled the space had been removed, and now the dining area was left completely open. Windows on both sides of the room covered most of the walls, allowing the gray light of the rainy Paris day to illuminate the contraption that was currently being constructed on the far wall of the room, which covered the entire back of the room; with only one door on the left side, the rest was normally bare. However, some sort of medieval device rested in the middle of that wall. It was large, metal, full of gears and cranks, and had what looked to be two identical and extremely large pinpoint spears facing each other on the left and right sides of it. They were like gigantic needles made of steel, and they were pointed at each other. An open space in the middle of them revealed straps, more like leather restraints, attached to the wall. Men were hovered around the contraption, working diligently to ensure that everything was in place.

The door on the left side of the wall opened, and three men walked inside. The supervisor of the project immediately diverted his attention from the workers to the men who had walked through the door. Two of the men, both Caucasian were dressed in button-down shirts and dress pants and carried oversized briefcases in their hands. The man the supervisor addressed, however, was in stark contrast to them. He was Middle Eastern, dressed in what looked like a black cotton robe. He was fairly tall with a solid muscular frame, and he wore a turban on the top of his head. His caramel-colored face and dark eyes looked over the construction as he stroked his goatee, admiring their work.

"Everything is going according to plan," the supervisor offered.

The man in the turban took a step toward the contraption, giving it a more scrutinizing inspection. "How long until it is finished?" he asked as he stroked the steel gear on its left side. He moved his hand along the massively oversized stainless steel needle, feeling its tip and giving a satisfied look when he felt how outstandingly sharp it was. The workers halted their jobs so the men could speak without raising their voices. The man in the turban raised his hand and addressed the workers. "Please, continue."

The men did as he asked, and he turned back toward the supervisor.

The supervisor replied, "Fifteen, maybe thirty minutes, tops." The man was French, his accent thick.

The man in the turban nodded, waved the supervisor away, and walked from the construction to the middle of the open room. There, he looked up at the ceiling. There was a gold chandelier hanging from the black ceiling tiles that stretched the length of the room.

"Place them here," he said to the man on his right. "I want multiple cameras here. I want the ability to show a wide view and a close-up view simultaneously. Just make certain the wide view does not extend farther than the wall. We do not want anyone watching to discern our location from anything they could possibly be able to see if the windows are in view."

"Of course," the man agreed.

"This will be a live video feed. Make sure there is nothing that can keep this broadcast from airing live. I want a backup camera on each side wall as well, both of them solely focused on the machine."

"No problem. We will connect the cameras wirelessly so there will be no feed to cut. You'll have twenty-four hours of continuous footage on these cameras. Will that be long enough?"

The man in the turban smiled, more to himself than to the man who asked the question. "Oh yes. That will be more than enough time. The show will long be over by then. Now, get to work. I want to see everything up and running in one hour. It is time to make history."

Just then the phone belonging to the man in the turban made a sound. He walked away from the two men as they began to install the cameras and opened his phone. It was a text from Melania. The man hadn't known her very long, but she seemed to share his wishes for the end of Xander King. He didn't like working with women—it was very foreign to him;

37

however, he would do anything to destroy King. When Melania first contacted him a week ago, she had told him about Vitalii Dragov's plan to put an end to Xander. The man was skeptical, so he continued his own planning. But when she called him yesterday afternoon, explaining that Xander had managed to escape, he immediately put his plan into motion. He sent some of his men to kill the horse and leave the message on the wall. He sent some of his men to kidnap Natalie Rockwell, and he flew Melania to Paris from Moscow, on her promise that she knew Xander well enough to put an end to him once and for all. She had said Dragov wouldn't listen to her. She had said Dragov underestimated how dangerous Xander and Sam could be. Melania told him that if he brought her on board, she would ensure that they would be able to outsmart Xander by playing on his weakness: his loved ones.

Melania still was not proven to him, but so far she had helped him orchestrate what he knew was the perfect plan to exact revenge on Xander, and send a message to America that the world would no longer allow the US to keep the world under its thumb. He opened the text from Melania.

Xander is here. We have him cornered at the warehouse. How shall we proceed?

He typed his response and closed his phone. He turned back toward the men finishing up the construction of his machine and glanced at the men installing the cameras. He had Xander right where he wanted him. He knew his brother would be proud. Not only was he going to make Xander pay, but he would be able to finish what his brother had started. Better than that, he knew that when America saw their beloved movie star murdered live on the Internet, their fear would rise to a whole new level. The recruits to the cause would be much easier to gain, and it would be the very thing to build the army that could finally teach the world the way life was supposed to be lived.

His way.

And if his intel proved right that the President's daughter was really coming to Paris and if he could manage to find where she was going, he could possibly even bring America to its knees, tonight.

A smile once again grew across his face. His chest swelled with pride. It was going to be an incredible night. America's sweetheart, America's hero, and quite possibly the President's daughter, all squashed under his power.

The new world power.

It's Your Lucky Day

Xander took a deep breath, raised both his Glock 19 and Joe's pistol out in front of him, one aimed to the left and one aimed to the right, as he stood up straight behind the chest-high cubicle. He had the entirety of the open room in his view. He immediately squeezed both triggers when he saw movement coming down the left and right sides of the room. Bangs from his pistols echoed through the warehouse. Both men dove behind the makeshift cubicle walls, and Xander zeroed in on the group of people in the middle of the opposite side of the warehouse. Four of them. As soon as they heard Xander's pistols, they ducked for cover.

"Come out and play, Melanie," Xander said in a singsong but sinister voice.

"Hold your fire!" Melania shouted. "Xander, I do not wish to kill you here." The elevator at her end of the warehouse binged, and the door opened. "Check your phone. My boss wishes to speak with you. I just sent you his location."

"Why did you bring me here if you didn't want a fight?" Xander shouted, confused.

"To make sure you were stupid enough to come alone."

"I am single, but I don't think it would work out for us. It's not you, it's me."

"Just be at the coordinates I sent you in two hours. Then maybe you will get to see your precious Natalie before she is dead."

"If you touch her—"

"What?" Melania interrupted. "You will what, Xander?"

Xander didn't finish his sentence. Instead, he jumped up on the desk and then over the wall of the cubicle. He sprinted around the right side of the last row of cubicles. The man he had shot at a moment ago stood up, but Xander put two bullets in him before the man could even lift his arm. At the sound of Xander's gun, the group of men and Melania made a break for the elevator. Melania was in front, and she made it in. Xander hit two of the four men who followed, but because he was sprinting, he didn't think they were kill shots. The elevator door began to close as Xander began to close the distance. He was about twenty yards away. He wasn't going to make it to stop it from closing. Out of the corner of his eye he could see the man from the left side of the room running for the elevator. They had left him behind. Xander slid feetfirst on his right side, his pistol extended in front of him. If he couldn't keep the door from closing, he could at least get a shot off inside the elevator. As his eyes met the six-inch open slit left in the closing door, he fired inside and heard a man squeal in pain.

Bingo.

As he continued to slide along the slick concrete floor, he rotated 180 degrees and shot the man left behind in the

41

warehouse, right in the stomach, just before he fired a shot at Xander. Finally, Xander came to a stop as his feet hit the brick wall at the end of the room. The gunman dropped to the floor holding his stomach, groaning in pain. Xander got to his feet, holstered one of his pistols in his waistband, and walked over to the man he had just shot.

"Well, apparently she didn't think much of you, huh?" Xander stood over him as the man writhed in pain. He was wearing blue jeans and a black T-shirt with a brown leather jacket. The man didn't speak; he just scrunched his face in pain and continued to try to catch his breath. "Ouch. Looks like I got you good there."

"Fuck you," the man said with a French accent.

Xander looked around the empty room. "Who? Me? Wow, okay. I thought we were going to be friends, but—"

Outside Xander could hear sirens coming down the street. Whatever he was going to do, he was going to have to hurry.

"Fine," Xander said to the man. "I'll let you live if you tell me where Melanie is going."

"Fuck you."

"A man of many words."

Xander put his foot on the man's stomach, directly on top of the bullet wound, and pressed his weight upon it. The man let out a mighty scream and then began to plead. His face turned pale and sweat began running down his face.

"Fine! Okay! I don't give a shit about her, I just met her. I don't know where she is going! I swear!"

Xander pressed harder.

The man screamed in pain.

"I swear! I don't know! All I know is that there is parking below us. That is where the elevator goes. But I don't know where she is going!"

The sirens drew closer, and Xander believed the man. He removed his foot from the man's stomach and backed away toward the elevator.

"It's your lucky day. But if I find out you knew where they were going . . ." Xander didn't finish his threat; he just punched the button on the elevator and backed his way inside as the door opened. He waved his gun at the man on the ground and made a tsk-tsk gesture. The door closed in front of him, and he hit the button with the letter P on it. The elevator lurched downward, and Xander could see blood on the floor below him. He had definitely hit someone with his slide shot a moment ago. The door opened in front of him, and with his pistol extended he gave the empty parking garage a once-over. There was nothing but pavement and concrete all around. Not a single car. They had gotten away. Xander put away his gun and pulled out his phone. When he turned it on, he saw the message from Melanie. He didn't recognize the location she had sent, and he didn't have time to look it up. He could hear commotion above him. Just then, two police cars came swerving around the corner of the parking garage and squealed to a stop in front of him. Four men posted up behind the opened doors of their patrol cars, and one of them shouted for him to put his hands up. Xander didn't speak French, but he was sure that's what they had yelled. He did as they asked. Other than killing them, there was no other option. And he wasn't going to do that. Getting back in the elevator wouldn't help either; he knew that by then they would have the upstairs covered as well. As he raised both hands, he managed to finger his way to Sam in his text list. And he managed to text her the word *Jail*.

Xander hadn't wanted to involve his friends, but he knew

43

they were already on their way. That's what they did. And he knew if he wanted to see Natalie alive ever again, being stuck in a jail cell in Paris, France, sure wasn't going to get the job done. He just hoped that Sam could once again work her magic, and he hoped she could do it fast.

Cause for Concern

Sam, Kyle, Zhanna, and Sarah had been in the air for more than four hours. Only Zhanna had been able to fall asleep. As Sam looked around the cabin of the CIA's private jet, she felt good about the team that had organically come together. Sure, she didn't know Zhanna very well, but they had only known each other for a couple of days, and it wasn't like they'd had time for tea. Or vodka, which Sam assumed the Russian would most likely prefer. So would she, for that matter. Zhanna was a beautiful woman, and according to the old CIA cowboy, Jack Bronson, she was equally as adept at fighting. Sam hadn't seen it yet, but as she looked over at Sarah Gilbright, she knew you couldn't judge such a thing like fighting by the way someone looked. Because as pretty as Zhanna was with her long red hair and perfectly curved body, Sarah Gilbright made her look like the spokeswoman for average. Sarah was a knockout. And because they had already been through a couple of battles together, she knew Sarah was also a badass. A wolf in model's clothing. Sam definitely understood how Xander could fall for the buxom blonde. The bravest blonde Sam had ever met.

Then there was Kyle. Until the last couple of weeks she only thought him to be an immature playboy. And most likely that is still all he was, for the most part. But she did get to see the heart in the man. The heart that reminded her of Xander. Most people would think Xander heartless because of his ability to take a man's life. But Sam saw it as the opposite. His ability to risk his own life for those he didn't even know was as noble a thing as a man could do. And she had seen Kyle take up arms in much the same way now. For Xander, for her, and for the rest of this merry little band of misfit killers. Sam had found herself in private moments thinking of Kyle in a way she hadn't over the last few years she had known him. His adorable and frustrating charm had always been there, but mix that in with a man who would lay down his life for you, and you have a recipe for disaster. Disaster, because Sam thought all relationships of the love/lust variety to be a terrible idea. Xander was the perfect example right now. If he had not let his feelings for Natalie Rockwell blossom, he would be at his home celebrating the end of the search for his murdered parents' killer. Instead, he is in Paris, throwing caution to the wind, willing to do anything to ensure Natalie's safety. Sam never approved of mixing business with pleasure, yet here she was, contemplating such notions for Kyle.

Stupid.

She should be on her couch reading the latest Stephen King novel, but no, here she was on her way to war because of feelings. Xander's feelings for Natalie. But she knew she was being a complete hypocrite, because if she got a call that Kyle was in danger, she would come running like a devil for his due.

"Everything okay, Sam?" Kyle asked from the seat beside her.

Sam jumped a bit, not prepared to hear anything but the hum of the jet engines. She turned in her seat toward Kyle, tucking her right leg under her left, and let out a sigh.

"Not really. I can't for the life of me imagine who could have taken Natalie. Haven't we rid the world of Xander haters yet?" She recovered quickly, not letting on that she had been thinking of Kyle.

"I know what you mean. I've been racking my brain. But I don't know the people Xander has been involved with over the years like you do. I was hoping you would have an idea." Kyle leaned toward her. Concern for his friend hung heavy on his face.

Sam wasn't sure that she had ever noticed the scar that ran through the dark hair of his left eyebrow. It wasn't very big, but it was definitely there.

"It could be a number of people, Kyle. We have taken out some of the worst human scum on the planet. They are bound to have some disgruntled family, right?"

"I was thinking the same thing. You think it could be someone in Dragov's camp?" Kyle asked.

Sarah leaned in now from the chair across from them. Her concern was evident as well.

Sam answered. "I really don't think so, Kyle. I believe this had to have been planned. Think of the orchestration of coming to Lexington and killing King's Ransom, and simultaneously kidnapping Natalie in Paris. That couldn't have happened in

47

twelve hours. Someone has been considering this for at least some amount of time now."

"I think you're right, Sam," Sarah chimed in. "I've been running this through my head since we took off. I e-mailed Marv and told him to check into the background and family of Sanharib Khatib. I just have a feeling it could have to do with him. This feels like revenge."

Sam nodded. "It certainly does. Marv will find something if there is anything. Xander has said on multiple occasions that he is the smartest man he'd ever met."

"What about Jack?" Kyle asked. "Have you heard from him?"

"Not yet," Sam said. "But he could have already been in the air when I messaged him. I don't have the number to the phone on the chartered plane, but I have messaged the charter company to get it. It's probably too late now, though."

"Damn it." Kyle was clearly dejected. "Do you think Xander is okay? I know he's Xander, but he isn't himself. He's running on rage right now. And while I wouldn't want to be on the other end of that rage, I do worry that it could cloud his judgment. Why didn't he just come and get us when he found King's Ransom?"

Sam let out another sigh as she readjusted her ponytail. "You know how he is. He thinks he has endangered us enough. He—"

Before Sam could finish, her phone chirped a text alert.

"It's Xander."

She unlocked her phone and went to his message. Everyone else leaned toward her in anticipation.

"What's it say, is he all right?" Sarah asked.

"Jail."

Kyle's face scrunched in confusion. "Jail?"

"Jail?" Sarah repeated. "What else?"

"That's it," Sam said. "It only says the word *Jail*."

"You think he's been arrested?" Kyle asked.

"I don't know, but I don't know what else he could mean," Sam answered.

"What the hell?" Kyle squirmed in his seat. "If he's been arrested, that's good news for him, safety wise, but that is terrible for Natalie. Sam, do you know anyone in Paris?"

"I do, but let's just say, an ex-MI6 agent isn't exactly a friend. More of a rival. I don't think I can get far."

Sarah said, "I'll call Director Hartsfield. The CIA is bound to know someone who can let Xander get a phone call to us at least."

Sam nodded. "Good idea. I'll try Jack again, and Kyle, you give Marv a heads-up and get him working on this. Xander needs our help now more than ever. Whether he wants it or not."

First Time for Everything

"Well, this is a first," Xander said aloud to the small empty room. It could not have been bigger than twelve by twelve, with a metal table in front of him and two metal chairs, one of which he was sitting in while the other sat across the table from him. And behind the empty chair was a massive rectangular mirror; through which Xander could feel eyes watching him.

"You want to get this show on the road?" he asked the mirror. "Seriously, you have to get me out of here." His last few words were tinged with panic.

He didn't know exactly how long it had been since Melanie had told him that he had two hours to reach the coordinates, but his best guess was about an hour. The panic sank deeper into his nervous system. Time to get things moving.

"I need you to send someone in here now! I have

information about the kidnapping of Natalie Rockwell!"

The words left a bad taste in his mouth and a helpless feeling in his gut. He didn't have to stew in it for long, however, because the mention of Natalie's name almost immediately led to the opening of the only door in the room. Xander knew that it was no coincidence.

"Okay, Monsieur King," a slightly round and partially bald Frenchman said as he walked into the room. "We need you to tell us what happened at that warehouse earlier." The man in the pale-yellow, short-sleeve button-down shirt and light-brown slacks turned the chair around backward and straddled it to face Xander.

"Listen, a woman's life is at stake here. You have got to let me out of here."

"Are you talking about Miss Rockwell? Is that the woman in danger?"

"Cut the shit . . . Detective?"

"Detective Beaumont."

"Cut the shit, Detective Beaumont. You know I'm talking about Natalie, and I know you know who I am."

"Yes, you are a rich American man whom my officers found armed in the parking garage of a warehouse where two dead bodies were found just upstairs. But I don't understand what this has to do with Miss Rockwell."

"Look, call Mary Hartsfield in Langley, Virginia. Her number is in my cell phone. Every second you hold me here is a second closer to you having the murder of a famous actress on your hands."

"So you know something about the disappearance of Miss Rockwell?"

Xander couldn't hold back. He slammed his still-cuffed

hands down on the table in front of him. "She's going to die if you don't let me go!"

The door to the room opened, and two armed police officers walked in. Detective Beaumont held up his hand to let them know it was okay.

"Look, Mr. King. I suggest you just relax and give us all the information you have, because you are not going anywhere for a while."

"The hell he ain't."

Just then a real-life cowboy walked into the room.

Jack Bronson.

"Jack!" Xander would have jumped up and kissed him if he hadn't been chained to his chair. He had no idea how Jack came to be in Paris when Xander needed him most, but he had a feeling it couldn't have been because of anyone but Sam.

The detective turned with a look of astonishment on his face. "And who the hell are you?"

"I'm the man who's taking this pretty son of a bitch outta here right now. If you could have someone get his things, we'll be outta your hair in a heartbeat."

"Officers," Beaumont said to the two policemen, "get this man out of here."

One of them reached for Jack's arm, and Jack retracted it with astounding speed for an older man. He may have been retired CIA, but Xander knew from what he had witnessed in Tuscany and Moscow that the old man still had a few rounds left in the magazine.

"If you wanna keep that hand, you'll keep it off of me," he said to the tall, bald-headed officer. Then to the detective he said, "Call your boss, he'll fill you in on what he and I already discussed."

Beaumont looked at the officers, then to Xander, and then to Jack. "Officers, watch these two while I step out for just a moment."

They nodded to him. Beaumont got up and walked out into the hall, pulling his phone from its clip. Jack stepped closer to Xander, wearing a sorrowful look on his face.

"I'm real sorry to hear about King's Ransom, Xander. Kyle told me how much that horse meant to ya. And I'm real sorry about Miss Rockwell too."

"Thanks, Jack. What have you learned?"

"Honestly, I hate to tell ya, I don't know a damn thing. I just got a message from Sam a while ago asking me if I would divert to Paris. When I landed, I called her and she said you were here. Said Sarah had Director Hartsfield call the chief here to tell him I'd be coming to get you. Guess that news didn't make it to the detective here yet. You find out anything while you been here? How the hell did you end up in here anyway?"

"Long story, Jack. Let's talk about it when we get out of here. But we don't have much time, I know that much for sure. What time is it?"

Jack checked his watch. "Right at eight p.m."

Just as Xander thought. It was seven when Melania explained that he only had two hours to reach the coordinates she had sent him.

Detective Beaumont walked back into the interrogation room. He didn't seem happy, but he was also clearly resigned to the fact that he had lost this one.

"Monsieur King, I don't know how you did it, but you are free to go."

Jack turned to Beaumont, a smile on his face. "God works in mysterious ways, Pepe, and so doth the CIA."

53

Beaumont walked around the table and began to unshackle Xander. "Your things will be at the front desk. We'll be watching you, Mr. King."

"Do me a favor, spend your time on something worthwhile, like, I don't know, finding a famous actress or something." Xander's tone was accusatory.

Beaumont had no words, but his face showed he wasn't pleased by Xander's insinuation that nothing was being done about the matter. "Let us handle the dirty work, Mr. King. Your fancy hands are not cut out for this sort of thing."

All Xander could do was smile. "Thanks for the ride from the warehouse, *officer*. I'll take it from here."

After a five-minute shouting match with the officer on duty, Detective Beaumont, and anyone else who would listen, Xander and Jack walked out of the police station, Xander without his gun. He didn't figure they would give him back the gun that belonged to the now-dead Uber driver, but keeping his Glock was Beaumont's way of sticking it to him. At some point Xander knew he would have to learn how to keep his mouth shut. It was that last comment, calling the detective "officer," that cost him his weapon.

They walked out to the curb. Xander found their location on his phone. The police station was on Avenue Mozart in the sixteenth arrondissement—which meant nothing to either Jack or Xander.

"I'm assuming you don't have a car," Xander asked Jack.

"I don't, but while I was bailin' you out in there, I had him go get one."

Jack nodded his cowboy hat toward the street where a navy-blue Mercedes sedan squealed to a stop in front of them.

"The son of a bitch wouldn't take no for an answer. Said you promised him a job or somethin'. You shoulda seen his face when I said we was turning the plane for Paris and that you needed our help."

The Mercedes door opened, and a man sprang out of the door, hair wild, grinning from ear to ear.

"Viktor." His name slipped out of Xander's half-smile.

Viktor was the crazy bastard who had come and picked up Xander in his daddy's helicopter, in the middle of the mountains of Ukraine. He was completely off his rocker, but he saved Xander's life. That is something you never forget. His goofball personality wasn't easy to get out of your head either.

"Boss," Viktor said; his Russian accent was as thick as ever. "Can't you stay out of trouble? For even little while?" His smile grew even larger.

Xander began to walk the thirty feet to the car. "If I did, what the hell would you do with yourself? Start a new Call of Duty clan on Xbox?"

They hugged.

"Viktor doesn't need Call of Duty, or Xbox. Viktor work for Xander King now. Real-life Xbox soldier."

Jack opened the back passenger-side door of the Mercedes. "You all speakin' some kinda foreign language? If so, stop it, I'm gettin' a headache."

"Cowboy is old school, boss," Viktor laughed. "He is not cool like you and Viktor."

Xander smiled. "Yeah, Viktor, because only cool people speak in third person."

Jack laughed and slid himself inside the car.

Viktor didn't get it. Xander didn't have time to explain. Viktor walked back to the driver's side and Xander got in beside him.

Jack spoke up from the backseat just as Xander was getting ready to speak. "Save your speech, Xander. We know you're glad to see us, but let's not waste time on all that. Let's go get your damsel out of distress."

Xander's gut rolled, first from the thought of Natalie still being held captive and second from immense gratitude for people he barely knew laying their lives on the line to help him and Natalie. He did as Jack asked and saved the speech. He opened his phone with the directions to the coordinates from Melanie and showed the map to Viktor.

"Get us here"—he pointed to the green pin on the electronic map—"as fast as you can."

Viktor threw the Mercedes into drive and fishtailed sideways out into the street. The sun was on its way down, and Xander was determined that whoever was behind the killing of King's Ransom and the kidnapping of Natalie was on their way down as well.

A Thread of Hope

Around the time that Jack was busy bailing Xander out of jail, Natalie's darkness was once again interrupted. Three men in black ski masks entered the room and turned on the hanging yellow light. Once again, she was surrounded by death. She did her best not to look at the photos on the walls as the three men surrounded her. This time, there was no man in a turban. She could tell they weren't there to take pictures either. They hoisted her up, two of the men held her up under each armpit, and they pushed her forward toward the door. The man in front of her turned to have a look, then stopped immediately. He shouted something in French, and the next thing Natalie knew, everything was dark again. They covered her head with some sort of knit sack and once again moved her forward out of the room. She had no idea where they were taking her, but still her mind searched for clues. Being an actress as well as an avid movie fan, her mind drifted as the air now felt slightly cooler. She couldn't see through the sack, but she could tell the light was brighter. As she noticed a cool, smooth material under her feet, she thought of the movie *Taken 2*. She remembered the scene where Liam Neeson's character was kidnapped and how he used the sounds, smells, and other triggers to help him tell where he was. The only problem for Natalie was that she wasn't Liam Neeson, and there was no movie magic to be had. The best she could do was imagine that it was marble under her feet, and once they took her outside, she could tell it had been raining. Some detective she was.

Other than the area directly around her hotel, she knew nothing of Paris. So it didn't help her to hear people bustling and dogs barking. That didn't clue her in on what part of Paris she was in. She may as well have been back in California. All except for the cool temperature and the rain, that is. No, there wasn't anything she could do that was going to help her in this situation. She would just have to hope that whatever reason they were taking her for, they would get what they wanted and then let her go.

She heard a car door open, then the two men forced her into a vehicle and slammed the door behind her. The upholstery on the seat was cloth and smelled heavily of smoke. No one said a word, but she heard two more doors close; then the vehicle started and was on its way. Somewhere. At least they hadn't stuffed her in the trunk, and at least they hadn't already killed her. She did find it odd that they would be driving her around in a car with a bag over her head. That would be sort of incriminating if she were easy to see. Then she figured it was probably a dark-windowed van. She did have to step up when she got in. Natalie knew she was worthless at trying to be a detective. Fear began to set in. Where could they possibly be taking her? What were they going to do to her when they got there? What did they want?

Not knowing any of the answers or the reason for any of this made her feel utterly helpless. Completely alone. She could feel the fear wrapping around her as the realization set in that this probably had nothing to do with money. If it did, they would have been trying to talk to her about it. Trying to find out whom to call at her bank or something. Anything. This wasn't about money. This was about those pictures on the wall in that room. This was about revenge. Which meant that this was about Xander.

It was at that moment when a small thread of hope began to wrap around the outside of that fear that was creeping up her spine. A man's voice, seemingly from the front of the van, interrupted her thoughts. "Boss . . . Yes, boss . . . Yes, we have her, and we're taking her there now."

A man in a black turban sat at a desk; two men sat opposite him—one French, one Middle Eastern. He finished up the phone call he was on. "Good. Make certain no one sees her. Sebastian will meet you there and explain how to proceed."

The man ended the call and addressed the Frenchman sitting in front of him. "Tell me that everything is ready."

The man sat up in his chair, cleared his throat, and eagerly explained. "Everything is ready, Akram. It is exactly how you wanted. The cameras are all set and everyone is in place."

"Perfect. I will be in touch. You can go now." Akram nodded toward the door.

The man left the room. Akram stood from his desk and went to the window that overlooked a garden. The light of day had faded, and only streetlights beyond the grass aided his visibility. He stroked his black scraggly goatee as he turned back to the Middle Eastern man.

"Now that I have everything in place, Hanan, we must make certain that there will be an audience."

"Yes, Akram, my men have hacked the social media accounts of Natalie Rockwell. When the video feeds go live, it will quickly spread across the Internet. We have e-mails with links to the live feed prepared for all of the news outlets as well."

"And if they are able to cut the feeds on the social media sites?" Akram asked.

"By the time they do this, *if* they do this, it will be too late. All of the media will have picked it up, and it will be on every news station across the web and traditional media. However, as a precaution, once the link is clicked, every feed will have a URL that will automatically open on computers and phones and take them to our site, which is secured beyond a twenty-four-hour hackable measure. Everyone will see exactly what you want them to see. What happens after that is up to you, sir."

"Excellent. And where is Xander?"

Hanan squirmed a bit in his seat. "I didn't want to tell you this, but he was arrested at the warehouse."

"Arrested? What? This means nothing without him!" Akram came away from the window and stalked right up to where Hanan was seated. Madness swirled in his dark eyes.

Hanan leaned back in fear of the man and held up his hands. "It's all right! He's out!"

"Out of jail? But how?" Akram softened a bit.

"I don't know, but I have a man tailing him. He is on his way to the stadium now, just as you wanted. Everything is okay. That is why I didn't tell you!"

Akram grunted in frustration as he kicked up on the bottom of Hanan's seat, sending him crashing onto his back against the hard floor. Akram then rounded the toppled chair and kicked Hanan in the jaw. The force of the blow severely jarred him, and before he could turn to look up at the fierce Akram above him, he spat a string of blood onto the floor.

Akram backed away. "You will not underestimate Xander King as my brother did. He has the world's most powerful nation behind him."

Hanan sat up, spit more blood on the floor beside him, and wiped his mouth on his sleeve. He looked into his boss's eyes, and with all the conviction he could muster he told Akram what he wanted to hear.

"We will not underestimate him. And thanks to you, Akram Khatib, America will not continue to be the most powerful nation for long."

Funny Business

The jet carrying Sam, Kyle, Sarah, and Zhanna began to descend from its 35,000-feet cruising altitude, beginning its final approach into Paris. For the past thirty minutes of the flight, all four of them had been diligently reading a file that was passed along by Marvin. Marvin called Kyle back almost immediately after he had received Kyle's message telling him of Xander's troubles, and asking what Marv thought about who could be behind the kidnapping. The first name that popped into Marv's head after he read that Kyle thought it was revenge was Akram Khatib. There was little doubt in Marv's mind that the one behind this was the little brother of Sanharib Khatib. It was one of the biggest fears Marv had when he originally told Sean Thompson that Sanharib could be Xander's parents' killer. Marv had spent months in Syria gathering intel on Sanharib's operation. One of the main things he had learned was that

Sanharib was merely the face of the terrorist outfit. The public figure who put himself out there when claiming an act of terror. Much the way that Bin Laden had done before him. But Marv had seen on many occasions that in fact it was his little brother, Akram, who had actually been pulling the strings. Akram just wasn't old enough to have been involved with Xander's father, which is why Marv only mentioned Sanharib when telling Xander about him. As far as terrorists were concerned, Akram was the most evil of them all. He didn't just sit back and play the puppet master. He was deeply involved in everything; he actually loved getting his hands dirty. Sanharib raised his little brother Akram to be a killer. He had Akram trained in hand-to-hand combat, gunplay, and every other art of war since the time he was old enough to walk. Akram was notorious for being ruthless, killing many a man with just his bare hands. Just for the sport of it. All part of his relentless training.

Marv's first thought when he heard of the heroics that Xander and his team had pulled in Syria was of Akram. It had been told to him that Sanharib had been like a father to Akram. Marv had been meaning to have a talk with Xander about him, and the danger that could come in the form of retaliation. But with the madness of the past few weeks, he hadn't had a moment to bend Xander's ear. And he never would have dreamed that the retaliation would come so quickly.

After reading Kyle's message, he immediately pulled the file he had been building on Akram Khatib and sent it to him. He knew in his gut that this was who was behind all of the terror in Paris. And he had a sinking suspicion that there was something bigger in the works, and Natalie Rockwell and Xander might be nothing more than the icing on top of the terror-filled cake.

Kyle looked up from his iPad. "What do you think, Sam?"

"I think Marvin is right."

"This is really bad, isn't it?"

Sam made a "maybe not" face. "It is, but it is a huge help to know who is behind this. Even though we have no other information, at least Marvin is familiar with this man and his business. That may help us pick up on some details that otherwise would have been missed."

Kyle didn't respond. Sam could still see questions in his eyes. "But yes, as far as who this is? It's bad. Not only has he no regard for human life; according to Marv's file, he really has it out for the USA."

Zhanna leaned forward in her seat. "How this makes it worse? His hating your USA."

Sarah answered for Sam. "Because it means this could be more than just revenge on Xander for killing his brother. Sam, you think he will use this as an excuse to attack the United States as well, don't you?"

"Possibly. I'm afraid we might be walking into a plan that goes beyond Xander. In fact, I'm afraid this could all just be a distraction."

Kyle shrugged his shoulders. "This stuff must be over my head. I don't get it."

Sam said, "I think what Marv is worried about, and what I am now worrying about as well, is that if Akram Khatib is indeed behind this, we may be walking into something much worse than the kidnapping of a beloved movie star."

Kyle was catching on. "But what better distraction than to kidnap one of the most popular actresses in the world. He knew the media would go into a frenzy over this."

"Exactly," said Sarah. "And I think the very moment he

found out Xander was involved in what happened to Akram's brother in Syria, and he found out he was tied to Natalie Rockwell, a light bulb went on for a way to kill two birds with one stone."

"Avenge his brother by killing Xander, and killing a beloved American in Natalie?" said Kyle.

Sam answered this time. "No Kyle, avenging his brother by killing Xander, while the spectacle of kidnapping Natalie merely serves as a distraction for a much larger attack."

Kyle was still confused. "But what would make you think that? Nothing in Marv's file says anything about planning something against the US."

Zhanna fielded this one. "But Kyle, it *is* in there. It is just, how you say . . . between the lines."

"That's right, Zhanna," Sam agreed. "Kyle, men like Akram Khatib are always planning something against their enemies. And the United States is a terrorist's perpetual enemy. From the looks of our situation, it seems as though the perfect storm has gathered here in Paris."

Kyle was frustrated. "Well, I'll let the CIA and the US government worry about all that shit. The only thing I care about is helping Xander get Natalie out of here alive."

"That's what we all want, Kyle," said Sam. "What we are trying to say is that to find her, we might have to figure out what else Akram is planning. I know it seems that we are jumping the gun, and maybe we are, but all of us have been dealing with people like Akram for a long time. We understand the way they think. Right, girls?"

Zhanna and Sarah nodded.

Kyle shook his head. "I don't like this, Sam. This is way over our heads."

"Kyle," Sam said, resting her hand on Kyle's arm, "you couldn't be more wrong. This is precisely what we have all been trained to do." Sam glanced at Sarah and Zhanna. "And now so have you. Xander has been preparing you for this for years now. Against my many protests, I assure you. But you were there with me in Syria. You are ready for this too."

Kyle shuddered. "You think this will be like that?"

"I'm not going to lie, this could be worse. This will require us to use much more than just our combat skills. This will require brains as well."

Kyle's head dropped and he stared at the floor for a moment.

"Well, Sam, then how the hell are you going to be any help?" A smile slowly grew across his face.

"You and Xander, always trying to be the comedians."

The four of them broke the tension with a much-needed laugh. It would be the last laugh any of them would share for a while.

Strap In

Darkness had officially settled over Paris. As Viktor weaved in and out of traffic on the A1, on their way to the destination that Melanie had insisted Xander travel to, Xander's head was buried in his phone. He read headline after headline of all the major news stations, and all of the headlines were about the same topic: the kidnapping of Natalie Rockwell. Reality of just how bad the situation had become washed over Xander as he continued to read. There were still no leads, no new updates from the police, and what was far worse than that, Xander was flying blind. For all he knew he was leading Viktor and Jack to join him in death. That was more likely than not. From the very beginning of this, he should have pulled Sam in with him. He would be much further along than he is now. Natalie would have a much better chance at surviving, and he would have a much better idea what he was driving into. As the anger toward himself began to boil over, Viktor brought him back to the task at hand.

"Boss, Viktor is no expert, but same car has been following us since we left police station."

Xander turned and looked past Jack through the rear window. There were several cars, and without watching for a while, he couldn't determine if Viktor was right.

"Doesn't matter. They already know where we are going. I suspect there will be more waiting when we get there."

Jack spoke up from the backseat. "What's the plan, son? We're flyin' blind here."

"You two stay in the car while I go and check out the situation. No sense in all of us getting ambushed."

"No sense in one of us either. You go, I go," said Jack.

"Viktor not wait in car. Have to take piss anyway."

Jack shook his head in the backseat. "You see what I've been dealin' with, Xander?"

Xander turned and gave a quick smile. Then he gave Viktor a pat on the shoulder.

Viktor gave a goofy smile, then pointed for Xander to look ahead. "This is it, boss."

"You gotta be shittin' me," Jack said as he followed Viktor's finger.

In front of them was a massive stadium. The Stade de France. The premier soccer stadium in Paris. As they pulled into the large empty parking lot, the stadium towered above them. What looked like a ring from Saturn sat atop the concrete structure. There were no lights on from the outside, but something was glowing from within. As Viktor pulled the Mercedes sedan as close as he could get, Xander noticed there was a spot in the gate that had been left ajar.

"Looks like we're in the right place."

"I don't like this, Xander," Jack said, staring at the opened gate.

"I don't like any of this, Jack. But what did you expect? A welcoming committee with catered food and an open bar?"

Jack didn't answer. Viktor put the car in park but left the car running and the lights on after Xander suggested to do so. The three of them got out of the car and walked around to the front. Jack handed Xander a spare pistol.

"I never leave home without a backup."

Xander thanked him, but his mind was on the stadium. They walked through the open gate and stared for a moment at the Coca-Cola billboards that surrounded the entrance to a tunnel that undoubtedly led out to the playing field. All the smiling faces in the ads made Xander long for all of this to be over. But he quickly shrugged off the thought and moved on.

"You just gonna walk right in?" Jack asked. "Shouldn't we at least split up, take a different route? That way we aren't just sittin' ducks?"

There was a set of stairs that led up over the tunnel that Xander was eyeing. He pointed there. "Jack, you and Viktor go up that way and then split off to the right and left. If you see anything, just give a shout. We won't have any problems hearing each other."

"What if it's trap, boss?" asked Viktor.

"Then the two of you get the hell out of there and do whatever it takes to find Natalie." Xander turned to Jack. "If something happens to her, you know it will be far worse for me than if I don't make it."

"I know, son, but ain't nothin' gonna happen to you. I figure this is just another distraction. Otherwise they woulda just tried to kill ya at that warehouse. There is somethin' they want you to see. I'm betting that's what that glow is inside there. I just hope it ain't the worst."

Jack didn't need to elaborate. Xander knew exactly what he meant. If whoever was behind all of this really wanted to hurt Xander, showing something happening to Natalie would be the way to do it. Xander's heart sank. He could feel it in his bones that something terrible was about to happen.

The van rolled to a stop and Natalie's heart pounded in her chest. They had finally made it to wherever they were going, but it was all the same to her: black. She heard two doors open and close, and then the door beside her opened. She didn't know if the smell was that strong or if it was because her senses were heightened, but the scent of water hit her immediately. She felt hands grab both of her arms, and they pulled her from the vehicle. The smell lingered and soon was accompanied but a musty and muddy scent. It only took a couple of steps before she also heard the lapping of water against something solid. Fear jumped through Natalie's nervous system. Water? Did they mean they were about to drown her? Torture her? She didn't really know what waterboarding was, but she knew it included water. Is that what they were going to do to her?

Natalie stiffened her legs and dug in her heels. Her screams were muffled by the gag in her mouth, but that didn't stop her from trying. It was more instinct really. She had no other choice but to fight this. If they were going to kill her, they weren't going to have an easy time of it. It was then that she began to thrash violently with all that she had. Digging her heels, wiggling her arms, bucking with her lower back. But the hands wrapped around her arms only tightened their grip, and before she knew it, her feet were swept off the ground and she was being carried to what she was sure was her demise. That didn't stop her from writhing around, but it did release another level of panic. There was absolutely nothing she could do. The helplessness she was feeling was all-encompassing. Who were these people? What were they going to do to her?

"This will only be more painful than it needs to be if you do not cooperate."

It was the man in front of her. His accent was French and his tone was even. She fought against the men holding her as they set her back down on her feet. She kicked out in front of her and she connected with something. She got one of them! She kicked again and missed, then felt something hit her head. She was dazed for a moment. Purple bursts of light exploded in front of her eyes. She almost passed out. She longed for the escape. Instead, the sack was jerked off of her head and after a few blinks to clarify, lamplights overhead shined down over a long dinner cruise boat sitting in what she immediately figured was the river Seine. A tall man stepped in front of her view and pulled the gag from her mouth. His head was bald, and he was wearing a dark T-shirt and dark pants. His body was thick; he looked like a soldier.

"Are you finished?" he asked her.

Frantic, Natalie answered, "Who are you? What do you want from me? Money? I can get you money!"

"This is not about money, I am afraid. This is much more important."

The man motioned for his men to follow him toward the

71

boat.

"Where are you taking me? Just tell me what you want!"

The man didn't answer. She tried a couple more times to get his attention as they forced her over a ramp onto the boat. Her attempts to get some answers were only met with silence. They continued to push her through a doorway, and at first all she could see was an empty dining hall. There was a long hardwood floor in the large rectangular room with darkened windows on both sides. Then her eyes found the back wall. To tell you that fear invaded her would be a devastating understatement. It was something she'd never felt before. A feeling that stole her breath entirely and wobbled her knees as it shook her being. A spotlight shined over that back wall, which held a device that could not be mistaken, even though she'd never seen anything like it. Not in real life and not on any movie set either. In front of her were two large steel pieces that were wide at their left and right beginning, and a few feet later they gradually shrank to a needle-sharp point at their tips. In the three-foot gap between the two needle points were what looked like leather straps. They were in the position where someone's limbs would be. A strap clearly for a head, two for arms, and two for legs. At the fat ends of the two spear-like steel needles were what looked like the gears to a machine. The closer they forced her toward the contraption, the bigger the needle points became. The tips looked all the more sharp, and they were thick, unbreakable.

"What are you doing?" Natalie began to panic. "Please, let me go! I can pay you!" Once again she began to struggle against their grip.

"Strip her to her underwear, then strap her in."

The men immediately began to rip away at her pajamas.

"No! Please! I've done nothing to you! PLEASE!"

She was down to her white cotton bra and panties now. As she began to further plead, the man stepped in and replaced the gag inside her mouth. She squealed in fear as they strapped down her arms. She squealed in terror as they strapped down her legs. And tears streaked down her horrified face as the men strapped her head against the wall at her forehead. She was now suspended on the wall. Her left and right arms straight out to the sides, her legs spread out below her. She was shaped like a star on the wall. Just the way Akram Khatib had intended.

As Natalie continued a futile struggle against her restraints, the bald soldier pulled out a phone and dialed a number.

"It is done."

Looking for Trouble

"Ugh! I can't stand being the President's daughter sometimes!" Adeline Williams began to throw a mini tantrum in the middle of her suite at the Four Seasons Hotel George V, Paris.

Though Adeline had just turned twenty-one, when it came to being locked down by her travel entourage of Secret Service, she reacted more like a twelve-year-old. Her friend Karol sat silently on the bed while the fit continued.

"They can't *make* us stay in here. We are in Paris, for God's sake. They can't keep us holed up in this room! I don't care what is going on out there!"

Karol replied, "Don't you think it's best, though, Addie? I mean, if they kidnapped Natalie Rockwell, don't you think the President of the United States of America's daughter might not be too far off their radar?"

Karol attempted to be the voice of reason during these times when Adeline reverted back to her teenage ways. Karol had always been the more responsible of the two. Adeline had always been the one trying to test the boundaries. It was clear she even enjoyed driving her mother and father crazy. Part of that side of her was fun for Karol. There certainly was never a dull moment. She just didn't like it when Adeline didn't know when to quit.

"Oh please, Karol. No one knows I'm here. Not even the press. And what with all the hoopla surrounding Natalie Rockwell's kidnapping, no one would find out either. That's the entire reason we took Uncle Terry's plane to get here. So no one would know."

Adeline walked over to the bed and took a seat beside her friend.

"Karol, we are in Paris! Don't you want to go explore? Go dancing? If I wanted to sit in some tacky, overdone room I would have just stayed at the White House." There was pleading in Adeline's deep brown eyes. She tucked her blonde hair behind her ear and cocked her head to the side waiting for Karol to answer.

Karol let out a sigh. "Of course I want to do all of those things. But I don't want to get into trouble, Adeline. Not again. The only way I'll go is if you get Jeremy to escort us."

Adeline rolled her eyes and once again began to pace the room. "You know he isn't going to let us. He has to do what Daddy says. He's an ex-marine or something. They never go against orders."

Karol grabbed the remote and flipped on the television. "Then let's just order some room service and a movie."

Adeline stopped pacing for a moment. A look of deep thought held tight to her face. Then she went over to the closet, pulled out two dresses, and handed one of them to Karol. As soon as Karol took it, Adeline began to undress.

Karol held the dress with a look of confusion. "What the hell are you doing, Addie?"

Adeline just smiled and slipped her tight black dress over her head, then pulled it down as she shimmied it over her hips. "Go on, put yours on."

"I don't like this. What are you up to?"

"Would you just stop being a prude and get dressed? We are not just going to sit in this hotel room and rot."

Before Karol could ask how she planned on ditching Jeremy, their Secret Service guard, Adeline walked around the corner to the bathroom, then walked back out with her robe on. Not an ounce of her little black dress was showing. The rotten look on her face said everything.

"Get dressed, Karol. Tonight is going to be a blast!"

Karol reluctantly began to change into her going-out attire. She didn't like one bit where this was headed. But when Adeline Williams made up her mind that she was going to do something, no one could stop her. Not even the President's best men.

Adeline cleared her throat as she took out a bottle of Visine and used the eyedrops to smear her mascara ever so slightly.

"How do I look?"

Karol frowned. "Like you're about to get us both in big trouble."

Adeline waved her off and started for the hotel room door. She pulled the robe tight around her neck and put on her most worried look. She peeked through the peephole, and sure enough, her shadow, Jeremy Watson, was standing guard. For a moment a feeling of guilt washed over her. She liked Jeremy. He had been the first of her personal guards who treated her like a woman instead of a child. She didn't want him to get into trouble for what she was about to do, but she knew if things went the way she was planning, he and everyone else would be none the wiser. With that thought washing away her guilt, she removed the chain and cracked open the door.

"Jeremy?" Adeline made sure to throw a little extra tremble into her voice.

Jeremy turned toward her with a smile, but it quickly faded when he saw Adeline had been crying.

"Addie? What's wrong?"

She motioned for him to step inside. He obliged.

"Is Travis out there?" she asked, referring to the second man in her security detail.

"No, he's out front, why? What's wrong?"

"It's just really embarrassing and I don't want him to know. I don't want you to know either, but I really don't have a choice because I can't just walk and go get what I need myself like a normal person." Adeline made sure she sounded like she was rambling. What Jeremy couldn't see was that just around the corner, Karol was zipping up her little blue dress, rolling her eyes as she listened to her friend.

"Calm down, Adeline. What's wrong?" Jeremy looked concerned and confused.

Adeline turned away shaking her head. Then she waved him away. "Never mind, Jeremy. I shouldn't have called you in here. It's too embarrassing. I'll figure something out. Can you just leave us alone?" She buried her hands in her head as she turned away from him. She also managed to give Karol a wink

77

without Jeremy seeing. Karol knew exactly what Adeline was doing. This wasn't the first person she'd seen Adeline run this con on. It worked pretty much every time. Men didn't like the subject Addie was about to bring up, so they just instinctively did whatever it took to make it go away. Karol couldn't help but return Addie's wink with a smile and a shake of the head.

Jeremy reached out and put his hand on Adeline's shoulder. Adeline turned into him and wrapped her arms around him, burying her face against the lapel of his black sport coat. She let out a couple of muffled sobs and then spoke into his chest.

"Oh God, listen to me, I'm a mess! You promise you won't tell anyone about this? It's so embarrassing! I'm acting like a little girl!"

She was laying it on thick.

Jeremy gave her shoulder a squeeze. "It's okay, tell me what happened and we'll fix it. No problem."

Adeline pulled back; puddles of tears formed at the base of her eyelids. "I had an accident."

Jeremy clearly didn't have any sisters, because he had no idea what that meant. "Are you hurt?"

"Hurt?" Adeline said, confused. "No, an acc-i-dent." With each syllable she nodded her head toward the lower part of her robe.

Jeremy followed her nod; the gears turned in his head and then his eyes shot back up to hers. "Oh, shit. Uh. So, what does that mean?"

Really?

"Jeremy, I don't have any tampons, and neither does Karol. I wasn't supposed to start for a few more days, so I am completely unprepared."

Jeremy instinctively backed up a step. Not for any other

reason than he just got really uncomfortable. The exact reaction Adeline had hoped for.

"Uh, okay. I'll just radio down to Travis to bring some up."

"What? No!" Adeline gave her best horrified expression.

"O-okay, then just call room service, they'll bring some up."

"Do you have any idea what it is like to be a woman and have this happen to you? It's mortifying, Jeremy! It's mortifying enough to have to have this conversation with you, there is no way I would have it with a stranger!"

"Okay, well, what do you want me to do?"

"Go get me some tampons and some Advil from the sundry! Please!"

"Addie, you know I can't leave my post. There's no way—"

"You can't be serious!" Adeline forced her face to scrunch into a sob. "You aren't going to help me? Oh my God. I can't believe my life. This is ridiculous!" She paused for a moment to take a shuddering breath. "Fine! I'll just go myself, blood dripping down my fucking legs! I bet that will get the press off the kidnapping. I can just see it now, 'President Williams' Daughter Bloody in Paris'!" She turned away again and gave her best fake cry.

Jeremy looked up at the ceiling, checked his watch, then let out a deep sigh. "Fine. Don't answer your phone, the door, or anything else. I'll be back in five minutes. You hear me, Adeline?"

Adeline threw her arms around him and began thanking him. As she did so, she noticed in the mirror fastened to the door that the bottom of her robe had slid up and she could see her black dress. She quickly let go and wrapped the robe back

79

around her.

Jeremy said, "Okay. I mean it, do not answer this door."

He hadn't seen the dress.

"Okay, I promise. Thank you so much, Jeremy. You are a lifesaver!"

Jeremy started out the door and then turned back. Adeline interrupted him just as he raised his finger and opened his mouth. "I know! Answer for no one!"

As soon as he shut the door, Adeline threw off her robe and started jumping up and down. "Like a charm!"

"We are so dead." Karol took her and Adeline's shoes from the closet and handed Adeline her pair of black pumps.

"No." Adeline smiled. "We are so about to have the time of our lives!"

With that, Karol knew that Adeline wasn't a bit worried about the consequences, so it wasn't even worth broaching the subject. The two of them grabbed their clutches and snuck their way down the hallway and eventually out the back of the hotel.

The two of them were full of laughter and looking for trouble.

Showtime

Jack and Viktor did as Xander asked and left him at the entrance and went up the stairs to the second level. Xander wasn't sure what they would find inside the stadium. A lot of times the very worst thing you can do is speculate. If they were walking into a trap, it wasn't one that any of them would be able to walk away from. There were simply too many dark spaces for men to hide. But something inside Xander knew that they weren't in danger here. At least not physically. He was sure the glow inside was the jumbotron. If they even had jumbotrons in soccer stadiums in Paris. That wouldn't be something Xander would know. He was a fan of the NFL, UFC, NBA and any other American sport acronym that you could think of. But not soccer, or futbol, rather. One thing he knew for certain, however, was that whatever he was about to see, it wasn't going to be pleasant. And though it wasn't going to have anything to do with soccer, he knew it most likely would be the beginning of a game. A game of life and death that he had grown very tired of playing with other people's lives.

He had given Jack and Viktor time enough to find a good spot to perch. He steeled his nerves and stepped forward into the tunnel. The air was cool and damp, and his sneakers squeaked and echoed as he walked. The closer he came to the end of the tunnel, the brighter whatever was shining inside the stadium became. Dread slowed his pace. The best that he could hope for was to see anything other than Natalie dead. As the concrete walkway beneath his feet turned into a soft grass, he found that indeed the light they had seen was a gigantic screen glowing white. Like a flashlight in a tent, it illuminated the stadium, which was filled with row after row of empty seats.

There were no signs of anyone in the stadium. If Jack and Victor were up on the second level, they too were hidden. Without instruction of any kind, Xander did the only thing he thought to do and walked out to the middle of the field.

"Okay!" Xander's shout echoed throughout the stadium, reverberating his own word back to him. "I'm here! You got what you wanted!"

He let his voice finish its echo before turning to face the massive screen. The bright white light was almost enough to blind him. No one spoke back to him, and as he stood there in silence, he could hear his heart thudding against his chest. Instinctively he pulled his pistol. The cool steel felt good in his hands. Almost like a security blanket. He took a deep breath, then let it out slowly. It was so quiet in that stadium that he almost jumped out of his skin when the giant screen in front of him came to life and the roar of a crowd filled the entire stadium. Not a live crowd, but a crowd cheering through the speaker system.

The source of the crowd noise flashed onto the screen in front of him. He recognized the venue immediately: Churchill

Downs. The screen was replaying a video of that year's Kentucky Derby coverage. Xander knew it because there on the screen was a big black colt wearing the number six on his side.

King's Ransom.

Xander's stomach turned, and he felt hot saliva rush into his mouth through his jowls. The starting gate opened, and horses burst through and began racing down the track. For two minutes, Xander watched. He didn't know it, but his mouth was slacked open slightly as he watched his beloved racehorse come from behind and win the big race. This was the first time he had seen the race since watching it live. His reaction this time was much different than when he first watched. There was no celebrating this time. The camera then showed Xander, Natalie, Kyle, and Annie celebrating the win in the owner's box. The camera zoomed in on Natalie receiving a celebratory kiss from Xander; then immediately the screen went black. He was once again plunged into darkness, and the silence was deafening in the wake of the noise of the crowd. A myriad of emotions overwhelmed him. Then his stomach turned again.

Now on the screen was a shaky video of someone walking in the dark. He recognized where this video was taking place as well, because it was his own backyard. The person walking with the camera was approaching his own barn. In that moment he cursed himself for not having security posted outside. He knew what was coming next as the sound of horses whinnying and blowing air through their mouths reached his ears from the speakers. When he saw hands open the barn, he turned his back on the screen. There was no way he was going to watch them murder his horse. His breath was coming fast and thoughts were racing through his head as he heard a stall door open. As the footage continued behind him, Xander continued to beat himself up. Why didn't he have security by the stalls? Why didn't he have a better lock on the barn? Why hadn't he installed an alarm? His entire adult life he had been keeping strangers safe, but it never occurred to him to protect his own prized animals? Even after his home was invaded, he had been too distracted to put stronger security measures in place. It was a mistake that he would never forgive himself for. He put his hands over his ears, desperately trying to drown out the sounds that were projecting from the stadium's speakers. Tears came to his eyes. Even though he didn't watch them do it, he couldn't keep the visions of them killing Ransom from playing in his mind. His stomach rolled again, and he lost it on the ground in the middle of the field. The taste of vomit lingered on his lips as he wiped his mouth with the sleeve of his hooded sweatshirt. When he didn't hear any more sounds, he slowly turned his eyes toward the screen. The camera had stopped on the words that were written in blood on the wall of Ransom's stall.

Natalie Rockwell.

Then the screen went black. He could have spent years trying to prepare himself for what he saw next, but it wouldn't have helped. All the battles he had fought in the military, all the violent missions he had carried out, and all the horrible things his eyes had seen in war—all paled in comparison to the image that held his eyes at that moment. The massive screen switched into a split screen, the same image on each side, except the right side was zoomed in.

Zoomed in on Natalie Rockwell's face.

The speakers in the stadium popped, and then he could hear her sobbing, moaning, trying to cry out, but it was all muffled. On the left side of the split screen, a camera showed an empty room where on the far wall Natalie was strapped with her limbs sprawled into the shape of a star. He glanced back over the right of the split screen, and the zoomed camera showed tears running down her face and a gag fixed in her mouth. A brown leather strap was wrapped around her forehead, holding her head in place.

Xander was mortified.

He looked back to the left side of the screen and saw large gears on both sides of two huge steel rods with sharp points, each about a foot away from Natalie's ears.

"Hello, Xander," a man's voice boomed over the speakers of the stadium. The accent was clearly Middle Eastern. "So nice of you to join me."

Xander didn't say a word. He just stood, on wobbly legs, staring at Natalie as she writhed around inside the straps of the torture device. He couldn't imagine the fear she must be feeling. The hopelessness.

"I imagine you probably don't like what you see in front of you, do you, Xander? I wonder if the millions who will be watching all around the world will like it? I wonder what they will think seeing their beloved star in such distress? They are signing on to watch by the thousands as we speak. I imagine the number in the next four hours will grow well into the millions. But what will they find before it's all over? That, Xander, is entirely up to you."

Xander instinctively began walking toward the screen. It was then that the smaller screens attached to the concrete along the rail of the upper deck all around the stadium, spaced about thirty feet apart, came to life, each screen displaying a different image. Xander stopped walking and spun around slowly, seeing every single screen. Each screen showed a different picture, but they all shared one similarity: a dead man's body, laying on his back, dead eyes staring soullessly into the camera. All Middle Eastern men, wearing similar clothes, all covered in blood.

"The viewers will also see this, Xander. Your handiwork in my home country of Syria, outside my brother's home."

Xander's stomach dropped. Just as the image of Sanharib Khatib popped into his head, the real image of him dead filled every single one of the smaller screens around the stadium.

"They will see my brother. Dead at the hands of their real-life G.I. Joe. Americans and the rest of the world will see me give you what you didn't have the courtesy of giving me. A chance. A chance to save the one that you love. They will see that you are the real monster, and they will see the compassion that I have before I take her away from you."

Xander looked back to the screen that showed Natalie. A desperate and lonely ache crawled all through his body.

"But they *will* see her die. America must learn that there are consequences for their actions. The world will no longer stand by and let your tyranny run rampant in our cities and our countries. And when you don't make it to your precious Natalie in time, they will see that the power in the world has shifted, because the encore to that performance will hit even closer to home for your powerful America."

Xander had no idea what that meant, but he knew that terrorists weren't all that creative. He knew in that moment that he had been set up as a distraction for a larger plan. He hoped that this terrorist, apparently Sanharib Khatib's brother, was telling the truth about the broadcast. He hoped his government was watching and that they were immediately taking the steps to try to find out what else this monster was planning. Because Xander knew he would have nothing to do with that. If Khatib made the mistake of giving him a chance to save Natalie, he was going to use it, and he was going to save her. That much he knew for certain.

The man's voice continued. "You have four hours. I had planned on giving you six hours. But that was before you went against my wishes and decided not to come here alone as you were told. Consequences. Your actions have consequences."

Xander immediately set a timer on his Apple watch.

"I wish you no luck. I wish only that you find her dead, the way I found my brother. Then you will know only a small portion of the pain of losing a brother. But you had better hurry, before all hope of saving her washes away."

Xander stood in the middle of the field, his eyes watching Natalie suffer. He knew all too well what it was like to lose loved ones. No one knew the lasting hurt of such tragedy better than himself. And he wasn't about to feel it again.

Not tonight.

Not Natalie.

As soon as that thought rolled through his mind, the sound of a machine coming to life filled the loud speakers. Xander watched in horror as the gears on both sides of the giant steel spears began to turn. His heart sank as he took in the fear on Natalie's face as she watched the massive spears begin their slow and relentless motion toward her head. Her eyes were wide, her muscles taut, as she struggled against the restraints. Squeals of terror harmonized with the mechanical hum of the slowly grinding gears.

He heard the man's voice bellow out once more over the horrifying sounds of machine and Natalie's screams. "Four hours."

Anything Is Possible

Sam, Kyle, Sarah, and Zhanna sat in silence, staring in horror at the television fixed to the back wall of the jet. Just as they had touched down in Paris, they received a message from Marvin that something big was going on. He had received an official e-mail from director of the CIA, Mary Hartsfield, with a link embedded inside it. Sam paired her phone to the television and opened the link. For five minutes they sat in silence, watching the very same video that Xander had just endured at the stadium. The commentary from Akram Khatib and all. Now that it was over, every last one of them struggled to find words. As the machine turned the gears and the gears turned the spears aimed at poor Natalie's head, all of them were frozen in their seats.

"Holy shit," Kyle said, finally breaking the silence.

"Holy shit," Sarah agreed.

While the rest of them sat motionless in shock, Sam stayed

silent for a different reason. Her wheels were already turning. She listened intently to every single word Akram said. She listened for inflections placed on different words, and tried to find emotion in words that might lead to some sort of clue. She played it back in her head, looking for anything that may be of use. Akram Khatib was the brother of Sanharib. Sam had choked the life right out of the son of a bitch just a couple of weeks ago. No clues there. Akram went on to talk about showing compassion, about giving Xander a chance to save Natalie. Clearly, he wanted Americans to see Xander as the bad guy. To think that he was the reason Natalie was in this mess. Not likely anyone would fall for that, but he was giving conspiracy theorists something to grab on to. The only thing that Akram said that didn't mesh with the rest of his speech was . . .

"Washes away," Sam said out loud. She didn't mean it for anyone to hear.

"What was that, Sam?" Kyle asked.

"Washes away," she repeated. She took out her phone and scrolled to Marvin in her contact list.

"Washes away?" Sarah asked. "You think it could mean something?"

Sam looked up from her phone. "It just strikes me as an odd thing to say—'before all hope of saving her washes away.' Why would hope *wash* away unless it has something to do with water?" Sam finished her thought, not expecting an answer, then pressed call on Marv's contact.

Marv answered, "I heard it too," instead of hello.

Sam's next thought was of Xander saying how smart he thought Marvin to be. He'd caught the word "washes" in Akram's speech as well. They were on the same page. "I need you to check all security cameras surrounding the River Seine."

"Already have my team on it. How's Xander?"

"That is my next call. Let me know the moment you find anything."

"Will do. I have an SUV at the airport to pick you up. I had one of our local operatives stock a bag with toys that you'll find useful, along with Xander's standard go bag. I spoke with Director Hartsfield, you have the full cooperation of the CIA."

"Thank you, Marv. As soon as you have anything—"

"I know, I'll call you."

Xander dropped to his knees and took in a long cool breath of air. His chest was tight and his heart was heavy. He couldn't look up at that screen any longer. Watching Natalie strapped to that wall was literally breaking his heart. Usually, in times like this, he was able to channel the hurt and the fear into anger. An anger that usually fueled him to do some extraordinary things. At the moment, that ability escaped him. Maybe it was the sight of Natalie. Maybe it was the lack of having any idea where she might be.

Xander looked up, averting his eyes from the screen, and searched the stands for Jack and Viktor.

"Jack! Viktor!"

It was all he could do to shout their names. He had a new feeling, something he had never felt before, and whatever it was stole his ability to think straight. After a moment of hearing his own voice echo back to him, he forced himself to his feet. Even that was a struggle. From his right, he could hear the two of them making their way to the middle of the field. He took another deep breath, but this new feeling wouldn't leave him.

Helplessness.

That's what it was. Never in his life had he felt it, and it was quickly draining the qualities that made him who he was. His fearlessness was being overshadowed, and like an elephant standing on his chest, this sense of helplessness wasn't allowing him to recover.

"What are we going to do?" he asked Jack.

Jack immediately recognized the helpless feeling in Xander's eyes. He remembered seeing it in the mirror after he found out that his daughter had cancer. Jack knew all too well how that feeling could affect a man. That didn't make it any easier to comfort Xander, because he too had no idea what to do. But he had to say something.

"If what that man said is true, and all the world has access to this video feed, that means the greatest minds in our intelligence community are already workin' on this, Xander. The brightest of the bulbs are figurin' out exactly how to find her as we speak."

Xander immediately thought of Marv. And then immediately he thought of Sam. If Sam were there with him, she would know what to do. Or at least where to start. He nodded to Jack. And for once, he was happy that Viktor knew to keep his mouth shut. He just needed to think. He looked back up at the screen, back up at Natalie.

Use it, Xander. She needs you, get a good look at her. She is there because of you. Now figure it out. Talk to me, Natalie . . . Where are you?

As he spoke those words to himself, he also began to replay Khatib's words back in his head. He closed his eyes, and he could hear the man taunting him. Jack turned to Viktor and ushered him back a few feet. He was giving Xander a moment to work it out. Xander continued to flow through the words he had just heard, and then something hit him. Like a left hook to the jaw, the words "before all hope of saving her *washes* away," smacked his brain inside his head. He reached for his phone and dialed Sam. He sent up a silent prayer that she was already in Paris.

Sam answered the phone. "Xander, where are you? Are you all right?"

"Sam! Where are you?"

Just the sound of her voice felt like a warm blanket being wrapped around him.

"We are just getting into our SUV. Tell me where you are and we will be on our way."

For the first time that day, Xander felt his first twinge of hope.

"We're at the Stade de France. Sam, please tell me you saw—"

"We saw it. I'm so sorry, Xander. But we are going to find her," Sam told him. She said it with such matter-of-factness that the helplessness he was feeling took another blow and felt like it just might be on its way out.

After a pause, they both said the same four words in exact unison.

"She's near the water."

They couldn't see each other, but a thin and hopeful smile grew across each of their faces.

Akram Khatib's game had seemed unwinnable just

moments ago. But now that the undefeated team had just pulled itself together, anything was possible.

Wanderlust

"Where to, ma'am?" The Middle Eastern cab driver asked.

Adeline wore a huge smile. "I was hoping you could help with that."

"I'll try. What do you want to do? Party?"

"Is it that obvious?"

"Maybe it's the way you're dressed," he said.

"Where do all the young people go to party here? Is there one place that stands out?"

The cab driver smiled at Adeline in the rearview mirror. "Wanderlust."

"Wanderlust?" Adeline smiled back at the cab driver, though she didn't really like the look he was giving her. "Wanderlust, that's so weird! That's the one I got an e-mail from earlier! Let's do it!"

She tried to sound excited, and she was, but the cab driver kind of creeped her out. Normally, Adeline would have called Uber. She had no idea how cabs even existed in 2016. But she also knew they were far better for what she and Karol were getting into. She could pay the cab driver cash. Uber didn't even accept payment outside of their phone app, and it tracked every move she made. Adeline thought she was being smart in using this mode of transportation. She thought she was outsmarting the Secret Service. Her miscalculations began when she left her cell phone powered on. The driver began to pull away.

"Wait! Wait just a second please, sir," Karol said to the cab driver. Then she just stared at Adeline expectantly.

"What?" Adeline asked.

"You think a cab will keep them from finding us?"

"Like, totally. I'll pay with cash. Come on, Karol. We've got to think like outlaws to keep them away from us long enough to have a little fun." Adeline was glowing with pride.

Karol rolled her eyes. "Then you'd better let me do the thinking. You've been far too sheltered under the presidential umbrella, girl."

Adeline looked confused. That look turned to shock when Karol snatched Adeline's phone from her hand, rolled down the cab window, and tossed both of their phones into a nearby garbage can.

"Karol! What the hell are you doing?"

"Addie, wake up. They can totally track us through our phones. As long as we have them, they will know exactly where we are."

Adeline's expression morphed into one of wonder. Karol watched as her friend's pretty face slowly revealed the understanding that her brain finally tapped into. "Good thing you have me around, girl."

"You are good, Karol. I'm super impressed!"

Poor Adeline knew she had always been more beauty than brains, but that had always been part of her charm. The cab pulled away from the trash can and on toward Wanderlust. After Adeline received the e-mail earlier, she googled top places to party in Paris, and the warehouse-style nightclub overlooking the river had been amongst the first to pop up. So she knew immediately which club the cab driver was talking about. She remembered the club touted itself as the largest nightclub in Paris. It had an outdoor music plaza, restaurants, several bars, and an indoor nightclub as well. The DJ advertised on the website was one Adeline hadn't heard of, but Karol said he was "totes amaze." The pictures made it look fun. They were all filled with people their age packed in by the hundreds. It seemed a perfect place for the two of them to blend in and get lost for a while. And maybe even meet a couple of hot guys.

As the cab sped through the crowded streets of Paris, Adeline turned to Karol, an excited smile on her face. "Okay, Vodka Red Bull's to get us started, and maybe a shot of tequila?"

"Tequila?" Karol made a sour face. "I can't do tequila. Not after my disaster at prom. I'll puke for sure."

"Okay, we'll do like a Washington Apple or something. You think bartenders in Paris know how to make shots like that? OMG, I wonder how many cute guys will be there? Let's not pay for a drink all night!"

Karol smiled. "When was the last time you paid for a drink at a bar?"

"Never! Being a girl is so awesome!"

The two of them shared a laugh. Their spirits were high. They were in a cool new city, headed toward a night out, and they had managed to ditch their supervision. They were riding high, and a feeling of invincibility washed over both of them.

"Wanderlust," said Adeline as she stared at the lights of the city that were shining just outside her window. "What a perfect name. I have a feeling tonight is going to be a wonderful adventure."

The feeling of freedom that came over the young woman was a feeling she didn't get all that often. Most twenty-one-year-olds went away to college and freely explored who they were and what they wanted to be. That exploration came in many forms. Of course, there were classes, books, and grades to worry about. But it was the time being free with your friends that she thought helped you most figure it all out. Though she was away at college, the President's daughter never went anywhere alone. And that, unfortunately, meant parties as well. She never cared about trying drugs, getting wasted all the time, and sleeping with a bunch of random guys. But the fact that she couldn't even entertain those notions made her feel as though she was missing out. She figured that was the draw of sneaking out. She didn't want to cause worry. She didn't want to cause trouble for her SS guard, Jeremy, but she had to go and let her hair down. She wanted to be able to tell a story or two of how she got out and made a few bad decisions when she was young. Isn't that how you learn?

She knew her thinking was silly. But a part of her believed that times like tonight were necessary. She decided that she would let "Future Adeline" worry about the consequences tomorrow. And there *would* be consequences. For now, however, she and Karol were free.

A Different Kind of Bad Guy

Akram Khatib took the last sip of his coffee and sat the mug down on his desk. He didn't like to drink coffee, but he knew it was going to be a long night. He didn't like putting anything but the purest of things in his body. He didn't smoke, didn't drink, and only ate the healthiest of foods. He treated his body as his temple. And it showed. He loved the way that other men looked upon him with envy when they saw his physique, and he loved it even more when the women couldn't look away.

He walked to the center of the room, dropped down and ripped off fifty push-ups with ease. He did this a lot when he was anxious. There was a lot riding on this night. When most others would become weak and reach for a drink to calm their nerves, Akram worked it out through exercise. He was much too strong to give in to those weak-minded urges. He had always felt anyone who did was certainly inferior to him.

He popped up from the floor, his breathing as normal as it would be if he had never even done the push-ups. He walked over to the small bathroom, flipped on the light, and gazed at himself in the mirror. For a moment he saw his much older brother staring back at him. He looked away, then looked back and was happy to see himself again. Though he looked like his brother, he was nothing like him. Sanharib was weak. He was old school as well. That is why it was difficult for them to get along, until of course Sanharib needed some dirty work done. He had felt much older earlier in the day when he wore the abaya and the turban. He only wore it to help conceal his identity. He hated wearing those traditional garments. Now that he was back in his tactical gear, a long-sleeve black T-shirt tucked into his black military cargo pants, he felt like himself again. And he felt ready for whatever the night might bring.

"Revenge," he said aloud to himself. His jaw clenched and his muscles tightened at the thought of Xander King. His brother's murderer. So full of all that American arrogance. They all thought they knew everything. How every country and every religion should go about their business. Akram knew that is what brought Xander to take it upon himself to murder Sanharib. That American attitude of "I can come and go as I please." Bullshit. He felt himself swell with rage as he thought about the audacity of the American soldier. He wanted not only to teach him a lesson by taking away what he loved—the horse, Natalie Rockwell—but also to teach him cause and effect on an even larger scale. And he also wanted to get his own hands on Xander. He didn't want one of his men to kill him, and Akram didn't want to simply shoot him from across the room. He wanted to take the arrogant man on and show him that American legends pale in comparison to the likes of a *real* soldier like himself.

Just as a sinister smile began to show itself in his reflection, his cell phone began to ring and he walked back over to the desk to answer it. It was Tristan, a detective in the French Police Nationale he had paid off. He was hoping there would be good news.

"Tristan. What have you learned?"

"A lot," Tristan answered in a thick French accent. She was brought to the Four Seasons Hotel from the airport, along with a couple of guards and a friend.

Akram stroked his beard in delight. "Good, good. I have a contact in that hotel. I'll have them get to work on a distraction."

"No need, boss."

"No need? How else will we get to her?"

"She is no longer at the hotel. You won't believe this, but my partner and I just watched her and her friend run two blocks from the hotel and get in a cab," Tristan explained.

"What? You are joking me. Just her and friend?" Akram was excited. His pulse quickened at the thought of the President's daughter alone. He couldn't believe his luck. But then again he didn't believe in luck. Luck was for people who couldn't *make* things happen.

"Just the two of them. They were looking all around as they ran. She must have found a way to sneak away. The e-mails we've been sending about the club must have worked."

"Club?"

"Nightclub. A place to party," Tristan clarified.

"Yes, of course. Young women in America like to party. This is perfect. Follow them and coordinate with Sebastian. We are going to bring the President and America to their knees!"

"We are a couple of cars back now. They are headed along the River Seine. They are headed toward Wanderlust."

Akram leaned against the desk. "Will there be a crowd?"

"There will be hundreds of partiers there. It is biggest nightclub in Paris."

Akram couldn't believe his good fortune. Everything he was doing was meant to be. Allah had blessed the mission from the start. It was then that he realized why his brother had to die. It was for the greater good. The greater good that he now knew was his destiny.

Tristan spoke up after the moment of silence. "It will be packed in the nightclub. Are you sure you want us to let her make it there?"

"Oh yes. Very much. The more people there, the better. You just cannot lose sight of her."

"No chance of that, boss. I brought in a few more men. There will be several of us there. We will wait for your signal."

"Perfect," Akram said. "Sebastian will have his team setting up. They will come in by boat. Just make sure she doesn't leave."

"They are going to Wanderlust, so don't worry. They won't be leaving for a while. There will be too much partying."

"Make sure there is."

Akram ended the call. The night could not be going better. He had America's sweetheart broadcasted live to the entire world, strung up on a wall, death closing in on both sides. He had America's G.I. Joe, his brother's murderer, right where he wanted him. And while Xander chased his tail trying to find his love, things were all set up to deliver the strongest blow to the US that had ever been dealt. The murder of the daughter of the President of the United States himself. The hundreds of others who would die with her would just be the icing on the massive publicity cake. The only thing that would make the night perfect would be if he got the chance to kill Xander King himself. He most likely wouldn't make it past Akram's men, but if by some miracle he did . . .

Akram had a plan for that as well.

Disconnected

Xander, Jack, and Viktor walked out of the stadium, but not before Xander took one long, final look back at Natalie on the big screen. She continued to struggle against the restraints, the gears continued to turn, and the metal spears proceeded to inch their way toward her beautiful face. Xander could live a thousand years, and he would never forget that sight.

"Sounds like you and Sam hit on somethin', did you?" Jack asked. The massive stadium looked a bit fake looming over his shoulder in the night. The sound of the live feed still played over the speakers inside. The grinding away of the machine, the sobs from Natalie.

"I think so. It isn't much, but it is certainly better than nothing."

Viktor straightened his pants, then rubbed his fuzzy beard. "Boss, if Natalie is on water, how will we get to her?"

"A boat, Viktor," Jack answered. "Why don't you leave the thinkin' to Xander and me."

"I don't do boats," said Viktor. "Only helicopter."

Xander nodded. "Thanks, Viktor."

Xander's phone rang. Sam. He answered. "Everything okay?"

"It's fine. We are about halfway there, but Marv is on the line. I'm going to patch him through."

Xander waited. He hoped Marv had already found something. The CIA didn't mess around when it came to locating people.

The phone clicked and Sam spoke up. "You still there, Xander?"

"Here. Hey Marv, what have you got?"

"Hey X-man. Sorry about all this, my friend, but I think we can find Natalie."

"I like the sound of that."

"Fortunately, there isn't a lot of traffic on the river right now, so it didn't take long to find what we were looking for. About a half an hour ago, a camera on the Seine in the fifteenth arrondissement picked up a group of men carrying a woman on board a dinner cruise."

"You're sure of that, Marv?" Xander asked. "You could tell they were escorting a woman?"

"The footage is grainy, Xander, but it's pretty clear that is what was happening. I have to keep studying the footage to see the details on who else got on and off the boat, but I'll have that and the boat's proximity on the river in just a few minutes. Hold tight and—"

Xander heard a loud noise, almost like glass smashing, right before the line went dead. Xander took the phone from his ear, looked at it as if that would provide an answer for what he heard, then put it back to his ear.

"Sam? Sam, are you there?" He looked at Jack. "Something happened. I heard a crash or something and we were disconnected."

"Hold tight and—"

Marv didn't get a chance to finish his sentence. Well, at least Sam didn't get to hear him finish before a van came careening out of a side street and smashed into their SUV. The crash was so loud and so full of force that for a split second everything went black. The next thing she knew, their SUV was on its side, airbags deflating after deployment as they were being pushed across the road, metal scraping, glass smashing, Sarah and Zhanna screaming, and her ears ringing with a high-pitched zing. In the moment they were being shoveled across the highway, it reminded her of last Christmas when she and Xander were turned over in their Hummer on that snowy night in Lexington. She remembered having to shoot her way out then, and that thought brought her hands to her pistols, readying them for the shoot-out she was sure was about to ensue.

"Ready your weapons!" Sam shouted over the scrape of fiberglass and asphalt. "Whoever this is will be trying to kill us as soon as we come to a stop!"

Her last four words—"come to a stop"—were across dead silence because the SUV had already done just that. There was no time to make sure everyone was all right. Sam knew the men who slammed into her would already be coming out of the van, and the best way to make sure her team was okay would be to provide cover while they regained their wits. With her pistols at the ready, she put her feet past Kyle and stood on the asphalt through the smashed window of the turned-on-its-side SUV. Still inside the SUV, she reached out through the window above her, and blindly aimed in the direction of the van as she began to squeeze the triggers. She tried to make sure the spray was no wider than the van; that way a stray bullet would be far less likely to clip an innocent bystander.

As Sam continued firing her pistols, she shouted instructions to the rest of the team. "If you're conscious,"—POP-POP-POP—"get out through the sunroof and"—POP-POP-POP—"make sure they don't make it to this side of our truck!"

POP-POP-POP!

Sam could see movement from the backseat. Kyle was helping Zhanna and Sarah maneuver around her legs and out through the sunroof. She glanced to her left and saw no movement from the agent who had been driving. He was slumped against his door, a pool of blood under his head. She fired a couple more blind rounds before she heard backup gunfire from behind her. It was just in time because she had just fired off the last of her ammo. She crouched beside the seat in front of her, found the black bag of ammunition the CIA agent had brought along, and scooped up two fresh magazines. She loaded them into her pistols, racked both slides, and made her way out the sunroof. The air was cool and smelled of burnt rubber and gunpowder. Horns were honking; off in the distance she could hear screams and sirens. Those sounds were all surrounded by the blasts from guns and the crashes and clanks their bullets made as they burrowed into vehicles, concrete, and glass.

Sarah and Zhanna were posted at the rear of the SUV on Sam's left, and Kyle was to her right huddled down, popping up momentarily to fire off a few rounds. She sidled up to him and took up the defense against their attackers, as well as the eight more who had pulled in behind them in two all-black stretch SUVs.

Sam checked on Kyle, straining her voice over the violent sounds that surrounded them. "Are you all right? Are you hurt?"

"I'm fine! We need Xander! Is he on his way?"

"I'm not sure! We got cut off before we could finish our conversation!" Sam shouted over the automatic gunfire that erupted about twenty-five yards from them. She fired four shots back at two men on the right flank of their van. In the streetlamp's beam, she could see that one of them went down.

"What—" POP-POP. Kyle had fired his weapon in between words. "What are we gonna do? We'll run out of ammo before we fend them all off!"

Kyle was right. Sam had already gone through two full magazines just making sure all of them could exit the vehicle safely. She watched the slide kick back on Kyle's now-empty Glock, and she handed him her last spare magazine. She had only eighteen bullets left herself, and she knew the girls only had one pistol each. She raised up from behind their overturned Chevy Tahoe and caught two of the gunmen behind the van that hit them as they were reloading. Four squeezes of the trigger later and both of them were down, leaving her with only fourteen rounds. There were at least seven or eight men left, maybe more. She couldn't tell exactly how many they had eliminated. It was dark, cars were still rushing by, and the side where Sarah and Zhanna were shooting was obstructed by the van that was still in T-bone position in front of them. She couldn't see exactly how many were opposing them, but she knew one thing for certain.

The four of them were in trouble.

Sam looked back over her shoulder, away from the road where gunfire was raining down on them. She saw a row of storefront buildings. Just beyond those she could see railroad tracks. If they could make it there, they might have a chance. But there was no cover in the stretch they would have to run to get there. Nothing to keep the bullets off of them. Even the buildings that were closer than the tracks were too far to make it safely. Sam glanced back over at Sarah, the slide of her pistol locked back: empty. Sarah's face was full of concern, an expression that Sam was certain her own face mirrored. Gunfire continued behind them.

They weren't going to make it out of this without creating some sort of distraction.

Did Someone Order a Distraction?

Sam ducked down behind their overturned SUV, gunfire echoing in the night behind her as she continued to stare toward the train tracks, hoping an answer would come to her. They were two hundred yards from a chance at getting lost amongst the railcars that sat idle in the dark, but it may as well have been two hundred miles. The crackle of the automatic weapons was beginning to drive her mad.

The sniper rifle and Xander's go bag.

Just as that thought came to Sam's mind, out of the corner of her eye she noticed the slide on Zhanna's pistol lock back. Their last line of defense was however many bullets she had plus however many remained in Kyle's last magazine.

Sam turned toward Kyle and shouted, "How many bullets?"

Kyle fired a shot to drive one of the men back, then shouted without looking, "Seven, maybe six!"

"Hold them back, but only shoot when you have to!"

Sam tucked both her pistols behind her back and entered the SUV through the sunroof on her hands and knees. The driver was still unconscious behind the wheel. She reached into the large black bag where she had grabbed the extra magazines earlier, dodging shards of window glass as she fingered for the butt of the rifle. She heard Kyle fire twice more. Their time was running out. Fast. As the fingers of her left hand danced through the dark and found the sniper rifle, her right hand grasped the nylon handle at the top of Xander's go bag. After Kyle fired twice more, Sarah knelt down beside Sam as she backed out of the sunroof.

Sarah's voice was hurried. "Sam, we've got to go, they're closing in on our right. We gotta go!"

Sam nodded, then handed Sarah her pistols. "Hold them back, there are about seven rounds left in each!"

Sarah took both of Sam's Glocks, and as soon as she stood up and handed one to Zhanna, a man jumped out from the side of the van in front of them with his gun raised. Sarah flinched as she raised her gun, but she heard a shot fired behind her and the man in front of her dropped. Sarah glanced to her left and found Kyle, his face wrought with worry but his gun trained on the dead man. Sarah gave him a nod, and Kyle managed to duck down behind the SUV just as someone fired at him in the distance. Sarah took up his position just as Sam locked the magazine in place on the M24 sniper rifle.

"I'm out!" Kyle said. Fear was visible in his weary eyes.

The sirens were getting closer, but she knew they wouldn't be much help. These men were professionals. They would dispatch the police in seconds. As Sarah and Zhanna fired off their last few rounds, Sam stood, turned the rifle in the direction of the gunman, and peered through the scope. There had been at least one other van full of men that had already pulled in. They were severely outnumbered and, worse, completely out-ammo'd. She could manage to get a few of the men with the sniper rifle, but with only Xander's Glock and two magazines in the go bag, this was a battle they couldn't win.

But she wasn't going down without a fight.

Sam shouldered the sniper rifle, peered down the scope, and as she swept from right to left, it found three men crossing the road, hunched over, guns out in front, coming straight for them. She gently wrapped her finger around the trigger. She heard Sarah and Zhanna shouting that they were out of ammo, and shouting at her to run, but it was muffled. Like their voices were a mile away. Sam inhaled sharply as the world outside of her scope faded away. As she let out a breath and just as her finger twitched, a sedan came out of nowhere from the left side of her scope and drove right through the three men stalking toward her, crashing into the SUV beside them. Before she pulled her rifle down, the door of the sedan opened, arms pushed the deflated airbag to the side, and a man rose quickly from the door and began to fire at the men who had been firing at Sam and the others.

Xander.

As soon as she saw him emerge from the car, firing away, she took down her rifle, threw his go bag on her back, and began backing away from the SUV toward the train tracks.

"Let's go!" Sam shouted to Kyle, Zhanna, and Sarah. "Let's regroup in the rail yard!"

The three of them looked at Sam, then glanced back toward the road where Xander was glowing under a streetlamp, his pistol blasting red-orange bursts of light from its tip. Kyle pumped his fist, then quickly sidled up to Sam, and the four of them moved for the tracks. Zhanna, Sarah, and Kyle went running, while Sam backed her way there as she brought the rifle's scope to her right eye. She found Xander, noticed two more men emerging from his sedan, and swung her rifle to the side of the road where the three of them were firing. Her scope found one man aiming at her from the side of the van. She saw a quick burst of fire from the barrel of his gun and squeezed the trigger. She didn't feel any bullets hit her, and before she turned to make sure none of her crew had been hit, she watched the left side of the man's neck explode from her rifle's round.

Sam glanced behind her as she opened and closed the bolt, chambering a new round, and saw the three of them still running for the train tracks. None of them were hit. She was in between the shops now. Xander, and she assumed Jack, were still firing away. She brought her rifle back up and saw Xander throw his pistol to the ground—out of ammo—then make a break toward her. A man wearing a cowboy hat—it was indeed Jack—continued firing behind him as he moved toward Sam as well. He was trying desperately to hold the gunmen off while they ran her way. As Xander approached the overturned SUV, she swung her rifle back to the right and fired after her sights found two gunmen rounding the vehicle at the same time as Xander. The man flew backward off his feet, but as she went to take out the second gunman, the heel of her boot caught on the curb and she slammed onto her back; the rifle clanked against the blacktop and slid several feet away from her. The last thing she saw was Xander hurdling the overturned truck; at the same time the gunman rounded its other side. Her heart dropped to her stomach. She knew Xander was unarmed, and the van that had T-boned them would block any chance Jack might have of taking out the gunman for Xander.

Without looking, she dove back behind her, and with the rifle in her hands she rolled back over. Her heart was racing as she moved the scope toward her eye, and she heard the rapid tat-tat-tat of an automatic rifle echoing toward her. Fearing the worst, she audibly inhaled as she brought the rifle to her shoulder and dropped her head in place for a look through the scope. Her mind flashed the sight of Xander going down in front of her, but her eye found reality, and it was Xander tearing the rifle from the gunman's grasp, hitting him with a front push kick, and turning the gun on its owner, dropping him with a short burst. Xander then turned his back to Sam and took two more gunmen out on the opposite side of the van. It was then that Sam realized she had been holding her breath. She finally released the air, and through the scope she watched Xander turn back toward her. He shrugged his shoulders as if to say, "What can I say?" as he jogged toward her. Jack and another man ran not far behind him.

Sam let her arm that held the sniper rifle relax and collapse against the blacktop. As she exhaled, her mouth formed into a half smile of relief.

She said aloud to herself, "Cocky bastard."

The Band Is Back Together

Xander watched as Sam jumped back up to her feet. When he glanced over his shoulder, Jack and Viktor were right behind him. Over Jack's cowboy hat, in the distance, he saw two more SUVs screech to a stop under a streetlight. Whoever was holding Natalie certainly didn't lack resources. He motioned for Jack and Viktor to speed it up, then continued to jog forward, and Sam let him catch up. They were in an alley between storefronts. In front of them it was now pitch black. The tracks that Sam had seen a few moments ago were no longer visible.

Sam said, "Good timing, old boy."

"Good to see you, Sam. Thanks for coming. I'm sorry—"

"You left without telling us, I know." Sam waved away his words. "You're an idiot. But we're here now and now Akram Khatib knows exactly where we all are."

"Where does this alley lead?"

"Train tracks. I remember from studying a map that it is a massive abandoned railway. We can definitely lose them there."

Xander asked, "Abandoned railway in the middle of Paris? Where have I heard that?"

The two of them made it to the end of the alleyway, and just as Jack and Viktor reached the drop-off into the gravel, gunfire erupted from the street behind them.

Sam answered, "Maybe on the news. Parisians are fighting over whether to develop it or use it as green space."

Xander looked down and kicked at the gravel under his feet. "Green space, huh?"

They heard a clanking noise a few feet away from them. The four of them turned toward it, and Sam turned on the flashlight of her phone. "That must be Kyle."

Emotion welled up inside Xander when he saw Kyle's face in the bright white light. He was peeking out from behind an abandoned railcar, banging a pistol against it to get their attention. Xander had never been so happy to see his friend's face. Kyle came out from behind the railcar and met Xander halfway with a massive man hug.

"Goddamn, it's good to see you," Xander said.

"I'm sorry, buddy. We're gonna find who did this. They're going to pay for what they did to Ransom."

"And for taking Natalie," Sarah said.

She and Zhanna walked out from behind the same railcar, both shading their eyes from the flashlight. Xander let go of Kyle and walked toward them. Sarah wrapped her arms around him. The smell—her scent—of lavender and honey filled his senses. It made him long to be in a much different place, under much different circumstances.

He said, "Thank you for coming."

115

"I'm sorry about King's Ransom, and I'm sorry about what is happening to Natalie. I know what she means to you. I saw it in both of your eyes back at your place in San Diego. Don't worry, we'll find her."

"I hate to break up the reunion," Sam interrupted. "But we've got gunmen bearing down on us, and we've got to get somewhere that I can call Marv back. Maybe by now he knows which way we should move."

Xander knew Sam was right, but he didn't want to let go of Sarah. After just a moment longer, she pulled away. Xander located Zhanna and gave her a nod just before Sam turned off the flashlight. When Sam opened her phone, the glow from its face was much softer.

Sam handed Xander his go bag. From the outside it looked just like a standard backpack, but Xander knew the contents weren't quite so ordinary.

"Marv had this prepared for you prior to my arriving," Sam told him. "It's got your Glock 19, two extra mags, a suppressor, a Marfione Halo 4 OTF knife, a SAT phone and a burner phone, two flash and two smoke grenades, a flashlight with an IR strobe, an IFAK, a class-three body armor vest, and a night-vision/IR monocular."

Kyle said, "So, basically a fuck-shit-up bag?"

"Basically," Sam answered.

Xander dug inside the bag and pulled out the Glock and the flashlight. Then he retrieved the knife, unzipped and placed it in the pocket of his joggers, and, finally, replaced his hoodie with the protective shirt-vest. He handed Sam the SAT phone, strapped the go bag on his back, turned on the flashlight, and started jogging.

"Call Marv on this," he said to Sam. "Let's move north.

Everyone but Sarah, lose your phones."

"But Viktor just bought new iPhone," Viktor said in a whine from the back of the pack.

"Sorry, Viktor," Xander replied, no sympathy.

"But why does Barbie get to keep phone and Viktor does not?"

Sarah answered, "Cause *Barbie's* phone is a CIA-encrypted phone."

Viktor groaned, then tossed his phone to the gravel. "Boss, when we get back, you get Viktor phone like Barbie?"

"Yes, Viktor."

There were three more phones that cracked against the gravel below them as everyone did as Xander asked, followed by men shouting from the spot behind them where they had entered the rail yard just a moment ago.

"There is flashlight!" one of the men shouted.

"Follow me!" Xander said to his ragtag crew as he zagged over a few sets of tracks, putting a long stretch of interlocked railcars between them and the gunmen. As soon as they moved out of sight, the pop of gunfire erupted behind them and the clank of bullets rocketing through metal crashed into the railcar beside them.

"Let's put some distance between us and them." Xander said. And before they kicked it into gear, he broke out into a sprint, he and his flashlight moved quickly away from them in the dark.

"Don't you know you got an old man with ya?" Jack shouted.

Xander didn't slow down for a second.

117

Partying Does Pay Off

Xander stopped at the open doorway of an abandoned railcar. He had been sprinting for nearly a full minute. The others were coming, but he used the seconds of solitude to form a plan. His mind was focused on locating Natalie, but he was forced to push that aside for the moment. If they didn't survive and dispose of these gunmen, there would be no point in a plan to find Natalie. He had to work on this situation first. He shined his flashlight around him. There was nothing but rows of tracks running vertically over gravel. The occasional abandoned railcar scattered here and there. He needed his team to distract the others.

His team?

Until that moment, he hadn't really categorized them as such. It had always just been him and Sam. Even Kyle was a late addition. But it was undeniable that the rest of them were part of a full-scale team at this point. None of them, with the exception of Sarah due to her CIA obligations, had any reason to be there. Other than they wanted to fight for what was right.

For Xander.

For Natalie.

More gunfire erupted behind *his team.* As Sam approached, she was ending a call.

"Marv?" Xander asked.

"Yes. He has a good lead. Let's get out of this situation and then go save your girl."

"Sam, have I told you lately that I—"

"That you love me? Too bloody much. What's the plan?"

As the others caught up, Xander quickly explained the play. They all got into place. Sam, Zhanna, Viktor, and Sarah pulled themselves up into the railcar. Xander found one not far away on the right, and he had given Jack the sniper rifle and directed him to another railcar over to the left. Both Xander and Jack climbed to the top of their railcars and lay flat, heads down, feet flat out to the sides. Seconds later, they heard the crunch of gravel. Xander had given Sam his Glock and the go bag. She would know exactly when to use the smoke grenade. Jack was positioned about fifty yards from Xander, with the railcar full of the team in the middle. The clouds of the day had cleared a bit, and the moon showered its dim white light over the empty tracks.

Xander heard a man's voice dole out an order: "Spread out. They can't be far."

He couldn't have been more than thirty or so yards away. Slowly, Xander pulled the SAT phone from his pocket. He had predialed Sarah's number, so to call it he just needed to press call. He moved without noise and with minimal movement. As he slid his thumb to the call button, Xander closed his eyes and let the men tell him where they were.

Paris was quiet. Off in the distance he could hear traffic coming from the road. The occasional horn. And sirens, most likely at the crash site by now. A cool breeze blew across the top of the railcar and slipped under the collar of his protective shirt-vest. Goose pimples stood across his arms, and he pricked his ears to hone in on his enemy. Gravel crunched under several different footfalls. Some were farther away, but a couple were close and moving to his left. This is exactly what Xander had hoped for. With minimal ammunition in the Glock, and not knowing exactly how many men they were facing, he needed to separate them. From the sounds of it, they had done it for him. The crunch of the gravel grew closer, and they were just to the left of his railcar now. He glanced to his right, in the direction of the team in the middle, and then out in front of their railcar. It was dark, but the flashlight attachment on the assault rifles of the oncoming gunmen would be like target practice for the accomplished sniper that Jack was known to be. It was time. Men were right below him, and they were getting too close to Sam and company out in front of him.

Xander pressed call.

Sarah's phone rang in the middle railcar, and immediately the gunmen's attention were drawn there.

One of them shouted, "There! The car in middle!"

A split second before their guns blasted Sam's railcar, Xander watched her throw a smoke grenade right at their feet.

Perfect.

The grenade hissed, and a cloud of white smoke rose between the gunmen and the railcars. As Xander slid the SAT phone back into his pocket and slithered to the edge of his railcar, he heard the distinct pop of the M24 sniper rifle. Jack had begun to pick them off, finding them by their flashlights through the smoke. Below Xander, two men reacted to their compadres' gunfire by turning back toward them and giving Xander their backs. Xander slid his hand inside his pocket to his knife, and as he dropped down behind the gunmen, he pressed the auto-release button, ejecting the blade from the handle of the knife, and drove the blade down into the first man's neck, just above his protective vest. The knife sank into his skin with zero resistance. Xander knew it was the man's carotid artery, and after he gave the blade a twist and removed it, blood shot out onto the railcar. The gunfire continued all around him. The rapid fire of the enemies' automatic weapons, the distinct sound of Sam shooting his Glock, and Jack shooting the sniper rifle all came together in a horrifying symphony.

The moment Xander pulled the knife from the man's neck, the gunman in front wheeled around and Xander, with his left leg, front-kicked the assault rifle from his hands. Immediately, Xander crouched and twisted his body to the right, then sprang up and uncoiled back to his left, bringing his knife hand around like a right hook, his blade sweeping through the gunman's throat. He quickly pressed the button on the knife, pulled back the charging handle retracting the blade, and clipped it to his waistband. He then picked up the dead man's assault rifle, an HK MP5 submachine gun, and moved toward the cloud in front of him.

"Move in! Move in!" a man shouted from inside the cloud of smoke.

Instead of getting in the middle of the cloud and possibly catching a friendly stray bullet, Xander climbed back up the ladder and crouched atop his railcar. The smoke began to dissipate, and he could just make out two gunmen walking out of the cloud. Xander tapped the trigger on the MP5—at nine

121

hundred rounds per minute, it didn't take much—and a short burst of nine-millimeter bullets landed in what Xander thought should be the man's chest and neck area. He then heard a couple of pops from the Glock from inside the railcar, and both men were down. He remained crouched, listening for more gravel-crunching steps.

There were none.

Xander slowly and quietly descended the ladder at the back of the railcar and rushed across several tracks and to the back of the car where his team was positioned. He looked into the darkness, in the direction of where Jack was supposed to be, and that's when he heard a man grunting and gravel being kicked around in a scuffle. Xander didn't hesitate. He bolted across the tracks. Gunmen must have flanked Jack's railcar as they had his, but Jack must not have seen them. Another grunt of pain echoed to Xander's ears, and as he turned the corner, one man had just thrown Jack to the ground, and the other leveled his assault rifle on him as Jack slid across the gravel. Xander quickly raised the MP5, but when he squeezed the trigger all he heard was a click. The damn thing had jammed. The two gunmen whipped around, not hesitating to fire. Just before he heard the blast of their guns, Xander threw himself backward onto the gravel and behind the back of the railcar.

"Get him!" a man yelled.

Xander kicked back up to his feet, ran around the opposite side of the railcar, and collided head on with the second gunman as he rounded the front end. Xander instinctively lowered his level, picked the man up with a double-leg takedown, and drove him down into the gravel. As soon as they landed, Xander's right hand found the man's side piece, removed it from his hip, rolled onto his back as he racked the slide, shot the other gunman twice around the throat and head as he rounded the railcar, and in an axe motion drove the butt of the pistol down onto the top of the nose of the man he'd just tackled. The man wailed in pain and grabbed for his face. Xander pistol-whipped him once more on the forehead, and the man went limp. A flashlight came around the corner in the distance, and again Xander raised his pistol, ready for who was next.

"It's Sam!" She held up her hands. "It's me! This end is secure. Are you all right?"

Xander lowered his gun. "All clear!"

When Xander rolled to his left to check on Jack, and the cowboy was already standing over him, holding out his hand.

Jack said, "What kind of SEAL don't check his magazine before he shoots?"

Jack pulled Xander to his feet; Sam's flashlight shone on Jack's smiling face.

Xander answered, "You and I both know that wouldn't happen. The damn thing jammed on me."

"Are the two of you all right? We couldn't see a thing," Sam said as she and the rest of the team caught up.

"We're fine," Jack said.

Xander dusted the gravel off himself and nodded toward the unconscious gunman. "When he wakes up, let's see if we can get him to talk. In the meantime, what did Marv say?"

He didn't waste any time. Now that they weren't in imminent danger, Xander's mind immediately shifted to how to find Natalie.

Sarah's phone rang. "It's Langley. I have to take this. Go ahead, I'll catch up in a sec." She walked away from the group and answered the call.

Sam said, "Marv is sending a possible location for where the dinner boat is located, which he believes they forced Natalie onto. He knows where we are. He is sending two cars for us, away from the crash site that will surely be crawling with police by now."

Xander said, "There are too many of us. I'd feel more comfortable if it were just you and me going after Natalie, Sam. Maybe the rest of the team can work on finding Khatib?"

"You're right, there are too many of us," Sam agreed. "But I believe we need Jack as well. Since we have a sniper rifle and we are likely going to have to board a boat in the middle of the river, he would be able to help keep the deck clear for us from shore."

Xander looked to Jack. "Suits me. I'll let you young'uns do the chasing," Jack said. "I'll pick these bastards off from afar. It would help if I had a spotter with good eyes."

Xander turned to Viktor.

"Not that crazy bastard," Jack scoffed. Then he said to Viktor, "Don't get me wrong, I love your enthusiasm, but I ain't good at baby sittin'."

"Viktor not baby. And Viktor have perfect vision. Good enough to see your wrinkled old face from long way off!" Viktor puffed out his chest.

Xander knew that Viktor just wanted to help. Since there were no helicopters around, this was as close to helping as he was going to get.

Jack bowed up. "You better watch your mouth, Vik. I may be old, but I can still put you on your ass!"

Viktor shuffled toward Jack. "You wish, you old—"

Xander grabbed Viktor with force by the collar of his raggedy T-shirt. Viktor went silent. Xander said, "This is what

Jack is talking about, Viktor. If you're coming with us, I can't have any of this Xbox bravado. You are going to have to respect what Jack says and do everything he asks. This man is a seasoned warrior. You hear me?"

Xander let go of Viktor's shirt. Viktor cleared his throat and straightened out his shirt. "Yes, boss. Sorry, Jack. I have good eyes and can help get pretty actress back safe."

Xander looked to Jack and nodded. Jack returned the nod. Principal King to the rescue.

"All right, time to move."

Kyle stepped forward. "I'd rather stay with you, X."

"I know. And I want you there, but Khatib is going to be hard to find. I'm going to need you and Zhanna to work with Sarah and Marv all you can to help find him. It sounds like he is planning something else, I don't know what—"

"I do," Sarah interrupted. She ended her call and walked over to the group. Her tone was worried and the moon's light revealed the worried look on her face as well.

Kyle said, "That doesn't sound good."

"That was Director Hartsfield and Marv. She's tasked Marv to coordinate with me for help, and she's requesting the help of your team, Xander. If there is anyone to spare."

"There isn't," Xander answered quickly.

Sarah continued, "Marv thought you might say that, so he told me to let you know that he believes what Director Hartsfield called about is directly linked to Akram Khatib."

"I'm listening," Xander said. "But make this quick. Every second that we waste standing here is a second closer those steel spears get to Natalie's head."

"The President's daughter has gone missing," Sarah blurted.

125

"What?" Kyle reacted.

Sam put her hand on her hip. "All right, that is terrible. But what can you do about that?"

"Sorry, she's gone missing, here, in Paris."

"Holy shit." Kyle turned toward Xander. "You think it's Khatib?"

Sarah interjected, "Marv does. He believes if we find Adeline Williams, it will lead us to Khatib."

Xander huffed. "Well, that's quite a leap. But regardless, it's the President's daughter. You have to find her. If it leads to Khatib, great. If not, that just is what it is. We can't have something happen to her. It will open up a whole world of terrorists believing they can take shots at America. So, quickly, what do we know?"

Sarah relayed Marv's words from the phone call. "All we know is that a half hour ago, maybe less, the Secret Service reported that Adeline had gone missing. When Marv's team checked the CCTV cameras outside the hotel, Adeline and a friend were seen running from the hotel and getting into a cab. Apparently, she put the slip on her Secret Service guards. The reason Marv is concerned that Khatib could be connected is because his team checked the cameras up the block from the hotel and as soon as the girls pulled away in their cab, two suspicious-looking men across the street jumped into their vehicle and sped after them. After running their plates, the car is connected to a known radical Islamic group here in Paris. Not coincidentally, known to be funded by factions in Syria. Marv believes they are here working for Akram Khatib."

"Jesus," Kyle said. "So what can we do? Or how would *I* be able to help? I know nothing about counter-terrorism, or finding missing people."

"I don't know," Sarah said.

"Any idea where they are going?" Sam asked.

"Not yet, because get this, the cab they got into didn't have plates or a cab number on the side of the car."

"Because it wasn't a cab," Sam registered.

Sarah nodded. "That is the other reason Marv thinks it's Khatib's men. They must have intercepted their cab call, or paid the operator to dispatch one of their men."

"Shit." Xander hated hearing this. He needed to stay focused on Natalie. But this was the President's daughter. This was National Security. Now his mind was focusing on how to find Adeline, and he needed it not to be.

Sam stepped forward and addressed Sarah. "Wait, so how old is this Adeline?"

"Twenty-one. Why?" Sarah answered.

Sam couldn't help but smile. "Is she pretty? Does she have any history of liking to party?"

Sarah nodded. "Yes, and yes."

Sam's smile widened, and she looked at Kyle.

"What?" Kyle shrugged.

"You don't see? This is perfect for you, Don Juan."

"Don Juan? What is this, 1989? I don't get it."

Xander walked over to Kyle and put his hand on his shoulder. "You know all those nights we spent chasing women at bars?"

Kyle was still clueless. "Yeah. So?"

Xander couldn't help but smile himself. "It was practice."

"Practice?"

"Yeah, practice for the moment you had to go find the most important pretty girl you would ever have to find."

Kyle was quiet for a moment. Then the light bulb went on.

127

"They snuck out to party."

Sam said, "You've found your true calling, Romeo."

Jack hiked up his pants at the belt buckle. "Excuse me for being the old, out-of-touch guy here, but I don't get how Kyle knowin' how to party and pick up women helps here."

Everyone turned and looked at Kyle.

"Well, Jack. If I was hot, twenty-one, and never allowed to let my hair down, I'd go to the biggest party in town."

"Which is?" Sarah asked.

Kyle looked at Xander with an ornery smile. "Has to be that place we took those ladies we met in the cafe when we were here a couple of weeks ago. That massive place on the river. What was it called?"

Xander thought for a moment. "Wanderlust?"

"That's it!" Kyle pumped his fist.

Jack spoke up again. "I hate to be Negative Nancy, but out of all the places in Paris they could go, why do you think it's that one they're goin' to?"

Sam walked around Xander, unzipped his go bag, pulled out the burner phone, and handed it to Kyle. "Because, Jack. That is exactly where Kyle would go."

The Big Picture

"Ooh, can you turn this up please?" Adeline asked the cab driver.

The Middle Eastern man did as she asked, and an English lady's voice filled the interior of the cab.

This is a BBC world news report. Paris, France, is the talk of the world this evening. American superstar actress Natalie Rockwell was kidnapped from her hotel suite in Paris this morning. No information on her whereabouts was known until just a short time ago, and now everyone all across the world has a front row seat to the terrifying live feed that was brought to seemingly everyone's attention no more than an hour ago. If you haven't seen it, consider yourself lucky you're listening to the radio. The live feed is of Natalie restrained against the wall in some sort of medieval torture contraption, the monster in charge of this terrible act saying she only has hours to live. The contraption has two sword-like spears moving slowly toward her head. It's truly a ghastly sight. I had a brief conversation with a spokesperson from America's CIA, John Haversmith, and this is what he had to say when I asked him what was being done . . .

Adeline looked to her friend Karol, and with a shocked expression she mouthed the letters, "OMG." A man's voice came across the radio. His tone was solemn but confident.

This situation with Miss Rockwell is deplorable in every way. I assure you that the monster responsible for this heinous act will be dealt with swiftly. We have our best men and women on the ground in Paris as we speak, tracking her down.

The lady came back on and continued to report.

When asked if he thought there was hope for Natalie, John replied a resounding "yes." I also asked what we should do about the live feed, and he told me the best that all of us can do is be human and shut it off. I imagine that will be very difficult for her fans as they sit on pins and needles, waiting to see how this real-life drama will play out.

"Here we are," the cab driver announced.

"Thank you so much for the suggestion. This place looks outrageous!" Adeline's eyes were fixed on the crowd of young Parisians milling about outside the entrance to the nightclub.

"No problem. Have fun."

Adeline paid the fare and stepped out into the cool Paris night. She shut the cab door after Karol exited and shook her head when her friend looked at her. "Can you believe that news report? Poor Natalie. I mean, who would ever do such a thing?"

"You sure we should be doing this?" Karol said.

"Are you kidding me? Look at this place!" Adeline practically squealed as she swept her hand out in front of her as if she were revealing the great secret to happiness.

The two of them could hear the bass thumping from the

street. A sea of young partiers spread out in front of them, packing the outdoor area at the front entrance, which was covered by a bright green tunnel, resembling the entrance to an alien world. For Adeline and Karol, it might as well have been. They didn't get out much, especially Adeline.

Adeline tugged at Karol's hand, and the two of them practically skipped toward the first bar they could find. They didn't have to go far; music, booze, and freedom were everywhere.

Sarah Gilbright ended her call with Marv. Kyle and Zhanna let her have a minute to collect her thoughts. Her head was spinning a bit, and she was trying to settle it so they could approach this situation the right way. Just moments ago she watched Xander and Sam drive off with Jack and Viktor in the other SUV. She hated to watch Xander go. Hated even more to watch him go through this situation. He had been through so much in the last few weeks. More than most could handle. Just when he thought—they all thought—things were over, someone else took two things that he loved. Sarah never had the opportunity to see Xander with his racehorse, but everyone had been emphatic about how much he loved him. And then Natalie being kidnapped? Sarah didn't know what to feel. Just a day ago Xander had made love to her, made her feel things she had never felt before. She could tell he was feeling it too, but no matter how much she wanted him, he didn't look at her like she

131

noticed him looking at Natalie in San Diego. Xander liked Sarah, she knew that—could *feel* that. But as much as she hated to admit it, it wasn't the same for him as it was her. His heart was with Natalie.

As she watched the city of lights pass by outside the rear passenger window, she figured it was just par for the course for her when it came to love. The entire reason she moved to Langley, Virginia, was for a man. It was a man who got her involved with the CIA in the first place. And it was the CIA that took him away. Xander was the first man she let herself open up to since Derek, and she knew it was a mistake the moment she watched him and Natalie together. As terrible as it sounded, she was glad she had this new situation to throw herself into. After this was all over, she needed to focus on herself. She had a lot of things left to work on there, before she could be with a man again.

"What's the plan, Barbie?" Kyle smiled at her.

Sarah made a "watch it" face, furrowing her brow and tightening her lips.

"Sorry, I couldn't help myself. I could tell it got under your skin when Viktor said it earlier."

"Anyway." Sarah moved on to his question. "Marv said we need to go in and get her out of there, without causing a scene, if possible."

Zhanna spoke up from the front passenger seat. "So we have confirmed that she is there?"

"Yes. Marv said CCTV cameras picked her up getting out of a cab in front of Wanderlust with her friend. He's sending pictures over now."

Kyle said, "I knew it! So what's the play? Why don't we just find her and carry her out of there to safety?"

"Marv is afraid they are watching her there. He's afraid if we make a scene, it could possibly trigger a shootout. And he said there will be a mass of people there, so that could lead to putting too many innocent lives in danger . . . Also, he thinks they're up to something bigger."

Zhanna turned around in her seat to face Kyle and Sarah. "Bigger than taking President's daughter hostage?"

Sarah frowned. "I know. But he's afraid they may be trying to make a statement here. You saw how much coverage the shootings at the nightclub in Orlando received. This place is at least ten times larger than that, Marv says."

Kyle was still confused. "I don't get it, why don't they just evacuate?"

"It's too late for that. If they have rigged the place somehow for a bomb, all of that is already in place. If they sense something fishy going on, they can just detonate it and move on. Marv said Wanderlust doesn't get its fullest for another hour. It will be then that they will be looking to do something."

Kyle said, "Okay, still seems dumb to me to not just evacuate, but you all are the experts. So, again, what's the play?"

Sarah put on a half smile. "I say we play to our strengths."

"Which is?" Zhanna asked.

Sarah looked at Kyle. "There any truth to this Romeo thing?"

"Romeo?" Kyle questioned.

"Yeah, everyone seems to think you're a ladies' man. Any truth to that? Can you really pull it in?"

"Pull it in?" Kyle laughed. "I don't even know what that means."

133

Zhanna let out a breath. "Cut shit, Kyle. You are handsome man. Built well, but can you talk good to ladies?"

Kyle smiled and looked deep into Zhanna's eyes. "Ever since the moment I saw you standing outside that helicopter in Florence, Italy, something in the back of my mind has been telling me that there is something special about you."

Sarah leaned back in her seat, taking in the show.

Kyle continued, "But it wasn't because you were one of the most beautiful women I had ever seen. And though you *are* absolutely stunning, it had nothing to do with the way you were dressed, showing every phenomenal curve on your body either. It was your eyes. There was this . . . sincerity in them. Like, no matter how far I traveled and no matter how many women I meet, I will never find someone who could ever reach the depths that is your soul."

Everyone was quiet for a moment. Sarah was desperately trying to contain her laughter, but she had to see if Zhanna was going to fall for it. It was a good off-the-cuff speech, Sarah had to give him that.

Finally, Zhanna smiled. "You are good bullshitter, Kyle. It is bullshit, but good bullshit."

The three of them laughed. Then Kyle became dead serious when he looked down at the clothes he was wearing.

"I can't go in there like this."

"Like what?" Sarah asked.

"If you want me to go into a club and charm the President's daughter, I can't be wearing this!"

The three of them laughed again. Then Sarah rolled her eyes and checked her phone. He had a point: he needed to fit in. She wished she was going to be able to watch Kyle in action, but she knew she and Zhanna were going to have to take this seriously. She pulled up the Yelp app on her phone, and it showed a men's clothing store nearby. She told the agent driving the car to stop there. As Kyle went inside and got nightclub ready, Sarah and Zhanna formulated a plan to find out if something much larger really was going on at the club.

Hoping for a Little Magic

The agent driving Xander, Sam, Jack, and Viktor pulled the SUV to the side of the road adjacent to the railing that overlooked a portion of the Seine River. Marv had directed them to a spot about a quarter of a mile downriver from the boat the men had forced a woman onto a little more than an hour ago. As they were driving, Xander had pulled up the live feed of Natalie on the SAT phone. Against the suggestion of Sam to leave it alone. But Xander wanted to study the room, even though on the feed, the room was empty except for Natalie strapped to the wall. Xander knew the boat would not be empty. He knew there would be men waiting for him. He was searching the empty dining room for clues as to where they may be hiding, but other than the door on the left side of the room, the video gave him nothing. Nothing but a broken heart and a sick feeling in his stomach as he watched the metal spears relentlessly rolling their way toward Natalie's head. They were much closer now, but he still had time. The toughest part would be boarding the boat; he could handle everything else.

The four of them exited the SUV. Sam instructed the driver to stay put and keep the SUV running. Sam had also told Marv to continue searching footage from the closed circuit-cameras around the river in case it could turn up any more clues. They walked over to the railing, and they found that it was a good spot for Jack to set up with the sniper rifle. Their spot looked down on the river, the wind was light, and there was a streetlamp just above them. Its light cast almost to the middle of the river. Good for Xander and Sam to get to the boat, and good for Viktor to help spot targets for Jack as the boat passed.

Xander opened his go bag and took out the night-vision/IR monocular. He gave a look down the river. He could see the front end of a dinner boat that matched the description Marv gave. It was time. He handed Viktor the monocular. "This will help you spot for Jack. He has a night-vision optic on his sniper rifle, so he'll be able to see what you see."

"Got it, boss."

Jack pulled the legs on the attached bipod that rested a few inches beyond the trigger guard of the rifle, and rested bipod on the thick rail that stood about waist high. "This is a good spot, X. We'll be watchin' your back. Now get out there and save that woman."

Xander knocked Jack's outstretched fist with his, and Viktor quickly punched at Xander's. He didn't want to be left out. Xander dug back inside his go bag and screwed the suppressor onto his Glock. After a press check, assuring he had a round in the chamber, he handed Sam an extra magazine for her Glock. He kept the last magazine in the bag, zipped it up, and strapped it on his back. He moved his knife that was clipped to his waistband to his zipped jogger pocket in case the water might pull it away. He then gave Sam a nod, and they walked around the railing and descended the stairs to the concrete riverwalk. The water was black outside the stretch of the streetlamp. This was ideal for Sam and Xander. They couldn't make out the boat down the river; it was too dark.

Sam asked. "How long do you think we have?"

"Five minutes, maybe."

"It's going to be cold, isn't it?"

Xander smirked. "Very. You gonna be okay?"

"Not everyone got tortured in the cold water of San Diego Bay, Mr. Navy SEAL. I don't do water without a wetsuit. Unless I'm in the Virgin Islands."

"Don't worry, Sam, I promise you won't melt. *The Wizard of Oz* is fiction."

Sam gave a fake chuckle. "You're calling me a witch?"

Xander nodded toward the boat. "I was kind of hoping for a magic spell."

"You've got all the spell you need there in your hand." Sam nodded to Xander's Glock. "You're pretty good with that magic wand."

Xander said, "You know it's best if they think I'm the only one coming for her."

"You want me to remain in the water? Bollocks." Sam shook her head.

"Okay, you don't have to stay in the water, but stay hidden."

"Don't worry, I'll pop out at the right moment."

"I know you will." Xander smiled. Then he walked to the water's edge. "Shall we?"

There was no hesitation in Sam's reply. "We shall."

The two of them lowered themselves into the water. Xander

was okay until he sank in past his genitals. He could literally feel them shriveling up. Sam let out an audible shiver beside him. It was miserable, but their bodies would adjust.

"You okay?" Xander asked.

"Let's just go," Sam snapped.

They both pushed off and floated out away from the concrete walkway. The Seine runs from the northeast and empties out into the English Channel at the left bank. The current began to carry Sam and Xander right toward the oncoming boat. They swam out closer to the middle of the river as they let it sweep them westward. Marv told them there would be a low rail that ran across the sides of the dinner boat. He had said the cabin was all windows on the sides, so if they wanted to remain incognito they would have to stay low once they pulled themselves up.

Floating in the cold water of the Seine reminded Xander of his training with the SEALs. So many freezing cold mornings in San Diego Bay. All of them were tough, but all of them were necessary. Many moments of the last ten years of his crazy life were spent on the way to battle. And the mental toughness it took to make it through training, though incredibly difficult, still wasn't the same as moving toward a real enemy, knowing this could be the last night you take a breath on earth. It was much easier for him years ago. It's always easier when you don't have as much to lose. He only had his sister back then, and Kyle. Now he had so many more people that he cared about. The people who help him run his companies, their families. All of his employees who count on him to feed their own families.

Xander glanced back over his shoulder. He could barely see Sam wading in the cold black water behind him. He didn't know what he would have done without her over the last few years. It started for them as a venture in justice. Now he was just as close with her—if not closer—than with his very own sister. And here she was again, risking her life for him. Xander knew if he brought it up, she would just tell him that she wouldn't be here without him. But Xander knew she had repaid that debt long ago. He didn't want to put her in danger anymore. He just couldn't seem to stay out of trouble these days.

"You okay, Sam?"

"No idea." She shivered as she spoke. "I'm bloody frozen."

"Almost there."

The boat was only about a football field away now. Xander thought about all of the people who were in Paris to help him. People who had zero skin in the game. They were just there to see that he was okay, and to make sure that justice was done to those who had harmed him and Natalie, whom they didn't even know. The fact that Sarah was willing to come all this way to help spoke volumes about her. He knew how hard this must be for her. To have feelings for him and watch him risk it all for another woman. A woman who, no matter how Xander tried to spin it, was the only one for him. As the boat approached, he made a vow to himself in that moment, that after he saved Natalie, she would never doubt that notion again.

Saved by the Belle

Sarah and Kyle stood on the street by the SUV, with the Wanderlust nightclub just down on the corner. Sarah finished helping Kyle adjust the earpiece in his ear, brushed a piece of lint off the shoulder of his new button-up shirt, and gave him a smile. She thought the powder blue he chose was a good look against his tanned skin.

Kyle grinned. "Well?"

"You clean up nice, Kyle Hamilton."

"These jeans aren't too tight?"

Sarah looked down, shrugged her shoulders, and widened her smile. "Maybe. But they look good on you. Besides, skinny jeans are on trend right now."

"You sure you don't want to grab a drink with me?" Kyle asked. Playful.

Sarah rolled her eyes. "Are you ever serious?"

"Um . . . No. Not really. What fun is that?"

Zhanna closed the door of the SUV and joined the conversation. "You look good, Kyle. I've seen lots of pretty young girls walk by. You are not going to get distracted, are you?"

"No, I know what this means. I'm going to find Adeline and, after I make her feel comfortable, try to get her to leave."

Sarah put her hands on her hips. "So he can be serious."

"Don't get used to it." Kyle wagged his index finger at her. "So, while I'm in here finding Adeline, you guys are going to, what, be looking for a bomb?"

"Yes. That, and anyone looking suspicious. We're going to be checking behind the club by the river as well. Make sure nothing *fishy* is going on."

Kyle looked shocked. "Sarah Gilbright has a sense of humor? You sure I can't buy you a drink?"

Another eye roll. "Just get in and out of there as quick as you can. I'll be in your ear to let you know if we find anything. Hopefully we won't, but Marv texted me while you were in the store and said his team saw a lot of suspicious movement on the river side of the club earlier. Be careful in there. The good thing is, if Khatib's men are here, they won't recognize you. So you shouldn't set off any alarm bells for them when you approach the President's daughter." Sarah let a wry smile grow across her face. "Any idea what line you'll use? Don't make it something cheesy."

Kyle smiled. "Hello has always worked pretty well for me."

Zhanna started down the sidewalk. "Oh please. Gag me with spoon."

Sarah and Kyle laughed. Sarah patted him on the arm. "Good luck. Hopefully by the time you walk out of here with

Adeline and her friend, Xander and Sam will have found Natalie. Then we can all get the hell out of this place."

"Your lips to God's ears."

Sarah started toward Zhanna but walked backward to look at Kyle. "No matter what you hear in that earpiece, stay with Adeline. Okay? No matter what."

"Got it. Be careful," Kyle said.

"You too."

Kyle began his walk down the street toward the large, open patio area where people were eating and drinking out in front of the nightclub. For the first time, the weight of the situation began to dawn on him. Here he was, *alone*, in Paris, the first line of defense against the *terrorists* trying to kidnap the President's daughter.

Terrorists trying to kidnap the President's daughter.

He stopped for a moment and took a deep breath. It didn't come easy. He felt he was way out of his league. He was happy to have Sarah and Zhanna with him, but they weren't really with him. Intel from Marv made it seem like the enemy was already here watching, and here Kyle doesn't even have a gun. All he was armed with was his charm. How the hell was that supposed to save him once they converged on him, even if he was lucky enough to convince Adeline Williams that she and her friend should leave with him. Highly unlikely. Maybe at the end of the night, after a few drinks and quite a few dances. But that would be too long. He had to think of something and he had to do it fast. But what? Sure, he had convinced women as gorgeous as Adeline to do a lot of crazy things, but not in a strange country, without a wingman, and without a place to take her to.

"Kyle, you're fine." Sarah's voice came in through his earpiece. "You look great, and I could tell by the conversation in the car that you are going to know exactly what to say."

Kyle took a deep breath. "Thanks, Sarah." It was exactly what he needed in that moment.

"Go get 'em. We won't be far. I'll be listening and we'll be right here around you if you need us."

Kyle felt his confidence returning to him. "I'll be fine. Just make sure you find out what else they're planning."

"Got it."

Kyle smiled. "Hey, Sarah? You ever see the movie *Four Christmases*. The one with Vince Vaughn?"

Sarah hesitated, not so sure where this was headed. Then she figured it out. "Uh, yeah . . . You want a safeword, don't you?"

"Ha-ha, yes. Yes I do."

Sarah laughed. "I don't think *mistletoe* will work in the middle of the summer."

Kyle smiled and began to walk onto the crowded patio full of young partiers. "Yeah, I was thinking . . . *menage a trois*."

"You're incorrigible."

"You love it."

Sarah ignored him. Kyle walked onto the plaza, adjusted his shirt, and did a quick scan. Out front there were a smattering of four-top tables, all full. A DJ stage at the back at the back of the plaza was situated by the large, bright-green, tunnel-like awning at the entrance to the club. Between the tables and the DJ stand encased by a long bar on either side was a crowd of dancers. As he walked to his left, around the tables and toward one of the bars, he had to fight his instinct to search the crowd for women he would want to take home with him. It wasn't easy to break a ten-year habit in only ten minutes.

What would Xander be looking for?

Kyle closed his eyes to clear his mind, and when he opened them, he saw the crowd in a completely different way. Almost everyone in the crowd was younger than he was. Twenty-nine wasn't old, but it was for this type of place. A young crowd was always a good thing in Kyle's mind, but especially good right now, because he figured if there were some of Khatib's men here, they would have to be older. Or at least the same age as Kyle. This would make them much easier to spot. There was always that crowd of drinkers who were just holding on too long, the sad ones who thought it was still cool for them to be in this type of environment. He would have to overlook them, but he figured that would be easy. The men who would be working for Khatib would be hard men. Killers. And usually that is a thing you wear on your face, whether you want to or not.

At the same time he was looking for possible enemies, he had to keep an eye out for Adeline—which was much more in his wheelhouse. But the first thing he needed to do was get a drink. It was like a weapon in a crowd like this. Without one, it was hard to feel confident in that intersexual battle. The line wasn't long, so he propped himself up against the bar and ordered a Vodka Red Bull.

After a moment, his drink arrived and he took a sip. It immediately made him think of Xander and all the times he and his friend had cheers'd these drinks and tore through bars together. The first sip went down cold, and it made him think of what Xander and Sam were doing at the moment. His heart jumped to his throat and began to beat as fast as the bass from the speakers around him. He knew he *had* to come through for his friend, because he knew Xander was going to come through for Natalie. He just wanted Xander to be proud of him.

"Hello, handsome."

Kyle nearly jumped out of his skin. He hadn't expected someone to approach him. He tried to recover quickly, but his mind was still divided.

"Hey—hey, how are you?" Kyle said to the brunette. She was tall, hair down below her shoulders, a bright-blue, tight-fitting bodycon dress, and if looks could kill, she would have been a shotgun. Normally, he would be ecstatic about her approaching him. But of course it happened when he had to stay focused. And there was no way he could stay focused if she remained standing in front of him. He needed an exit.

"I'm good. Better now," the woman said with a coy smile, her French accent thick.

Damn it.

Kyle took a sip. "Yeah? Listen, you are beautiful, but I'm so sorry, I am here with my girlfriend."

It was all he could come up with.

The woman squinted her eyes and gave him a suspicious look. "That's strange, because I saw you walk in from the street and you were alone. And here you are, only buying the one drink."

Shit.

She wasn't going to let him walk away.

He was going to have to be a dick.

"Listen—"

146

"There you are, baby!" Kyle heard a woman say, then he felt an arm slip around his waist. "I was looking everywhere for you!" Then he felt a kiss on his cheek. When he looked over, he was too shocked to form words. So the woman who had just wrapped her arm around him spoke to the dark-haired woman for him. "Who's your friend, baby?"

Before Kyle could speak, the dark-haired woman made a disgusted face, scoffed, and walked away in a fury.

Kyle turned to face the woman who had just saved him.

Adeline Williams.

All Aboard

Xander propelled his upper body up out of the water with a powerful kick of his legs, stretched his right arm as high as it would go, and wrapped his hand around the chrome guardrail. Before she could react, he snatched Sam by the back of the shirt and lifted her with his free hand until she too could reach the rail.

"Chivalry isn't dead," she quipped.

By the light shining on her from the top of the boat, Xander could see that her lips were blue and her face was pale. Yet her sense of humor remained. On the float to the middle of the boat, Xander had not seen anyone lurking. No shadowy figures with guns on the bow. It seemed odd. Sam pulled herself up and over the rail, then crouched down on the walkway to stay below the bottom of the window. Xander watched her do it but couldn't hear it due to the rushing of the water and the gurgle of the engine. That was a good thing. He pulled himself up and over, and crouched beside Sam.

Over the hum of the engine that rattled at the back of the long dinner boat, Sam whispered, "You see anyone?"

"Nobody."

Sam frowned. "I don't like this."

"No shit."

She glanced up to the top of the boat. "I'm going to make my way up there as you move inside from the back. I'll check the wheelhouse and see if there is anything suspicious. If it's just the captain, I'll move my way on over to the rooftop deck. We don't want the captain to alert anyone that we are here if we don't have to. I'll be able to cover you from the top."

Xander unzipped his go bag and handed Sam the SAT phone. "Take this. If something happens to me, call Sarah and get her to send a boat out here."

"If something happens to you, something happens to me."

"No, Sam." Xander took her forearm in his hand. "Not this time. If something happens to me, you have to get Natalie out of here. Promise me."

"Xan—"

He squeezed. "Sam, I can't have her get hurt. I can't let something happen to her because of me."

Xander watched Sam study his face. He could see her weighing the thought. "Fine. But, Xander?"

Xander just stared, waiting.

"This is the last time we do this to save a woman."

Xander didn't smile, and he didn't make a joke. His face was dead serious. "Sam . . . this is the last time we do this, period."

Xander let go of her arm and strapped the go bag back onto his back. As they parted ways, not another word was spoken.

Sam walked away toward the bow of the dinner boat. Xander duckwalked his way toward the stern. He stayed low in case there was an ambush waiting. He didn't want to alert them if they hadn't been already. Everything inside of him wanted to stand and see what he could through the window. But it was heavily tinted, and he didn't think it worth the risk. With each step closer to the back entrance to the dining room, his burning desire to catch a glimpse of Natalie seared through his being like a terrible itch that *had* to be scratched.

He came to the corner of the wall of windows at the back. He paused for a moment to listen. He couldn't hear a thing over the motor purring just below him now. He figured the boat was just about to come to the spot where Jack and Viktor were set up. It was time to make a move, but he didn't want to go in blind. Slowly, he inched the bend in his legs straighter as he gripped the bottom of the window. What he saw through that dark, tinted window felt like someone hitting him in the stomach with a tire iron. Though it was dark and she was at the far end of the room, Xander could see the dirty-blonde curl of Natalie's hair covering her face over the top of the restraint. Anger roared through Xander like a train through a tunnel. There she was, strapped to the wall, spears circling toward her head, just like he had seen on the live feed.

Only they were much closer now.

Xander swung the go bag around and unzipped it. He pulled out his Glock and a smoke grenade, then zipped the bag closed.

150

He felt for the knife in his pocket. And with a deep breath he rounded the corner and bolted for the entrance.

Sam jumped and grabbed hold of the edge of the roof that covered the front of the dining room below. She did a pull-up and swung her legs around behind her so she was lying flat on the top. Several feet away, the roof ended and the wheelhouse jutted out from the top of it. She stayed on her stomach and slithered her way toward the back of it. The windows were tinted much the same there as they were below, making it nearly impossible to see inside. She was careful, because she knew it would be much easier for the captain to see out. As she came to the first window, she held her left eye as close as she could without touching the glass, then cupped her hand over her right eyebrow to block any light she could. Like looking through a darkened filter, she could see the captain on the other side of the wheelhouse, with what looked like a coffee carafe in his hand. Nothing seemed out of the ordinary. She didn't know if that was good or bad. Could it be possible that the captain didn't know what was going on inside his own boat? She supposed so, especially if he was paid *not* to look; anything was possible.

Sam was about to slither back from the window when she noticed what looked like a monitor glowing on the right side of the captain. It had the four-quadrant video feed, where video of various spots of the boat should be, but instead the squares were all black; only the white line that separated them was glowing. It felt to Sam like the captain of this boat had no idea what he was carrying. Money has a way of eliminating questions.

Sam backed away and took in the rest of the top of the dinner boat behind her. The captain's view was blocked on the backside, so the rooftop deck would only be visible from the camera that she noticed on the back of the wheelhouse—the camera that was not currently broadcasting to the captain. A feeling crawled up Sam's spine, and it wasn't a good one. Something was off. She duckwalked along the roof and then hopped the rail onto the deck. It spanned from the middle of the boat all the way to the stern. She pulled her Glock and walked along the rail to ensure no one would be interrupting Xander.

Out of His League

Sarah and Zhanna walked around the block. The oversized nightclub and plaza encompassed the entire block and overlooked the river on the backside. The bright-green lighted roof covered the entire top of the club. It was glowing, and hideous—somewhat like a space-age, futuristic structure—but Sarah supposed it served its purpose of standing out. It matched the style of electronic music that was spilling out of the back deck of the place. When Sarah leaned over the railing, the smell of damp earth and mold greeted her. Below her there were quite a few boats tethered to a concrete walkway. Down that walkway toward the club, there was an entrance that boaters could use directly from their boats. A small dinner cruise boat looked like it had just docked, and young partiers filed out of it and headed up into the club.

"What are we looking for?" Zhanna asked Sarah.

"Anything out of place."

"Everything is out of place. This whole club is strangest

thing I have ever seen."

Sarah couldn't disagree with that. Most people, at least back in the States, didn't come to a place like Wanderlust from a boat. Mostly because this club was for younger adults. And most people who owned boats were older because it took a lot of money to keep up with a boat. But it made a little more sense seeing the partiers file out of the "party boat" down below them. The river did leave Wanderlust uniquely vulnerable. If you wanted to hurt a lot of people, you wouldn't even have to get inside the club. A boat full of explosives would do the trick.

A boat full of explosives.

Sarah pulled her earpiece out so she wouldn't confuse Kyle, took her cell phone from her pocket and dialed Marv.

Marv answered quickly. "How's it going out there?"

"How fast can you comb through CCTV cameras at the back of Wanderlust."

"Uh, five minutes."

Sarah looked up and down the row of boats below her. More intently at the few that were just under the large outdoor patio filled with people.

Sarah said, "See if you can find any boats that may have come in either looking suspicious or having suspicious individuals getting off."

"Will do," said Marv. "I'll get right back to you."

Kyle did his best to contain his look of shock when he looked over and found that the woman who had stepped in and saved him from the brunette was actually the woman he had come there to find.

What were the odds?

He took a quick breath and maintained his cool as he turned to face Adeline. He put his hands on his hips and smiled. "What makes you think I wanted to be saved?"

She mimicked his pose, placing her hands on her hips. "Please. It was written all over your face."

"That obvious, huh?" Kyle widened his smile and extended his hand. "Kyle."

Adeline took his hand. "Adeline. And this is my friend Karol. And yes, it was that obvious."

Kyle started to walk away. "Well, thanks. Have a nice night."

That wasn't what Adeline had been expecting. She was even better looking in person. Kyle only made it a few steps away before stopping, then turning back around. "Wait, I feel like I'm missing something."

Adeline and Karol shared a glance but said nothing.

"Someone is supposed to do something else here . . . maybe . . . buy someone a drink or something? Help me out, I'm really not good at this sort of thing."

Adeline smiled a knowing smile. "Oh, you aren't, are you?"

He walked back over. "I'm really not. I know you already saved my ass from certain disaster with that other woman, but I could use a little more help. Can you walk me through exactly what a man in my position is supposed to do when a beautiful woman does what you just did?"

"Poor, inexperienced Kyle," Adeline said as she took him by the arm. "Sure, don't worry your pretty little head. Karol and

I can help." She winked at Karol. "For starters, every time I have saved a guy like you in the past, the least they did was buy me a drink."

Kyle smiled. "And the most they did?"

"Well, the night is young. So hopefully you'll be able to tell me that yourself soon."

"Drinks it is."

The three of them laughed, but Kyle's smile quickly faltered. As they turned to the bar, Kyle noticed two men over Adeline's shoulder looking their way. It may not have registered to him at all if they hadn't both turned away so suddenly at the exact time he had looked at them.

Khatib's men.

They were here.

Kyle suddenly felt completely alone and entirely out of his league.

Riverboat Gamble

"You see anything, Viktor?" Jack asked. Jack had the bipod extended and resting on the metal rail as he peered through his night-vision scope. The scope gave everything a green tint. The river was a dark green, the sky a slightly lighter shade, and the boat that was approaching almost looked like an alien spaceship. "Viktor?"

Jack pulled his eye away from the sniper's scope. Viktor was gone.

"Shit, son! This ain't no time to be disappearin'!"

Jack swiveled his head from left to right, his vision a little distorted after peering through the green-tinted night-vision scope. He didn't see Viktor at all. Anger moved through the old cowboy. He had been putting up with this crazy bastard for days now. Which was fine, because he did help Xander out when he needed it, and he had his own kind of charm. But when you are out in the field, you have to be able to count on someone. And right now, this was the very worst of timing to disappear. Sam's and Xander's lives were at stake. Finally, he noticed a tree branch jostle to his right. "Viktor! Get your sorry ass out here right now!"

Viktor emerged from behind the tree, his zipper in his hand, and the streetlight showed a bewildered look on his face. "What is problem? Viktor haven't taken piss since plane!"

"I don't give a good goddamn, soldier. You piss your pants if that's what you gotta do. The boat is here!"

Viktor's face morphed into surprise. "Boat is here? Why you not just say so?"

Viktor pulled the night-vision monocular from his pocket and ran to Jack's side.

Jack just watched Viktor for a second, in awe of his obliviousness.

"Knucklehead," Jack said under his breath.

"I thought Xander was going inside boat, why he up top with Sam?" Viktor asked. He was staring toward the boat through his monocular.

Panic flooded Jack, and he dove his head back to the rifle's scope. "He ain't supposed to be up top."

As soon as he said it, smoke plumed inside the windows of the dining area of the boat. Jack knew that was Xander. What he didn't know was who was walking toward Sam as she peered over the opposite side of the boat.

Xander inched open the door to the dining room as gently as he could. He didn't want to draw the attention of others who were surely lurking somewhere on the boat. And he didn't want to draw Natalie's attention either, because she might make noise herself and trigger the unwanted company. It was unlikely they would be heard over the boat's engine, but it would be nice if he could get in and out of there without resistance. He knew that wouldn't be the case. Khatib would never just let Xander walk in and walk out without a fight. This was his "statement to the world," after all. Xander looped his finger through the ring of the M18 smoke grenade. He would have to move quickly once the smoke started, because it would completely engulf them in a matter of seconds. The smoke could complicate things for him if he couldn't see Natalie's straps to undo them quickly, but he felt the smoke could be a lifesaver at his back if Khatib's men approached while he was focused on freeing her.

Xander gave the pin a yank, waited until the bottom popped, and as soon as the white smoke began to rush from the bottom of the grenade, he rolled it inside and charged into the dining room. As soon as he cleared the smoke that was filling the room at a rapid rate, he was taken aback now that he was closer to Natalie. Everything was a blur. The coming through the smoke, the dim lighting, the fact that no one had tried to stop him. Something had to be coming, but he jogged toward her, so close now to getting her out of there.

"Natalie!" Xander shouted. He was right in front of her now.

It wasn't until she began to raise her head that he noticed she wasn't actually strapped to the wall at all.

Weird.

The straps were there, at her ankles and her hands, but they weren't fastened. Instead, Natalie's wrists were resting on pegs and she was standing on two foot-sized platforms. And now that he was close, that didn't look like her hair. It didn't look like her body either. Xander knew every inch of Natalie, and when her face was finally revealed, it was clear they had been set up.

This wasn't Natalie.

It was Melanie.

The wig had been convincing enough from a distance, but up close, Xander felt like a fool. The shock of seeing Melanie's sinister smile instead of Natalie's innocent face had almost been enough to get him killed. Melanie reached behind her back, and when she brought her hand around, it held a pistol.

"You move and you die."

Sam's body froze in place when she heard the man with the French accent behind her.

He said, "Drop that gun in your right hand. Then turn around very slowly. No sudden moves."

Sam did as he demanded and dropped the gun. She began to raise her arms toward the black sky above her. As she did, she started to turn toward him.

"Slowly," the man reminded her.

Sam's mind spun as she evaluated her options. If she pushed off hard enough, she could make it over the rail of the boat below her and into the water. The problem was, she would have to squat first to gather enough power for the dive. She would be dead by then. Rushing him wouldn't help either, because now that she was facing him, she could see he was holding a submachine gun of some kind. Even the worst shooter would be able to hit her at least once before she could reach him. However, there were no other options. If this was it, she wasn't going to go down without a fight.

The moment Sam dug her foot into the flooring of the rooftop deck and squinted her eyes in preparation of the gun going off, she heard a crack in the distance, and with almost zero lag time, the entire top half of the gunman's head disappeared in front of her. She had already begun her dive toward him, so she used his lifeless body as a tackling dummy, and as she landed on top of him, blood hemorrhaged from the top of where his head used to be. She glanced up to where the sound of the rifle had come from, and underneath a streetlamp at the river's edge, she could see a figure hunched over the rail—Jack—and a figure beside him, the shadow of his arms over his head, jumping up and down—Viktor. Before Sam could register an emotion, she heard a gunshot blast directly below her.

Xander.

In the Thick of It

As they approached the bar, Kyle heard Adeline saying something but couldn't make out what she said. His mind was on the men across the plaza watching him. The same men were now walking toward him. They didn't belong with this crowd. It was clear that this was going down, and it was going down now.

"Sarah, they're coming. I repeat, they are coming!" Kyle's voice was urgent.

Adeline and Karol looked up at him like he was crazy.

Adeline took a step back. "What did you just say?"

No time to sugarcoat. "Adeline, I need you to trust me, okay? We have to get out of here right now."

"What? Kyle, you're scaring me. Who are you?" Her face turned from confusion to fear.

"I don't have time to explain. I know you're the President's daughter and you both are in danger. You have to come with me now, Adeline!"

Adeline recoiled from Kyle's outstretched hand. The men over her shoulder were working their way quickly through the crowd.

"What's that behind the bar?" Adeline pointed. She looked worried.

Kyle's stomach turned just before he turned his head. But he didn't know what she was referencing; there was nothing but a couple of bartenders pouring. Kyle whipped his head back to Adeline, but all he saw was her tugging at Karol as they pushed their way through the crowd, toward the entrance of the club. This club was so big that once she made it inside, she would be almost impossible to find.

Kyle bolted for her, pushing one skinny partier to the ground.

"Adeline! Adeline, wait!"

Out of the corner of his eye he saw two more men making their way toward Adeline from the street. If they didn't run into a block by the crowd, they were going to beat Kyle to the girls.

"Adeline!"

She didn't turn; she was fighting her way through to the entrance now. The men behind him were no longer a concern, but the two men closing from the side were gaining faster than he could. Kyle continued to push forcefully through the crowd.

"Sarah! Damnit, Sarah, are you there? Four of Khatib's men are closing us in. Adeline is running inside the club, I need help getting to her!"

Sarah didn't answer.

Kyle didn't have time to worry about her and Zhanna too.

163

He could feel panic trying to overwhelm him. It was like a rising tide, pushing and pulling at his wits. Adeline and Karol made it inside the club. He was only twenty feet away now, but Khatib's men were only ten. He saw a small gap in the dancers, and as the bass from the speakers rattled inside his chest, he felt like his heart was going to explode. He made a final push and closed the distance fast. One of Khatib's men pushed past the bouncer at the door, but just before the second man could make it, Kyle dove through two females and barely sank his fingertips inside the collar of the dark-haired man's shirt, pulling him down to the ground with him.

Unfortunately for Kyle, because of the way he had to dive, the man ended up on top of him. The man immediately raised his fist and brought it down on Kyle's forehead. Black spots floated in front of his eyes, and a sharp pain stoked at the back of his head where it had been driven down hard onto the concrete beneath him. Through the swirling dark flashes, he saw the man raise his fist again. Instinct derived from hours on the mat with Xander kicked in, and Kyle shrimped out and away from the man while putting his bent leg in between the two of them for separation. Simultaneously, he moved his head to the right, and when the man's punch missed, Kyle trapped the man's arm in between his left arm and his rib cage. In one motion, Kyle kicked his right leg, the leg that was bent between them for separation, out and around the man's neck while he brought his left leg up and hooked it around his own ankle where his leg was draped along the back of the man's neck. Kyle had trapped the man's head, as well as his right arm at the shoulder, inside the triangle he purposely formed with his legs. The man was trapped in a triangle choke, but all Kyle could think of as he pulled the man's arm across his chest and the man's head down toward his groin, tightening the choke, was Adeline in the hands of Khatib's other goon.

No time for the choke.

As the man writhed in between his legs, desperately struggling for air, for freedom, Kyle let go of his head, and in three powerful and quick motions, he drove three head-splitting elbows into the man's forehead. After the second elbow, the man's body had gone limp. But Kyle's third one landed before he could stop it. Kyle unwrapped his legs, and the man collapsed to the concrete, blood leaking from his battered face. Kyle hopped up to his feet, and as soon as he turned for the door, the bouncer held up his hands—"I'm not going stop you"—and Kyle pushed into the club.

The club was packed full of people.

The music blared through the massive warehouse of a room.

The darkness was only highlighted in a few places by glowing, colored florescent rope lights.

Adeline could be anywhere.

Sarah practically pulled Zhanna to the ground as she ducked behind the boat.

"Do you think they saw us?" Sarah asked Zhanna.

"I don't think so. It's dark."

Sarah and Zhanna had walked down the steps from the street onto the concrete riverwalk where the boats were docked for their owners to enter Wanderlust. Marv hadn't called back, but Sarah didn't want to stand around and wait. As soon as they started to snoop around the boats for anything that looked suspicious, a fishing boat, like a mini version of one you would see in the ocean, pulled up to the dock. Sarah could have sworn that the man that ducked back into the cabin had a machine gun strapped around his shoulder.

"Did you see what I saw?" Sarah asked.

"Man with gun? Yes, I saw this."

Sarah's phone began to vibrate in her pocket. She didn't answer. One, because she didn't want anyone from the boat beside them to hear her. And two, because she knew it was Marvin, and she already knew what he didn't about the boat. It had to be Khatib's men. Unless it was a police boat and she just thought it was a fishing boat. Sarah was no sea woman. The closest she had come to hanging out on a boat was a Disney cruise for her nephew's birthday—oh, and killing some Russian thugs on Xander's yacht.

Zhanna whispered, "How is Kyle doing?"

Kyle!

"Shit!" Sarah whisper-shouted. "After I called Marv, I forgot to put my earpiece back in!"

"I am sure he is okay," Zhanna said.

Sarah fumbled in her pocket and replaced the earpiece. As soon as she put it to her ear, two men rushed off the suspicious boat, and it was clear from their attire that they weren't there to party. Both were dressed in all-black tactical gear. Sarah, Zhanna, and Kyle had walked right into the middle of a war.

"Kyle! Kyle, are you there?"

For a moment, all Sarah could hear in her right ear was the sound of obnoxiously loud music.

"Kyle!"

"Sarah?"

Sarah's stomach did a flip when she heard his voice over the music.

Kyle shouted, "Where the hell have you been—"

"Kyle! Listen to me! You have to get out of there! Get Adeline and get out of there, there are men coming for you!" Sarah said as loudly as she could while trying not to let anyone that might still be on the boat hear her.

"What?" Kyle shouted.

Shit. The music enveloping his voice seemed even louder. She had no choice but to shout.

"Get out of there! There are men coming for you!"

The music continued to play without a response. Had Kyle heard her?

Finally he responded. "No shit, Sarah! I've been trying to tell you that for five minutes now! I lost Adeline in the club and there are—"

"Hey!" a man shouted from the direction of the suspicious boat.

Kyle continued talking, but Sarah didn't hear what he said. She was forced to focus on the man shouting at her. She poked her head above the bow of the small boat she was hiding behind, and as soon as her eyes crested the wood, she could just make out a man staring back at her.

"Hey, who are you?" the man asked.

Sarah looked at Zhanna's clothing, then down at her own. There was no way they could pass for club goers. She wanted to tell Kyle again that men were after him, but it sounded like he already knew. She and Zhanna needed to get in there, fast. But she had to get by this man first.

"Help!" Sarah shouted. Then she stood, letting the man see her. "Please! Help me! My friend, she isn't breathing!"

Zhanna didn't miss a beat. She immediately lay back on her back and splayed out her arms and legs. Sarah ran around the front of the boat she was hiding behind.

"Please, can you please help me?"

The thin, dark-haired man said, "Sorry. I can't help. I'm sorry."

Sarah thought quickly. "Can you please call for an ambulance then? Please?"

"No—I mean . . . Hold on, I'm coming," the man said.

Sarah knew that would do the trick. She knew attention would be the last thing he would want to be drawn to this area right now. The man exited the boat and began walking toward her. As he came into the light, she could tell by the bulge in his pocket he was carrying a gun.

"Oh, thank you. Thank you!" Sarah said to him. "I don't know what happened, she just collapsed."

The man rounded the boat and saw Zhanna lying on the ground. Sarah moved in behind him, ready to knock him unconscious when the time was right. But she didn't have to. As soon as the man knelt down, Zhanna brought her right shin to the side of his head with an impressive force for a woman on her back. The man toppled over and face-planted on the concrete. Sarah pushed out her bottom lip and raised an eyebrow, impressed.

Zhanna jumped to her feet and shrugged her shoulders. "What? I thought he was going to try to give mouth to mouth."

Sarah pulled out her gun and spoke into her earpiece. "Kyle, where are you? We're coming!"

She waited a moment to hear Kyle's voice.

The only thing her right ear heard in return was music.

Where There's Smoke

Melanie fired the gun as soon as she brought it near Xander's head. With no time to spare, Xander was able to shoot his left arm up to meet hers, and the gun went off right beside his ear. He couldn't help but recoil from the painful sound. When he did, Melanie jumped from her foot pegs and drove Xander to the ground. He managed to get his hand on her wrist that held the gun, and he banged it as hard as he could against the hardwood floor. She punched him in the face, and through the smoke he grabbed for her, but he only came away with the wig. He slammed her gun hand against the floor again, and this time she let out a yelp as the gun skittered across the floor.

Now she was in trouble.

The white smoke was so thick at that point that his eyes began to water and his lungs began to burn. Xander reached up and grabbed her by the throat. She wrapped both her hands around his wrist as he squeezed, but there was nothing she could do. He was too strong. With the force of a car accident, Xander slammed her down to the floor beside him, removing her from her straddled position over him. When her shoulder smashed into the floor, all the air gusted from her lungs and she choked trying to find a breath. He held his hand to her throat as he rose to his knees and began to apply downward pressure, taking his grip from painful to excruciating.

"Where"—cough—"is Natalie?"—cough, cough. His lungs were on fire, and his voice didn't sound like his own. The anger inside him was boiling over. Of course, Melanie couldn't answer with her throat being smashed in his grip, but he didn't let up. "Where?"

"Melania! Where are you?" a man shouted from the opposite end of the dining hall.

Xander released his hold on Melanie, took a deep breath, and rolled into the thickest of the white smoke. He didn't know how many would be coming in after him, but he was certain they would be armed, and you can't shoot what you can't see. He unzipped his pocket, pulled out his Marfione OTF knife, put his gun in his pocket, zipped up his pocket, and pressed the button on the grip, releasing the blade from its sheath. All he could see was red. He turned over and dropped to his stomach. The smoke wasn't quite as thick there. To his left, he could just make out Melanie, holding both hands to her throat, still trying to catch her breath from the squeeze of Xander's grip. Back to his right, he could see boots. Three sets of them. The smoke swirled from the doorway and around the movement of the men who were entering the dining room. Xander put his mouth down to the floor, sucked in the cleanest air he could, then rose to a crouch, knife at the ready.

After hearing the gunshot below her, Sam pushed herself up off the half-headless gunman, commandeered his MP5 submachine gun, gave it a press check, and took a deep breath before making her way to the side of the rooftop deck. She wasn't going to go barging into the dining room. She knew Xander could defend himself. And she knew she wouldn't be able to see inside with all the smoke. The best thing she could do was scour the outside and make sure she at least kept as many bad guys away from him as she could. She jogged over to the starboard side of the boat, and just as she looked down over the edge, she heard another rifle shot from the distance, and the man below her went down instantaneously. Jack had that side of the boat covered for at least another minute as the boat floated by his position on the river's edge.

Something moved in the corner of Sam's eye. Her reflex automatically brought the MP5 to firing position, and just as another man pulled himself up on the roof, Jack put a bullet in him as well. Sam quickly looked down below that man and squeezed off a quick burst of rounds, dropping the gunman just below his ally. She then moved immediately to the other side of the boat where she saw the tail ends of two more men running around the corner to the front of the boat. They were moving toward the men she and Jack had just taken out. If they continued to run around to the other side, they would be dead in Jack's range.

Sam shouldered her weapon, hopped the rail, and dropped

down to the walkway, trapping the men between her own gun and Jack's sniper rifle on the other side of the boat. She stalked toward them as they disappeared around the front. She glanced behind her to make sure she was alone. That was when she heard the blast of Jack's sniper rifle again. She brought the butt of the MP5 to her shoulder, and as the second gunman rounded the corner back toward her, just as his face registered the shock of looking down the barrel of her gun, she put a three-round burst into his chest, dropping him face-first to the floor of the boat.

From above her, a man shouted down to her. She swung her gun in the direction of the wheelhouse and found a man—not the captain—holding a pistol on her. He had her dead to rights, so she released her grip on the MP5, and it hung down by her side from the shoulder strap.

The man extended his arms, making sure Sam could see the gun. "Keep your hands up. Who are you?"

Sam raised her hands, once again calculating her options.

From the front of the boat a man walked out of a door and shouted, "Hold it right there!"

In one motion, Sam spun toward the man at the front of the boat, took the MP5 in her hand, and as she fell onto her back she fired at the man who stood outside the doorway some thirty feet away. Before she could see if she had hit him, she looked straight up from her back, and as the man from the wheelhouse leaned over the rail to take a shot at her, she squeezed the trigger and a string of bullets blasted the man in the chest and neck. She had no time to do anything but jump to her feet and jump forward out of the way of the man's body falling straight for her from the railing. A bone-cracking thud hit the deck beside her only a millisecond after she moved. She immediately turned back toward the man at the front of the boat, expecting to see yet another gun trained on her, but instead the yellow light from the side of the boat showed her a man on his side, crawling toward his gun that had fallen from his hands. She must have hit him somewhere in the leg because the arm that wasn't reaching for the gun clutched at his right knee.

"Don't move," Sam warned. The man stopped reaching.

In a French accent, he pleaded with Sam. "Please. Please do not shoot me. I was just hired for security. I do not know the men who chartered this boat. Please, you must believe me."

Sam didn't believe him.

She walked toward him, and he quickly reached for his gun. That was when Sam shot a hole in the man's hand. His hand recoiled from the gun, and he let out a scream of agony that echoed across the river and bounced back to Sam's ear from the riverwalk.

Sam moved over to him, kicked him in the side of the head, then put her boot to his wrist, trapping his injured hand against the boat's wood-planked flooring. The man let out another awful scream. Sam leveled the MP5 at his head and cleared her throat.

"If you think this is pain, wait and see what I do if you don't tell me where is the man is who's behind all of this."

The man looked up at Sam, searching her eyes for a hint of mercy.

He found none.

Getaway Clean

Kyle frantically searched the dark, overcrowded, and overly loud nightclub. He couldn't let Khatib's men get to Adeline and her friend before he did. And he couldn't continue to bowl over the people dancing in the club like he had been doing, or he would also have to deal with bouncers. He weaved his way through the sea of partiers like a boxer parrying punches. He came up on a woman with blonde hair, grabbed her shoulder to turn her around, and he only found a scowl from someone who looked nothing like Adeline. The way he was going about finding her was hopeless. The crowd was too large, and from the vantage point of being on the floor with them it was impossible to see more than three or four people in front of him. He needed a better spot to search from.

Against the wall on his right, a woman dressed in a black

leather bikini was dancing on a raised platform. Kyle had no time to be concerned with how ridiculous this place seemed. Instead, he pushed past several more drunken partiers and climbed up beside the dancing woman. She took it as him wanting to party so she began grinding up against him. To avoid causing a scene, he let her dance as he scanned the room all around him. Up ahead, about thirty feet in front of him, in the soft glow of the neon lights, he noticed Khatib's man push a woman into an area that disappeared around the corner.

The woman looked just like Adeline.

He was too late.

Kyle jumped down from the platform. The time for moving slowly through the crowd was over. As he pushed through, men and women alike were thrown to the right and to the left, and some to the ground. Kyle's heart was pounding. He may have just let the President's daughter be kidnapped, or worse, killed. He knew he wasn't cut out for this. He should have listened to Xander, to Sam. He should have just let them take on this part of Xander's life. He should have just stayed in his lane and watched over the King's Ransom bourbon company. He knew he wasn't much of a business man, but he had to be better at that than he was at this. At saving people. What happened in Syria had just been a fluke. Xander was going to be so disappointed in him—

When Kyle rounded the corner where he had seen Adeline get shoved, the butt of a gun came flying toward his face. Instinct made him parry to the left and the gun came down, grazing his ear, knocking his earpiece out before the gun banged against his shoulder. He immediately stepped inside the man's reach, put his hip against the gunman's, wrapped his right arm under the man's outstretched arm and on around his neck, and twisted hard to his left, throwing the man onto his back. With the man's arm still trapped, Kyle bent his wrist in a way that made him drop the gun; then he stomped down on the man's head with the heel of his shoe, knocking him unconscious.

Kyle looked up from the gunman, and his entire body relaxed when his eyes found Adeline and her friend staring back at him. Adeline threw her arms around him, relief rushing to her face, as she now knew Kyle could be trusted.

Kyle asked, "Are you all right? Did he hurt you?"

Adeline let go of him and stepped back. "We're fine, how did you know we were here at Wanderlust tonight?"

"Doesn't matter, we have to get out of here, now!"

Adeline nodded and grabbed Karol's hand with her left and Kyle's hand with her right. Just like that, the three of them were lost in a sea of people. Kyle thought for a moment that the best way to keep Adeline safe might just be to stay right where they are. Right in the middle of the hundreds of sweat-drenched, alcohol-dazed people who were so involved in trying to get high, or get laid, that they hadn't even noticed Kyle taking out the bad guy.

Taking out the bad guy.

Kyle liked the sound of that. Maybe he was pretty good at this, after all. The problem for him now was that he had no idea where to go. Here he was, in a place he didn't know, in a city he didn't know, and *he* of all people was the only thing standing between the daughter of the President and some crazy-ass terrorist with a hard-on for Xander. He knew there would be more men at the front of the club. That is where they saw him and Adeline run to. He remembered Sarah saying they would check out the back by the river. Kyle tugged Adeline toward the back wall where there was another hallway. A large bald man, built like the Incredible Hulk, stood guard. Kyle made his way up to the big man. He leaned down to hear what Kyle had to say.

Kyle shouted over the thumping music. "Does this lead out to the back?"

The man made no indication that he understood; he simply flipped his arm in a brushing motion, silently telling Kyle to go back the other way. Kyle then realized he was in France. He probably didn't speak much English. But there is one universal language that everyone speaks.

Cash.

As Kyle dug inside his pocket, Adeline tugged sharply at his arm, then began to pound on his back. He looked back at her, but she was looking back over her shoulder. Kyle followed her eyes, and his heart sank when he noticed two men swimming through the crowd just a few feet from them. Kyle tugged at his money clip, pulled out the hundred-dollar bill on top, and stuck it out toward the massive bouncer. It may as well have been a key. The bouncer immediately took the hundred, lifted the rope, and Kyle practically lifted Adeline off her feet as he ushered the girls down the hallway.

The hallway seemed more like a cave the farther they walked into it. It was a half-circle shape with only a few dimly lit sconces every few feet on the wall. After about twenty feet, the music began to fade and Kyle could finally hear himself think.

"Where are we going? Who are these people?" Adeline asked. Her voice was shaky; fear had settled in.

Kyle continued to pull Adeline and Karol along. "It's going to be okay. I have people with me outside. They're going to help us get out of here."

It was then that Kyle finally saw a door, marking the end of the tunnel. He looked back over Karol's head and didn't see anyone coming for them yet. Everything inside him hoped to see Sarah and Zhanna when he opened that door. He reached for the metal knob, gave it a twist, and when the door opened, a cool rush of air washed over them and along with it came relief.

That feeling of relief was short lived.

"Hold it right there!" a man told Kyle.

As the door shut behind them, Kyle hoped that the French accent meant the French police. But when he turned to his left to have a look, all he found was the end of two submachine guns, being held by two men who were clearly not police officers. Every muscle in Kyle's body knotted up when he heard the girls scream.

A man dressed in all-black tactical gear nodded toward Kyle. "Don't get any ideas. You play hero, you die."

The girls screamed yet again.

"Shut up! Stop screaming or I'll shoot you too!" the gunman shouted at Adeline and Karol.

That was when Kyle saw Sarah and Zhanna round the corner behind the men.

Sarah shouted, "Don't move! Put your guns down!"

As soon as both men turned toward Sarah's voice, Kyle didn't hesitate. Gunfire erupted, and he pulled Adeline in the opposite direction of the men and straight down a set of stairs that opened to a concrete walkway by the river. Adeline was sobbing. Kyle's heart was racing as he surveyed the boats tethered to cleats on the walkway. He pulled the girls toward the only boat that looked like it had enough motor to speed away, and after helping them over the rail on the bow, he untied the rope and pulled himself onboard. Kyle didn't know a lot about boats, but he did okay on one in Syria when he had to, so he figured he could do the same here. As he moved along the side of the boat, it was clear it was some sort of fishing vessel. He pushed the girls inside the open door of the cabin, then stepped up into the captain's chair. He searched the dash, and he audibly exhaled when he noticed the key still in the ignition.

"There's a key!" He couldn't contain himself. "Sit down, girls, I'm going to get us out of here!"

He gave the key a turn and the boat fired right up. Kyle looked back at Adeline and pumped his fist. She smiled through her tears and gave him a nod. Kyle glanced through the front window of the boat trying to see if Sarah and Zhanna were okay, but the back entrance to the club wasn't visible from the water. He sent up a silent prayer for them, threw the boat in reverse, and backed out into the river. Darkness swallowed them as they moved away from the lights on shore and the boat groaned when he pushed it forward, leaving Sarah and Zhanna to fend for themselves. Kyle had seen Sarah in action, so he had high hopes that she would be okay. He felt his body relax. Even though he had no idea where they were going, at least they were safe.

"Uh, Kyle?" Adeline spoke up from behind him.

"Yeah?" He didn't look back.

"What the hell is this thing?"

The relaxing of his body hadn't lasted long. At the worried tone in her voice, he didn't have to turn around to see before his body tensed up completely. He turned toward her. She had managed to find a light switch, and the light from the bulb shone directly down on a large metal trunk bolted to the floor. Kyle couldn't see what Adeline was looking at down inside the trunk, but every single fiber of his being knew it wasn't good.

No Respect

Through the white smoke, from his crouched position, Xander could see the three sets of boots spreading out. The men were coughing as they moved, frantically searching for him, and for Melanie. Xander tightened his grip on the knife as everything slowed down for him. A set of boots moved right toward his position, another set a couple of feet away moved closer to the middle of the room, and the last set of boots moved a couple more feet beyond those. He saw the entire thing happen in his mind before he made his own move. He would rise up, stab for the groin and the neck area of the first set of boots. A quick one-two. Then he would spin clockwise, cover the distance between the two men, wheeling the knife around out in front of him, aiming for the second man's neck area, and in case he missed, he would immediately give three more quick stabs down the vertical line of the man's body. One-two-three.

Without any pause and maintaining the crouch from where he just made his last vertical stab, Xander would lunge forward, thrusting the knife toward the last man's groin. Then he would immediately remove the knife and give three more lightning-quick stabs vertically up the man's body, ending with the fatal stab wound in his throat.

Xander flashed back out of his mind's eye when it was time to execute the deadly choreography he just witnessed in his head. The boots of the first man were in perfect position, so he began.

Stab to the man's groin, stab to the man's neck.

Quick spin and a stab to the next man's neck, then one-two-three quick stabs down the man's body,

A powerful thrust forward with the knife, sinking it somewhere near the third man's groin—then one-two-three super-fast stabs up the man's body, the last one sinking in the soft skin of the man's neck.

Xander removed his knife from the man's neck, and hot liquid splashed onto his face. He instinctively shoved the man away from him, and his body landed like a sack of flour on the floor of the smoke-filled dining room. Xander didn't have time to relish in the three-kill move, because under the risen smoke, he saw a set of feet disappear through a window along the wall of the boat.

As Sam held her gun to the man's head, waiting impatiently for

him to tell her where she could find Khatib, she heard a thump behind her and what sounded like someone gasping wildly for air. She pressed harder with her foot down on the gunman's injured hand as she swung the MP5 around her body and pointed it toward the sound. Under a light shining down on the walkway from the rail of the rooftop deck, she could see a half-naked woman in a fetal position, back turned to her. Sam's immediate thought was that it was Natalie. She was so caught off guard that she momentarily forgot the man under her boot was not unconscious. That moment of lapse was enough time for the man to get his free arm wrapped around Sam's legs, and just as the half-naked woman began to get to her feet, Sam's legs were swept out from under her, and she fell to her stomach on the teakwood decking of the boat. By the time Sam looked back to kick the man in the face, the woman had turned toward her.

The woman with dark hair.

It wasn't Natalie.

Melanie.

A hundred thoughts swirled, but Sam's hatred of the woman who had betrayed her and Xander at the deepest level pulled her instinct through the maze of confusion, and she wrapped her finger around the trigger of her submachine gun. Melanie must have registered the danger immediately because she stopped dead in her tracks.

Sam shouted, "Where's Xander?"

"Dead, most likely."

Melanie having a Russian accent was still a shock to Sam's senses. She moved to one knee, never taking the MP5's aim from the middle of Melanie's chest.

"Don't forget the fact that I would absolutely revel in

184

killing you, Melanie. Now tell me where Xander is, or I will shoot you. With a smile on my face."

"I'm not afraid of you, Sam. You are washed-up agent riding on back of Xander."

"Not quite sure what that even means really. D'you mean riding his coattails? You always did seem a bit dim."

"Dim? You—"

"Oh shut it," Sam interrupted. "Tell me where Natalie is right now or I will shoot you. Do you understand?"

Before Melanie could answer, the SAT phone began to ring in Sam's pocket.

"Don't move, Melanie."

Sam glanced behind her; the man was still unconscious. She removed the phone from her pocket and answered.

"Marv?"

Marv was adamant. "Sam, don't approach the boat! We believe it's a trap!"

In an even tone as she kept the gun trained on Melanie, Sam said, "You don't say?"

"Shit, I'm sorry, is everyone all right?" Marv asked.

At that moment, Xander walked around the back end of the boat. Without realizing it, Sam let out a sigh of relief. "I don't really have time to talk right now. Would you please find out some real information? You're in danger of making Xander look bad for calling you the smart one of the bunch."

"I'm on it."

Sam heard Marv's words but didn't reply. She ended the call and rose to her feet, both hands on her weapon now.

Xander spoke up from behind Melanie, startling her. "Nowhere to go, Melanie. Tell us where Natalie is, or die. No more games."

Sam looked past Melanie and saw that Xander was holding a pistol. Melanie looked back over her shoulder at Sam, then back to Xander. Sam knew what Melanie was about to do, but there was nothing she could do to stop her. She knew that Xander would recognize the same thing.

Sam said, "Don't do it, Melanie. You won't get away."

"Fuck you, bitch."

That was when Melanie did what Sam and Xander were both expecting. She knew neither of them would shoot for fear they may shoot each other, so she took one heavy step and dove over the side of the boat. Sam ran to the rail and opened fire, shooting several rounds into the dark river water below. But she may as well have been shooting into a black hole. The lights of the boat didn't extend to the water. She shouldered the MP5, pulled out the SAT phone, and began walking toward Xander when she noticed him going for the rail.

"Xander, don't!"

Xander paused midclimb on the chrome rail. He then lowered himself back down.

"Did you hear what she called me?" Sam asked as she walked up to him. She secured the gun's strap around her shoulder and handed the SAT phone to Xander. "This bitch is mine."

Xander smirked. "That water is gonna be awfully cold, Sam."

"Just find Natalie. I have a feeling Melanie might just lead me straight to Khatib if I can stay on her."

"Fine, but keep the SAT phone. Get the agent's phone number that drove us here from Marv. I'll be carrying that. If she leads you to Khatib, you wait for me."

"If I can take him out—"

"Sam," Xander interrupted. "Promise me you'll wait."

Sam gave Xander a hug, then readied herself to jump from the rail. "Promise me when I call, you'll be ready."

Xander nodded, then turned and ran toward the back of the boat, and dove right over the rail to swim back to Jack and Viktor.

"He's like a bloody fish," Sam said aloud to herself. Then she dove toward the cold darkness below after Melanie— toward their best shot at finding Akram Khatib.

Getting Off the Boat Would Be the Bomb

"Adeline, come up here and steer the boat," Kyle said. "Just make sure to keep it in the middle of the river, and try not to hit anyone."

Kyle wanted to see for himself what Adeline had found inside the large metal case. Adeline didn't say a word; she just moved toward the captain's chair. Karol was frozen in place, in awe of the metal box's contents.

When Adeline took the wheel, Kyle could see the fear fully encompassing her eyes. "K-Kyle, please tell me you know how to fix this?"

Kyle didn't answer, because he didn't know what she was talking about. He walked over to the metal box and stood beside Karol. He took a deep breath and looked down.

"Holy shit" rolled slowly out of Kyle's mouth. He hadn't meant to say it. He hadn't wanted to react at all so as not to further frighten the girls. But with what he saw, he just couldn't help it.

"Holy shit?" Adeline began to panic. "What do you mean holy shit? You're CIA, aren't you, Kyle? Surely you've seen a bomb before! You know how to defuse it, right? Isn't that what they teach you? Please tell me that's what they teach you!"

Kyle didn't react. Again, not what he wanted. But the blocks of what he assumed were large piles of explosives, all stacked and tied together with a maze of wiring, had stolen his ability to speak. He had never seen a bomb in person before. But he and Xander rarely missed a movie. And they had seen many a movie that did have bombs, and one dead giveaway, above all others, was the little digital readout with red numbers methodically counting down toward what was always a massive explosion. And this countdown had just gone below the ten-minute mark.

"A bomb," Kyle said, almost unconsciously.

"Kyle! Hello?"

Kyle looked up at Adeline. He was certain that the fear he saw on her face paled in comparison to his own.

"Kyle!" Adeline shouted again. "You can fix this, right?"

"No."

Adeline made sure the boat was still moving straight, then turned to him.

"No? You can't fix this?"

"No, I can't fix this, and no, I am not CIA."

It was as if his mouth was on autopilot. Not only was he not in control of his mind, his words, and almost his bladder, he was actually saying the worst possible things he could at the moment. He took a deep breath and finally began to move past the shock and fear that had taken hold of his brain.

189

"Wait, you're not even CIA? We're screwed, Karol. We're dead."

Adeline's last words finally snapped Kyle back to reality.

"I can get us out of this," Kyle told her as he reached for the burner phone in his pocket that Sam had given him from Xander's go bag.

Karol spoke up for the first time since the discovery of the bomb. "You can? You can get us out of this?"

Kyle opened the phone and went to the contacts where Sarah's number was stored. As it began to ring, he walked over to Adeline and relieved her of her station at the wheel. He began to power down the boat's engine. He figured the only thing they could do was jump from the boat and swim for it. He didn't want to pull the boat toward land, because if the blast was as big as the bomb looked, more innocent people may be killed. He also didn't know if that would even make a difference. The bomb was massive. He had no idea what that meant as far a blast radius, but it looked like it was going to reach much farther than just the side of the riverbank.

"Kyle?" Sarah finally answered.

"Sarah!" Kyle shouted. He had never been happier to hear a woman's voice.

"You're okay! How is Adeline?"

"Sarah, I don't have time to explain, but the boat we jumped on has a bomb on it. A bomb! What do we do?"

"You must have jumped on the boat full of Khatib's men. Shit! A bomb?"

Sarah hesitated for only a moment.

"Kyle, get off the boat! Now!" she shouted.

It was obvious, and Kyle knew it. He also knew the answer to his next dumb question, but he asked anyway. "You don't know how to stop it? It might be a big one. Big enough to level a couple of city blocks, or worse!"

"Kyle, you can't stop the bomb. Get off the boat! I'll call Marv and tell him that the position where your burner phone is, is a bomb. We'll do everything we can from there! Call me as soon as you are safe. That phone was in Xander's bag, so it will be waterproof. Go now, Kyle!"

The urgency in Sarah's voice lit the fire in Kyle. He pocketed the phone and shut down the boat's engine.

Adeline shouted, "What are you doing? We can't stop in the middle of the river!"

Kyle walked over to her and ushered Adeline and Karol out of the cabin and moved them toward the back of the boat. "We have to get off here. We can't risk the bomb exploding close to shore."

The two of them didn't argue. Kyle glanced once more at the bomb and the red number ticked down to an even 8:00, then 7:59. They could swim to shore in eight minutes. The Seine River wasn't all that wide. But only if they hurried. The three of them arrived at the back of the boat, but instead of looking down over the end of the boat to the water they were about to dive into, all three of their sets of eyes were fixed on the two sets of lights that were speeding toward them out in the water.

Adeline turned toward Kyle with a look of hope in her eyes. "They're here to save us, right, Kyle?"

Kyle wanted to believe it was true, but deep in the pit of his stomach, he knew that the two boats speeding toward them weren't there to help. The only people who could know where they were that quickly were the people who had planted the bomb in the first place.

"Adeline, you and Karol have to run."

191

"What?"

Kyle could see the terror in her eyes now. "You have to go and jump off the front of this boat, swim to shore, and run."

Adeline panicked. "No, Kyle! We have to stay together! You have to keep us safe!"

The two boats were almost to them.

"I will. But I have to stay here to do it. Go now, Adeline. Go as fast as you can! I'll create a distraction from here. Just go!" he shouted, then shoved the two of them toward the front of the boat.

Karol stopped and turned toward Kyle. "Do you think these men know what Adeline looks like?"

Kyle was baffled. "What? It doesn't matter! Go!"

"Wait!" Karol shouted, holding her ground. "If Adeline gets captured, they can use her to really hurt the US, right?"

Kyle shoved the two of them again toward the front of the boat. "Exactly, now go!"

Karol turned to Adeline. "Addie, go now! Jump off the boat and swim as fast as you can. If they have me and Kyle on this boat, and they think that I am you, they won't keep looking for you."

Adeline's jaw dropped. "No way, Karol! You can't do that. I could never—"

"She's right!" Kyle interjected. "I know it's awful, Adeline, but she's right. I promise I won't let them hurt her, now go!"

Kyle knew he probably couldn't fulfill that promise, but he would die trying if that's what it took.

Karol shouted at her friend. "Addie, the boats are here. Go!"

Adeline grabbed Karol and wrapped her in a hug. Karol shucked her friend's arms away and pushed her to the bow of the boat. "Go, Addie. Now!"

Adeline turned, dove, and disappeared over the bow of the boat. Kyle immediately grabbed Karol and ducked back inside the cabin, frantically searching for anything he could use to distract the men on the oncoming boats. Or even better, kill them. He saw a harpoon fixed to the wall, but that wouldn't help. There were a few fishing rods, life preservers, and a net. No help. Then he noticed a locker in the corner of the cabin. He rushed over to it, and as he sent up a silent prayer that there would be something, *anything*, that he could use, he heard the boats' engines begin to slow. As he placed his hand on the metal handle of the locker, he knew that what he found inside might very well be the difference between life and death—for him and for Adeline's brave friend Karol.

Wild Goose Chase

"We have found the boat. I will call you as soon as we have them. There should only be about eight minutes on the timer—"

"Then you had better hurry! Stop the bomb, capture them, and bring them to me where I am holding the American actress. It will make the show far greater with President's daughter as part of the cast. Do not fuck this up!" Khatib ended the call and slammed the cell phone down on the desk.

Whoever had managed to retrieve the President's daughter *and* move the boat with the bomb away from the crowded nightclub had quite possibly ruined his big plans. Khatib sat in his chair, stewing. He figured the CIA must have had one of their best operatives in Paris. But he had no idea how they found out about Wanderlust. Khatib himself hadn't known it would be the bomb site until they found out that was where the President's daughter would be going. Having the bomb ready to be moved from the van to the boat had been a stroke of genius on his part, but he didn't care about that now.

Khatib opened the laptop on his desk, and the live video feed of Natalie Rockwell strapped to the wall immediately made him feel better.

"There you are," he said aloud to himself. "So what if I don't blow up nightclub? The President's daughter will soon be in my possession, and *you* . . ." He touched the screen where Natalie's face was, as if he were wiping her tears. "*You* are going to be all the publicity I will need."

Khatib moved his fingers to the keyboard, and after a few strokes the stats of who was watching the live feed on the website pulled up in front of him. He couldn't help but smile. Even he had underestimated just how much America loved their Hollywood star. The count for active users was now up to over two hundred million worldwide. Two hundred million people were going to watch live as the spinning spikes drove through the head of their star. And America could do nothing to stop it. He knew the trickle effect of that fear would shape the rest of the world's view of just how vulnerable the United States really was.

He keyed back to the live feed where the spikes were getting really close to their mark. But there was so much going on that he couldn't full enjoy it. He glanced back at his phone. Only an hour more and the spikes would reach their target. He had to make sure that it wasn't interrupted. And that was almost a foregone conclusion now as it would be nearly impossible— even if Xander knew Natalie's exact location—to reach her in time. Melania had just called to be picked up, so he knew that Xander had fallen for the trap. But somehow he managed to survive. Khatib wasn't the kind of man to sit back and wait. He had been careful when he had transported Natalie to where she was being held. And even though he interrupted the cameras around the dinner boat Natalie was actually on, he knew the CIA was scouring for clues. He knew they would be picking every little detail of the feed apart and searching every public camera in the city. That is why he went to such pains to recreate the boat's interior dining room where Natalie was. It matched perfectly the one where he had stationed Melania. That is why they sent Xander there. He knew the CIA agents, when they combed the CCTV cameras, would compare the live feed to old pictures of the dining room in the boat where Melania had posed as Natalie. And it had worked.

But Xander escaped.

Khatib knew Xander could never find Natalie. He had fallen for every bit of bait that had been laid in front of him. But he couldn't believe Xander had escaped the trap on the boat. Xander was the only thing that could possibly stand in the way of this working, so he needed to ensure that the wild goose chase continued to keep him and his team guessing. That is when his phone began to ring.

Khatib answered, "Melania."

"Akram, Xander's Sam is following me."

Perfect.

Khatib said, "She will relay where you go back to Xander somehow. We have them right where we want them."

"You should have let me kill him at warehouse earlier. It was mistakes like this that cost Vitalii Dragov and his partner, Martin King, their lives. I know you wanted to get his humiliation on camera, but it is games like these and this stupid thirst for revenge that will ruin this for you."

Khatib slammed his fist against the table. "You were supposed to capture him on that boat! I will be the one to kill him. He murdered my brother!"

The both of them were silent for a moment. Khatib's breathing was heavy. The anger he felt toward Xander had clouded his judgment. Melania was right. But Xander simply dying wasn't enough. The world seeing that America's best soldier could be defeated by a terrorist's own hands was far more important to Khatib. Showing the world that the days of their enemies hiding in bunkers and striking from afar were over was what would truly bring them fear.

Melania spoke up. "Where would you like me to lead them?"

Khatib stood from his desk and walked over to the window. "Lead them back to the warehouse."

Melania sounded surprised. "The warehouse where we had the Uber car bring Xander from the airport earlier?"

"Yes. I still have men there. Trap Xander and Sam there until I am finished with Natalie and President Williams's daughter."

"Xander will not just be trapped there. Not while he knows that Natalie's time alive on that wall will be coming to an end. I will have to kill him to keep him there." Melania did her best to explain.

Khatib let out a sigh. Everything inside of him wanted vengeance for his brother first. But he would not be like his brother and let other things get in the way of the larger plan. If Xander had to die by another's hand, at least he would still be dead. Vengeance would still be achieved.

Khatib finally let go of his own desires and did what was best for the cause. "Then you will kill him. You were right about what you said earlier. I cannot let revenge get in the way of my strike against America. It is far more important than

Xander King. Just make sure it is painful death."

Melania answered without hesitation.

"It will be my pleasure."

Khatib ended the call. It was time for him to go and pay Natalie a visit. And almost time to deliver his speech to America and the entire watching world while she died a violent death behind him. Bringing in Adeline Williams at the end would be the showstopper. Imagine the ransom America would pay to see her returned safely to their leader. A ransom far more valuable than money. They would be forced to break one of their most steadfast rules and finally negotiate with a terrorist. The American people's faith in their government would forever be diminished.

Kyle's Main Squeeze

"Sarah!" Kyle answered his phone.

"Kyle! Are you all right?"

Kyle was terribly out of breath, and his heart was racing. The two boats that had been speeding toward him had pulled up to the stern. He imagined they would be coming aboard at any moment. After finding only an iPad and a bowie knife in the locker inside the cabin, he and Karol made a break for the bow of the ship. As reality set in that he had no way to fight the men who would certainly be carrying guns, he considered jumping off the boat, and he and Karol would just swim after Adeline and take their chances. But he knew that would only get all three of them captured, or killed. He pulled Karol to the deck of the boat, and the iPad in her hand flashed a message notification on the screen.

Kyle finally answered Sarah. "No, I'm not all right! I'm on a boat, with a bomb, and some mercenary thugs after me!"

Sarah seemed baffled. What was he still doing on the boat?

"Then jump, Kyle!" she screamed. "For God's sake, they'll kill you and the President's daughter!"

"Adeline is gone. We made her jump and swim for it. Karol says maybe the men will think she's Adeline. You think that will work? You think that will keep them from searching for Adeline?"

"I don't know, but the two of you will be dead. Do you have any weapons? Is there any way you can take them out?"

Kyle heard Sarah, but he had no idea how to answer. He raised up from behind some sort of bolted container that he and Karol were hiding behind at the bow; he heard the voices of men shouting at the back of the boat. The men were boarding. Kyle and Karol had two choices: jump and try to swim to safety, ruining the iPad in the process and maybe Adeline's chances of escaping, or hold out as long as he could while the file loaded on the screen—a file that Kyle thought could be the very thing that might save Natalie—then take his and Karol's chances on trying to fight off the men who were after them.

Kyle whispered into the phone, "Sarah, listen, I found a file on the boat. I think it might be—" Kyle stopped talking when the file finally loaded on the iPad. It was a kill message. It was sent to a device to wipe it completely clean of all of its contents. Now he had no helpful information to pass along. He had nothing. Nothing but a knife. The voices were closer now, maybe even inside the cabin just around the corner from where Kyle was crouched. He could hear Sarah screaming his name through the phone.

"Kyle, Xander just called! I am going to merge the calls! Can you hang on? Maybe he'll know what to do!"

Sarah came back to the call. "Xander, are you there?"

Xander finished toweling off outside the SUV where Viktor and Jack were waiting with their CIA driver at the river's edge. Sarah had only told him that Kyle was in trouble before she switched over to his end of the call. She quickly stated that Adeline was trying to swim to safety while her friend Karol and Kyle stayed behind on the boat to be a distraction. Xander was so proud of Kyle. It took a lot of guts to hang around and wait for armed men to board your boat. All to give a woman he didn't even know a chance to escape.

"I'm here, Kyle, you there?"

"Xander!" Kyle half whispered and half shouted.

"Kyle, take a deep breath. Try to calm down and just listen to me. I'm proud of you. But listen, you can't fight the men boarding that boat."

"What? I have a knife, maybe I can—"

"Kyle, listen! If they think you are with Adeline, and those men will have no reason to think otherwise, they won't kill you. They will do what I need them to do. They will take you."

"Take us? But where?" There was fear in Kyle's voice at the thought of being captured again. Xander knew he still hadn't gotten over what happened last time he and Sam were captured in Syria.

"If they relay to Khatib that they have the President's daughter, I believe they'll take you right to Khatib . . ." Xander checked the timer on his watch, which read less than an hour before the four hours Khatib had given Natalie to live was up.

"And I believe that will also be right where they are holding Natalie."

"But Xander, I can't. And even if I could, how will you know where they take me? And what about the bomb?"

"If they are boarding the boat, they will stop the bomb. And we will know where you are by the phone you're using. Marv will track exactly where you'll be, and I'll be following alongside you on the road, right behind you."

Sarah jumped in. "All of that sounds perfect, Xander, but they will take the phone from him and destroy it. They might be Khatib's lackeys, but they will know to do that much."

"Not if you hide it, Kyle," Xander said.

Xander knew Kyle wasn't going to like hearing where he had to hide it. But this was the one chance Xander had to save everyone. It was their only lead. And with less than an hour, it was the only lead they were going to get.

Kyle said in a hushed shout, "Hide it? If you mean my ass, it will never fit up there. This is an iPhone, Xander!"

"Kyle, it doesn't have to go up your ass. Just pinch it between those big ass-cheeks of yours. When they frisk you, they'll pass right over it. I promise."

Xander couldn't guarantee that is how it would happen, but he wanted to give his friend reason for hope.

"Shit, they're coming," Kyle said. "You better be right, X. And you better come get us!"

"Oh, I'm coming, Kyle. And I'll be bringing Khatib's entire house down on top of him when I do."

Kyle ended the call, then immediately "rear-ended" the phone. Karol raised an eyebrow, but Kyle was not deterred. He stood from behind the box and squeezed the phone with the cheeks his mother had so graciously bequeathed him.

"Did you hear the conversation?" Kyle asked Karol as he took her hand and helped her up. She looked scared when she nodded.

"Do you have a wallet on you?"

Karol handed him her clutch, and he immediately threw it over the side of the boat. He knew if they found her ID, they would both be dead in seconds. Karol seemed to understand what he was doing, and she seemed resigned to the fact that there was nothing they could do to escape.

Kyle tried to console her as best he could under the circumstances. "I know this sucks. But that guy I was just talking to? He's the real deal. He *will* save us. I just need you to be brave and put on your best Adeline."

Kyle knew it didn't matter what Karol acted like. But he just hoped that none of these men were ever shown a picture of Adeline. If they were, this entire thing would backfire and they would kill them both on the spot.

"Just follow my lead," Kyle said to Karol. He put himself between her and the men who would be coming out of the cabin of the boat any minute. Karol just gave another nod. Sure enough, just then, two men came around the corner and immediately raised their guns, training them on Kyle's chest.

Kyle threw up his hands. "Do whatever you want to me, but let her go! If you do, I'll make sure the President knows you saved her life!"

One of the men walked forward. "This is President's daughter?"

Kyle nodded. "If you hurt her, you know our government won't stop until they kill all of you. So do the smart thing and—"

The man swung the butt of his assault rifle and busted Kyle in the mouth. "Stop talking." The man then turned to the other gunman. "Call him. Tell him we have stopped the bomb, and that we are coming with daughter of the President of the United States. He will be very pleased."

Kyle's mouth was on fire, and blood poured out onto the deck of the boat. But it seemed as though they had bought it. The man pulled Kyle back up to his feet and told him to spread his legs.

This was it.

The man began to frisk him. He started beneath Kyle's arms, then down his sides to his waist, then on down the outsides of his legs. Kyle continued to squeeze, but he didn't know if it would be enough. The man worked his hands back up the insides of Kyle's legs, then around his ass, patting at his back pockets.

"He is clear. Let's get them onto boat."

Kyle let out a sigh of relief but made sure not to relax too much. He still had a long way to go before he and the phone made it where they were going. But at least they were alive. For now. And at least Adeline had a fair shot at getting away. And maybe, just maybe, Xander was right, and wherever they were being taken, Natalie would be there too.

Staying on Track

"You still there, Sarah?" Xander asked.

"Still here. You okay? I'm assuming you didn't find Natalie?"

"It was a trap. Melanie was there instead. Sam is following her now. Are you all right?"

Sarah sighed. "No, I'm worried about Kyle. He hasn't had the proper training for this, Xander."

"I know. But I've seen him in worse situations, and he can handle himself. Can you patch Marv in real quick? I know he is already tracking Kyle, but I need that sent to this phone. And I need him to be following the SAT phone that Sam has. I have a feeling Melanie is going to lead her as far away from Natalie as she can get. And there is sure to be an ambush waiting."

"Of course, hold for Marvin."

Xander took the phone away from his ear for a moment and gave his head a slow roll to try and loosen up his neck. He was freezing. His clothes—the only clothes he had—were soaked through from the swim. And he had every one of his friends to worry about. If Khatib's men took Kyle somewhere other than where Natalie was, Natalie was dead. That thought forced Xander to begin pacing around the outside of the SUV as he waited.

"You okay, son?" Jack asked.

Xander stopped and covered the receiver of the cell phone. "You know, Jack, I have been through a lot of battles in my day. Been in some hairy situations. This scares me as much as any of them. I don't like being separated like this. Kyle on his own, Sam walking into God knows what . . ."

"I hear ya. But I've been around the block a few times, so you just tell me where you need me to be and I'll help make sure your friends have some backup."

Xander would have hugged Jack in that moment, wet clothes and all, but Marv came on the line. Xander gave Jack a nod of thanks, and Jack returned it with a knowing tip of his cowboy hat.

Marv jumped right in. "Xander, I've got tracking on Kyle and Sam. Kyle is on his way west, and I'll have a car to you in two minutes so you can get moving. Sam is headed in the opposite direction, more into the city. I'll send her coordinates to Sarah and Zhanna. Maybe they can help Sam if she gets into a spot."

Xander said, "Oh, she'll be in a spot. Melanie has had it out for her as long as they've known each other. Sarah, are you sure you don't mind?"

Sarah answered, "Of course not, Xander. We have two sets of agents on the way to pick up Adeline. They know around the area she jumped into the water, so they will be combing both sides of the river for her. Nothing more I can do. I'd love to help Sam kick a little more ass."

"You're the best, Sarah. I mean it," Xander said. He couldn't have been more sincere when he said it. Then he walked over in front of Jack. "Marv, cancel the car. Jack and Viktor are coming with me." Xander nodded to Jack. Jack gave him a wink.

Viktor was a little less subtle. "Jack! We are going to help boss get pretty lady back! Yes!"

Xander smiled. It continued to amaze him how these people who were mostly strangers continued to show up for him when he needed them most. Xander would not soon forget it.

Marv said, "Whatever you say, X. Be careful out there. I'll be watching and send any help I can from here."

"Marv, I love you," Xander said.

Marv chuckled, "You always were the sappy one. But I'll be damned if I wanted to be Akram Khatib right now. Do us all a favor and erase that son of a bitch!"

"Will do. And Sarah, be careful, okay?"

"You too, Xander. See you soon."

Xander ended the call. "Jack, you got that sniper rifle ready?"

"X-man, these bullets might as well already have names on 'em."

Xander's phone chirped. Marv had already sent the tracker following Kyle's phone down the river.

Xander looked back up at Jack and Viktor.

"Boys, let's go end this thing once and for all."

A Score to Settle

Sam was absolutely sopping wet and quite literally freezing, but she considered herself incredibly lucky to still be on Melanie's trail. She figured Melanie must have had a phone stashed in her knickers somewhere. That is the only way she would have been able to have a car pick her up. Though Sam imagined that there would be many Frenchmen willing to pick up a girl in her underpants. Even luckier was the cab Sam was able to find, and luckier still that the driver was so willing to follow another car for her. And the fact that he didn't see the MP5 she tried to hide behind her back was no small thing either.

Sam wasn't naive. She figured Melanie knew she was following her, and her instincts led her to assume that she wasn't heading anywhere near Khatib or Natalie. But Sam didn't really care. She knew Xander would be hot on that trail. For the first time in a long time, Sam had a score to settle for herself. Killing Sanharib Khatib in Syria could certainly be considered revenge after what he'd done to her, but this was different to Sam. Some scumbag terrorist doing what a terrorist does didn't hit that close to home. But Melanie infiltrating Xander's inner circle, and then betraying him, was deeply personal. It wasn't easy to fool veterans of the game like Sam and Xander. Melanie had managed to do it very well. It made Sam wonder what exactly her background might be.

As they wound around the streets of Paris, deeper into the city, Sam pulled her SAT phone and dialed Marv's number.

"Hello, Sam," Marv answered.

"Any idea where I am being led?"

"At first, no. But I checked a couple of points in the direction you are headed. For some reason something stuck out to me, because it is really sort of out of the way—"

"Marv," Sam interrupted, "I really don't have time for the long version."

"Right. I looked back and checked Xander's Uber ride from the airport earlier today, and I am confident they are taking you back to that same warehouse."

"Good on you, Marv. Xander may be right about you yet. How is Kyle doing?"

"You don't know, do you?"

Sam's stomach dropped and that forced a deep inhale. "Marv, please tell me he's all right. He's not dead, is he?"

"Oh God, Sam. I'm sorry. No."

A wave of warm emotion flooded through Sam.

Marv continued. "But he has been taken by Khatib's men."

Her stomach turned another one-eighty. She knew immediately how frightened he would be after what happened in Syria. "Please tell me we know where he's going."

"He managed to hide the burner phone. Xander is tracking him now. We think Khatib is having Kyle brought to him."

"What makes you think that?" Sam said.

"Well, they think he has the President's daughter with him."

"He doesn't?"

"No, her friend. Kyle managed to help Adeline escape."

Sam smiled. Kyle Hamilton was full of surprises. "Is she all right?"

"Well . . ."

"That doesn't sound good, Marv."

"We have men searching the area for her, but we haven't been able to locate her yet."

Sam said, "Khatib knows."

"What? Why would you think that?" Marv was surprised to hear the confidence in Sam's statement.

"You really think he would neglect to show his men a picture of one of his targets? They all have cellular phones, Marvin. This isn't the 1980s. He sent the men a picture of her. All of them."

"I hope you're wrong, Sam. But we have three teams searching now. Listen, you are getting close to the warehouse. I am sure that is where Melanie is leading you. You need to talk to Xander, he's been in there, maybe he can help."

"Connect me." Sam waited on the line. She was worried about Kyle. If Khatib gets his hands on him . . . She shuddered at the thought.

"Sam?"

"Xander! Please tell me you are staying close to Kyle."

"I've got him. Don't worry. Marv says you're heading back to the warehouse I was at earlier?"

"Seems that way, any pointers?" Sam asked.

"Yes. There is a parking garage under the building with an

elevator to the first floor. That floor is a large open room with temporary cubicles set up in the form of a large square in the middle, and more cubicles are lined all along the outside walls. But don't go in."

"All right, and why is that?"

"Sarah and Zhanna are on their way. I noticed a green dumpster half a block to the east. Wait for them there. They are bringing a few goodies that will help you," Xander explained.

"Now you're talking. But I want Melanie for myself."

Xander laughed. "Take that up with Sarah and Zhanna. I think they're still mad at her over the jet escape out of Moscow. She did try to blow them up too, you know. Don't be selfish."

Then Xander changed his tone. "Sam, I really don't know what Kyle and I are going to be walking into. If something happens, and you have a chance to save Natalie, forget about Melanie, will you?"

Sam's tone was sharp. "Don't talk like that, Xander. You'll figure it out, you always do. And don't tell me you love me, either. It gives me the creeps when you say that before you go off on a shooting spree. I'll see you in a bit when this is over. We can swap stories about how outstanding each other was in our victory."

"Fine, I won't say it. I like your version better. But Sam?" Xander said.

Sam rolled her eyes. "What?"

"I love you."

Sam heard the line go dead. She could hear Xander smiling through his words.

She said aloud to herself under her breath, "If he gets out of there alive, I'm going to bloody kill him."

What a Wonderful...ly Dangerous World

Xander ended the call with Sam. And though he was trying to keep it light so she wouldn't worry about him, his mood was as heavy as the SUV he had been riding in. He kept the call with Sam on speakerphone so he could continue to track Kyle. The GPS blip hadn't moved in a couple of minutes, and that was when Marv's number appeared on the screen.

"Where is he, Marv?"

"Port des Saints-Pères. It's a tiny little port on the river across from Le Louvre. Only room for one or two boats."

"I'm assuming you've already checked the cameras," Xander said.

"I have. They conveniently aren't working."

"Jesus."

"Xander, I have to call this in. I have to let the local authorities know that there could be terrorist activity going on that close to the museum."

"No way, Marv. It's late. The museum is closed. Khatib might blow up the entire thing if the police show up sniffing around. You have to let me handle this."

"X, I can't. If something happens, I won't be able to live with myself."

"Marv, who the hell are you going to call that is better suited to deal with this than I am? If you can tell me that, then you can call it in."

Xander let Marv sit with that for a moment. He already knew what Marv would say. Marv had been around at a time when the government was sending Xander on mission impossible after mission impossible. He knew there absolutely was no one they could bring in who would know better how to handle Khatib and his men.

Marv finally spoke up, resignation heavy in his voice. "Damnit, X. You and I both know the French couldn't find anyone better suited for this than you if they trained them from birth. Not to mention they are on boats, so let the frogman in you go wild."

"Will do. Jack Bronson is with me. He will help me establish a perimeter. He'll have my back with the sniper rifle. Marv?"

"Yeah, X?"

"Do you think Natalie is there? Do you think they never left the port?"

Marv let out a sigh. "I really don't know. But I think there is a good possibility. I'll keep an eye on all the surrounding cameras to see if I can pick up any clues. Kyle hasn't moved in five minutes or so now. So you'd better get in there."

"What, you aren't going to wish me luck?"

"If that son of a bitch Khatib is down there, you won't need luck. But you will need a spot on your office shelf for another award or two. I know that much."

"Awards are for the insecure. Seeing Natalie finish her movie in Paris will be all the *reward* I'll need."

"I hear ya. In that case, break a leg."

Xander ended the call. Their SUV was parked along the street about a block away from the X that marked Kyle's spot. A spot that hadn't moved in a while. Xander didn't like that.

He got out of the car and walked around to where Jack and Viktor were standing. "Jack, you know where you want to be?"

Jack pointed up to the building across the street. "Third floor, far left window. I'll be able to shoot the cherry off a kid's ice cream cone at the museum across the river from there."

"Works for me," Xander said. "You gonna be able to tell the difference between me and the bad guys?"

Jack smiled. "Ain't that what I got Viktor for?"

"Real comforting."

Xander loaded the last magazine from his go bag into his Glock, racked the slide, and gave Jack a nod. Then he turned toward the river and walked down the stairs to the riverwalk and into the shadows of the wall above him. There were a lot of things to think about, a lot of things to distract him. Natalie strapped to that wall, Kyle held captive, Sam and company walking into an obvious ambush. But Xander took one look at the timer on his watch—forty minutes remaining—and everything but what was right in front of him disappeared. With a deep breath, inhaling the stale and moist river air, he settled into the shadows.

His mind focused.

In front of him, along the wall to his left, was a row of thick leaved trees. The leaves helped block the lights of the city and would help him stay hidden. On his right was the river, and just beyond that, Le Louvre was lit up in the distance. The millions of people surrounding him had no idea how close they constantly were to danger. If people knew what Xander knew, they would be hard pressed to ever leave the house, for every dark corner had the potential to hold something sinister. And if you happened upon the wrong corner at the wrong time, you could be caught up in something as minor as a mugging or something as major as what was about to happen here. A full-on terrorist attack and hostage situation. He feared for his niece in that moment. Even though the world wasn't near as ruthless as it used to be, it was still unbelievably dangerous.

Xander walked slowly along the foot of the wall. Up ahead he could see a large dinner boat, just like the one he boarded from the water with Sam not long ago. He pictured the inside of the dining area, and unfortunately, his mind saw Natalie up on that wall. He shook this from his brain and trained his eyes on the right side of the boat. There was another slot in the concrete for another boat just like that one to be able to dock. Instead of a dinner boat, however, there were two smaller boats. Xander assumed one either had Kyle inside, or at the very least he knew the phone was there. There was absolutely zero movement on the dock. No people out for a stroll and no guards waiting to keep people away. A pit began to form in Xander's stomach. They didn't have time to be wrong about this being the right place. If Natalie and Kyle weren't here, it was over.

Xander gave a glance over his shoulder back up at the building Jack pointed to a moment ago. Sure enough, three floors up, back inside the far left window, he saw three quick flashes of light.

Jack was in place.

It was time to see if Akram Khatib was as well.

Girls' Night Out

Sam sent the cab driver away. She didn't have any money, but one flash of her MP5 submachine gun and suddenly that didn't much matter. He would live. She spotted the dumpster that Xander had mentioned almost immediately. The two beautiful women huddled behind it may have helped a little. Sam stayed close to the brick building as she approached Sarah and Zhanna, surprised at herself that she was happy to see them.

"You ladies have this figured yet?"

Sarah and Zhanna jumped and turned their pistols on Sam.

Sarah's face went from "shoot to kill" to complete relief when she realized who had come up behind them. "Sam! Jesus, you scared the hell out of me."

Sam said with a wry smile, "Hopefully Melanie will be as easy to sneak up on as the two of you are."

Zhanna got down to business. "There is definite movement

on first floor. And across street, there are two men on top of building."

"All right, any movement from the underground parking garage?" Sam said.

"Nothing," said Sarah. "That is definitely the way in. But how do we get up the elevator without them seeing us?"

Sam smiled. "Leave that to me. You girls ready for this? No telling how many will be waiting for us inside."

Sarah handed Sam an extra pistol. "Glock 19's your weapon of choice, right?"

Sam took the gun, gave it a press check, then smiled. "My kind of girl. What other goodies have you?"

"One smoke, one flash, and one frag grenade. Preference?" Sarah asked Sam.

"I like flashy. Xander is rubbing off on me."

"And we both have backup guns as well." Zhanna pulled her pistol and held it down by her side.

Sam smiled as she began to walk toward the exit of the underground parking garage. "Well, doesn't this bring a whole new meaning to girls' night out."

Sam pressed the button that called for the elevator. The parking garage had a couple of vans inside. While that didn't make the three of them nervous, it definitely helped them focus on what was ahead.

"So we're just going to let them know we're coming? Just like that?" Sarah asked.

Sam moved an orange construction barrel from outside the elevator over in front of the doors. "Just follow me."

The elevator dinged and the doors opened. After making sure the elevator was empty, Sam quickly moved in the barrel, hopped up on top of it, pushed in one of the tiles and climbed up through the ceiling. After a quick glance and a shrug of the shoulders between them, Sarah and Zhanna followed. The elevator doors closed and they began to move up to the first floor. Sam readied her flash grenade, while Sarah and Zhanna readied their pistols.

"According to Xander, there are cubicles that run along the walls of the space and more cubicles in the center of the room," Sam whispered. "When the door opens and they see the barrel, they will let off some rounds out of fear. When that stops, I'll throw the flash grenade. Cover your eyes and let's get behind the cubicles along the wall on the left. From there, we'll have some cover and can start to work our magic. Zhanna, if you see a cluster of men with guns, don't be afraid to use the frag grenade. No sense hanging on to it."

Zhanna nodded. The cables wobbled around them as they moved the elevator upward. Then the elevator came to an abrupt stop, jolting them as they crouched atop it. When the elevator dinged, Sam nodded to assure them she was ready. And just like she said they would, when the doors opened, blasts and pops came from the guns of the waiting enemy. Clinks and clanks and thuds rang out inside the elevator. Sam heard a man shout something, and before the last gun spit its last bullet, Sam had already released the flash grenade and it rolled out the front of the elevator, followed by a magnificent bright light. As the group that had been firing into the elevator reeled from the flash, Sam jumped from the top of the elevator, sprinted out the left side and dove behind the cubicles that were right where Xander said they would be. She immediately raised just her MP5 submachine gun above the top of the cubicle and let off a spray of bullets to serve as cover for Sarah and Zhanna. A split second later, they were on the floor beside Sam, readying their weapons for an attack.

"Melanie, give it up now and I promise I will only send you to prison," Sam shouted. "You can write love letters to Kyle from there."

A man spoke instead of Melanie. "Melania is not here. She had to retrieve something very important that we picked up for her. You are unlucky, you have to deal with Sebastian."

"Sebastian?" Sam laughed. She was stalling as she ejected the magazine on the MP5. By the weight of it, she felt as if she had ten or so rounds left. "You are in the wrong story, Sebastian. This is not a romance novel."

She had definitely spent far too much time with Xander. His dreadful humor was beginning to rub off on her. As Sebastian replied to her quip, she motioned to Sarah that she was going to move toward the back wall by the cover of the cubicles.

"Not many romance novels end with the pretty British woman getting her pretty little head blown off," Sebastian said.

By the time he finished his sentence, Sam had already moved to the back of the room. She raised her head above the cubicle just in time to see Zhanna toss the grenade into a group of three men standing close to the elevator. Two seconds later a nasty blast filled the warehouse, and as Zhanna and Sarah began to trade fire with the men who were left, Sam continued on around to the other side of the room. Now she had a fantastic angle from behind them. She traded the MP5 for the Glock. Trading volume for accuracy. She bounced up from behind the cubicle, aimed her pistol, and shot two men standing on the left side of the room, some seventy feet away. Four quick squeezes.

Sarah or Zhanna one-dropped another man who was closer to them, and Sam could hear groans from men who must have been hit by the grenade. Sam moved up to the first cubicle in the center of the room. When she peeked over the cubicle, she could still hear a couple of people firing from the front center of the room, but like her, they must have been ducked behind a cubicle wall.

Sam shouted, "Tell me where Melanie is, and we will let you live."

At the other end of the room, beyond where the gunmen were posted, Sam heard a door open and close.

"Sounds like a fair trade to me, Sebastian," Sarah shouted. "Your freedom for Melanie, who you probably don't really even know. You might want to consider accepting."

Then a female spoke up from beyond Sebastian. "You want me? Well . . . here I am."

Melanie.

That must have been the door that Sam heard open and close. A bolt of adrenaline flashed through Sam's body. She stood up and trained her gun on Melanie. But she almost dropped her gun when she saw who was with her. Sam glanced over at Sarah, and Sam could see the terror written all over Sarah's face.

This was bad.

Real bad.

While everyone held their weapons on each other, Sam reached her left hand into her pocket and slid out her phone. She thumbed to Marv's contact and typed a one-line text message:

Melanie has the President's daughter.

Visions of Violence Danced in His Head

As Xander crept his way to the water's edge from the shadows, for the first time he noticed movement. Beyond the dinner boat, near the exact mark on the GPS where Kyle's phone should be, two human shadows crossed in front of the boat. Xander had to be very careful how he approached. This was a heavily populated civilian area. These shadowy figures could easily be a couple of young lovers trying to—

POP-POP-POP-POP!

Four shots rang out, and Xander jumped onto the dinner boat for cover. One bullet ricocheted off the bow, then whizzed past Xander's head. After a glance inside the dining hall window showed him a completely empty room, he immediately jumped and grabbed the bottom of the rooftop deck rail above him. He fought the panic of Natalie not being there and pulled himself up and hopped over the rail. In five quick strides he was at the other side of the deck, raising his gun, and four shots later both unsuspecting men were on the ground. They had been expecting him to attack from the front lower level of the dinner boat.

Out of the corner of his eye he saw movement at the end of the dock. Xander dropped to his stomach on the floor of the deck just as two gunshot blasts echoed across the water. In front of him, in the open space between the deck floor and the first rail, he could see the man aiming in his direction. Just as Xander aimed his gun, he heard a crack in the distance and the man at the end of the dock jerked, then dropped flat on his face.

Jack.

Xander raised to a knee and scanned the area for any other possible gunmen. When satisfied the area was clear, he hopped the rail, dropped down to the lower level of the boat, then stepped out on the concrete dock that separated that boat and the two smaller boats, one a fishing vessel and one a speedboat. He took one last longing look back through the dinner boat's window. He knew he wouldn't see Natalie there, but hope springs eternal. And now he felt completely lost on how to find her. In a crouch he duckwalked over to the fishing boat and boarded. He quickly searched the outside and the cabin but found nothing. He did the same with the second boat, and just as he was getting ready to hop back out to the dock, something black on the white cushion of the outside bench caught his eye.

Kyle's burner phone.

Kyle was gone.

Natalie was nowhere to be found.

The feeling of failing her slowly began to creep into his nervous system. Instinctively, Xander grabbed a nearby towel, picked up the phone that had been stuffed between his friend's cheeks, and gave it a quick wipe down. When he unlocked the phone, there was a red alert at the corner of the messages icon. He tapped the icon, and it showed one text message that was clearly meant for him.

Captain America is always two steps behind Akram Khatib. Shame. I really wanted to play. Looks like that King's Ransom I told you it would take to get your Natalie back comes in the form of your good friend. Remember the good friend of yours my brother shot in the head? Your friend here will wish for such mercy. Happy Hunting. —AK

The vision of Sanharib Khatib shooting Sean Thompson in the face in Syria a few weeks ago flashed in his mind. Then a vision of King's Ransom dead in the stables, then one of Kyle being tortured, then a vision of those massive spikes being driven into Natalie's ears. Xander dropped to his knee. Saliva filled his jowls, and he lost it all over the floor of the boat. He wiped his mouth on his sleeve and took a deep breath. After another moment of those visions repeating themselves in his mind, everything went blank. He looked up at the fingernail moon that was half hidden by a moving cloud. He could hear his heartbeat in his ears, rapid and erratic. The sounds around him were muffled.

He felt lost.

It was then that a cool breeze blew gently across the back of his neck. He took a deep inhale and slowly began to gather his wits. He could swear that the scent traveling in the breeze was Natalie's perfume. He knew it was impossible, but the mind is a powerful force. A force he knew he had to harness to push him toward a different outcome. The smell of Natalie's perfume, though one he couldn't have actually detected, triggered a positive chain of visions that flashed before him.

His friend Sean Thompson smiling again. Spouting one of his off-the-cuff country-boy sayings.

King's Ransom running for the win at the Kentucky Derby. Xander rubbing his nose and patting his back in the winner's circle.

Kyle's blazing smile and infectious laugh as they clanked glasses on the back of Xander's yacht in the Virgin Islands.

Staring into Natalie's eyes just before she kissed him on the lips.

Adrenaline filled Xander's veins as he slowly rose to his feet. It felt like a high-octane sugar rush running through his system. The next vision he saw made him clench his jaw and ball his hands into fists. Before his eyes, in the dark water beside the boat, he could see Akram Khatib, blood leaking from his head as he lay on the ground. That was the vision he intended to see come to fruition next. Xander pulled out his phone and dialed Marvin.

"Xander! I was just getting ready to call you. I have eyes on Khatib! Cameras across the river show that he left where you are on a different dinner boat and is headed in the direction of the Eiffel Tower. I'm showing that you have twenty-five minutes to get to Natalie. You gotta get going!"

Xander didn't so much as respond. He hung up, walked around the center console, and fired up the speedboat. As he backed out into the middle of the river, he could see the Eiffel Tower's bright yellow lights off to his right in the distance. As he pushed the throttle forward, he heard Viktor shouting at him from the dock, wildly jumping up and down and waving his arms.

Xander didn't acknowledge him.

Instead, he pushed the throttle to the max, and the boat

lurched forward as he sped away toward his target.

Toward turning that last vision of Khatib dead into a reality.

Timber!

"What?" Melanie looked across the warehouse at Sam. "Have you nothing smart to say? Xander would make funny comment to try and throw me off. You should try this, Sam."

"Why don't you drop that fake Russian accent and go back to being my little assistant. Off you go, fetch me a coffee."

Melanie grunted in frustration and fired an errant shot in Sam's direction. Sam didn't even flinch.

"That the best you've got Melanie, or Mclania? Or whatever your name really is." Sam continued to goad her.

When Melanie turned her pistol from Sam to Adeline's forehead, Adeline squealed through her gag and struggled to get free of the two men holding her in place. "Actually, the best I have got is to put bullet in first daughter's head. Will this satisfy you?" Melanie said.

Sarah stood from behind the cubicle. "And what exactly would you gain by doing that? What is it that you want?"

"I have no allegiance. I do what I do for love of money, not country. I have been trained by the best in Russia. Vitalii Dragov is dead, so I move on to Akram Khatib. Information about your precious Xander is very valuable, and it pays very well to have it."

Sam replied, "Xander is worth far more than Khatib. He will pay you whatever you want if you let Adeline go."

Melanie laughed, glanced at Adeline, then back to Sam. "But then, I don't get to kill you."

"Oh, it's me you want, is it? Fine." Sam dropped her arms and tucked her gun in the back of her waistband. "Take me. Let Sarah have Adeline, and you can take me."

"Works for me, but you must come here first."

Sarah shouted, "Sam, no! You can't!"

But Sam walked around the corner of the cubicle and started toward the men holding Adeline. Adeline continued to thrash in their arms and whimper through her cloth gag. Her clothes were still soaked from being in the river, and the closer Sam got, she could see tears streaming down her face. Sam had a plan; she just hoped Sarah wouldn't jump the gun.

"That's far enough," Melanie said. She took hold of Adeline and waved for the men to go and see to Sam.

"Sam," Sarah begged. "Don't do this. They'll kill you."

"Better me than her. Just don't let them take us both."

Sarah took Sam's words to heart and refocused her gun on Melanie. "Let her go, right now."

"You are in no position to make demands, Barbie."

Just as the men began to frisk Sam, Sam whipped her head to the right to look at Sarah. She knew that was one of her triggers, and sure enough, Sarah broke. What happened next was a total blur.

Sarah shot Melanie in her arm that was holding the gun.

228

Sam forced her right knee across the left side of her body into the forehead of the man that was frisking her left leg. Just after the smack against his face, Sam spun behind her, whipping her elbow around, and it connected with the other man's jaw. Behind her she heard Zhanna shout, "RUN!" to Adeline, and as the man Sam hit with her knee rose back up to his feet, she brought her arm forward, the one that had just landed the elbow, and shattered his nose. She had to punch upward to hit him because he was so tall. Ruining his nose would hardly ruin his day; he already had a face that only a grandmother could love. The man didn't have any quit in him. After pawing at his bloody nose for only a second, he lunged at Sam. Sam stepped to her left—to the outside of his punch—and delivered a left hook to the kidney. As he staggered back in pain, she wheeled her left leg up and around in a full 360, and the heel of her boot connected with the big man's temple; and he toppled to the ground like a tree.

As she turned back to face the man she had hit with her elbow, out of the corner of her eye she saw Adeline running toward the elevator into Zhanna's waiting arms. And Sarah was closing the distance between her and the injured Melanie. The man in front of Sam reached for the gun inside his waistband. As he pulled it up to aim at Sam, she front kicked it out of his hand, and as soon as her foot tapped back down to the ground, she torqued her hip to the left, and the bottom of her shin bone landed flush against his jaw with the force of a Louisville Slugger. The instantly unconscious man did his best impression of his big friend, and Sam resisted the urge to yell, "Timber!" as he collapsed to the concrete below.

Sam turned her attention to Melanie and Sarah at the front of the room and stalked around the cubicles toward them.

Beyond where Sarah was grappling with Melanie, Sam saw Zhanna pull Adeline into the elevator, and off in the distance, she could faintly hear sirens closing in. If she didn't hurry, the police would steal her chance at returning the punch that Melanie had given her in Moscow as she was being held back by Dragov's men. Some people never forget a face; Sam had never been able to forget a punch.

Just before Sam could get there, Sebastian emerged from the cubicles and tackled Sarah to the floor. Sarah's gun skittered across the concrete, halfway between Sam and Melanie.

Sam said, "Let's see how fast you are, Melanie."

They both sprinted for the gun. After only a split second it was clear that Sam was going to get to the gun first, and Melanie decided to sidestep the gun and bolt for the door. Sam dove headfirst for the gun, grabbed it, aimed it, squeezed the trigger, and the bullet smacked against the door a millisecond after Melanie's shoulder turned the corner.

Sam popped up to her feet and noticed Sarah was in full guard on her back, holding Sebastian off with some jiu-jitsu defense. Sam walked over as Sarah trapped Sebastian's arm that was closest to Sam, leaving him completely defenseless against the kick that Sam delivered to the side of his face. Sebastian collapsed onto Sarah. Sam nodded to Sarah. Sarah gave the "I'm okay" nod in return.

Sarah said, "I'll call the police and make sure they pick up Zhanna and Adeline. Then I'll call Marv and have him coordinate a pickup for all of us. You go get that ugly bitch."

Sam barely heard Sarah's words. Her mind was already on running Melanie down. Finally, her body caught up with her thoughts, and Sam sprinted out the door after her.

A Quick Detour

Xander kept the speedboat at full throttle as he sped down the Seine. The river was nearly empty. The wind was cold in his face, and he squinted into the night, desperately searching for the first sign of Khatib's dinner boat. The hum of the boat's engine engulfed him. The slapping of the bottom of the boat against the tiny waves sprayed a mist of water all around him. He felt anxious. His mind continued to race, but he did his best to keep his breathing slow and his head clear. Worrying about whether Kyle was still alive and visualizing how he would pull Natalie from that wall were only clouding his mind. He needed now to rely on his instincts.

The Eiffel Tower's thousands of lights sparkled just around a left turn in the Seine now. The lights were casting their rays all the way down to the river below. Xander caught his first glimpse of the back end of the dinner boat rounding the bend up ahead just before it disappeared. His stomach clenched and his grip tightened around the steering wheel of the speedboat. He was close. Then his phone began to ring. He almost didn't answer it. He didn't want to hear bad news if that's what was calling. But it could be news about Natalie.

Xander shouted over the boat's engine, "Marv, I'm a little busy."

"Xander, we have a problem." Marv's voice was animated.

"No shit. Any other ways you want to try to blow my mind?"

"Xander there is a boat somewhere, the boat Kyle was on. It's got a bomb on it. Kyle told Sarah that the bomb on it looked big enough to blow up a few city blocks."

"I've kinda got my hands full here, Marv. Can't you let the French police look into doing something tonight? Call that George Costanza–lookin' son of a bitch detective that took my Glock at the police station earlier. Maybe he'll give a flying—"

Before Xander could finish his words, a boat came out of nowhere from his right side and smashed into the front end of his speedboat. It hit the boat so hard that Xander was thrown violently out of his boat and sent soaring through the air into the dark and cold water below. All he could see was darkness. Or maybe he wasn't seeing anything. The water wasn't nearly as cold as it should be. He felt like he was breathing fine. But he felt as if he were an astronaut floating in deep black space. No gravity, no sound...

Then he did hear a sound. It was like a fly buzzing around his head but very far away. He tried to move, but he couldn't. He tried to look, but he couldn't. Then he felt something burning. Not his skin, not from a fire, but it felt like fire in his lungs. He desperately tried to take a breath to extinguish the flames that grew inside his chest, but nothing was working.

Then, it seemed the fly was getting closer, and closer, right up on him now. He tried to swat the fly away, but he still couldn't move. Then, the fly was gone. Complete silence followed. Blackness.

Then, as suddenly as he had been thrown from the boat a moment ago, his head was pulled up out of the water by his hair and the world came crashing in on Xander. Pure instinct made him shoot his hand right for the throat of the man who was leaning off the back of the boat trying to pull him in. Simultaneously, Xander pulled in air through his mouth so hard that he nearly choked, and as he coughed out river water, his grip tightened as if it were a reflex around the man's neck, and he pulled the man into the water with him. Xander managed to get his elbow up on the top rung of the ladder hanging from the swim platform at the back of the boat. As he let go of the man's throat, he wrapped his legs around his body with the strength of a boa constrictor. As he squeezed with all his might, he forced the man underwater, holding him there as he uselessly writhed and bucked between Xander's legs. Xander glanced at his watch; he only had twenty minutes left before Natalie was dead. As the man's movements underwater eased to a halt, Xander regained his breath.

When the man was finally still, Xander opened his legs and the drowned man floated away. As soon as Xander turned and hoisted himself up onto the swim platform, he was forced to flatten to his back as the driver of the boat fired at him from inside the cabin. Xander quickly unzipped his pocket, pulled his knife, hit the blade release button, and, as the man stepped down on the swim platform, Xander drove the knife into the side of his calf muscle. The man screamed in pain and bucked backward, sending the bullet meant for Xander's head somewhere in the direction of the Champs-Elysées. Xander removed the knife as he scrambled to his knees, then jammed the blade between the man's fourth and fifth rib, straight through to the heart.

The man grunted, then collapsed after Xander twisted and removed the knife. Xander stood and then nudged the man's lifeless body out over the edge of the swim platform where he could join his friend in a float-off to see who could reach the Eiffel Tower first. Xander wouldn't be there to see who won; he immediately jammed the throttle and turned toward the dinner boat. He noticed a cell phone sitting in the cup holder beside the captain's chair. He picked it up and dialed Marv.

"Who is this?" Marv answered.

"Do I have to do everything?"

"X? What the—whose number are you calling from?"

"Long story short, I found the bomb."

"What? How could you possibly—"

"The timer isn't running, but you have exactly sixty seconds to tell me which wire to cut so they can't set it off remotely. Starting now."

"You crazy son of a bitch. I'll call you right back. Don't you leave that—"

Xander ended the call and sped away toward the boat that he hoped would be holding Kyle, Natalie, and that dead-man-walking son of a bitch, Akram Khatib.

She Started It

Sam sprinted out the door of the warehouse and down the side street in the direction Melanie ran. For a side street it was fairly well lit. Yellow lights hung from the brick buildings, shining over intimate little cafes and bistros. At first, Sam didn't see anything that resembled a cowardly woman running away from her like a little bitch. Then she thought if she were being chased by herself, she would run like hell too. But up ahead she noticed a shadow move to the left. Sam found another gear and dashed toward it.

She pulled to a stop at the street where she had seen the movement. It was much darker there. More like an alley than a street. There were plenty of nooks and cafe awnings to hide inside and behind. This was a dangerous game. Sam was exposed and at a major disadvantage. She searched the dark street for clues, but nothing turned up. She was surprised at just how empty it was. It was a nice enough night; people should be out and about. Maybe this wasn't the best neighborhood for that. Sam took a step forward when she saw a glimmer of dark liquid on the ground, reflecting the only light nearby. She bent down, and upon further examination, she discerned it was definitely blood. She was in the right place.

Sam continued forward. She jumped when she heard a couple laughing as they passed on the street behind her. She managed to avoid swinging the gun around when she turned to look. The sirens she had heard earlier seemed right around the corner now. A few steps forward and she noticed another cluster of blood drops settling down into the seams of the cobblestone. Goading her worked once, so why not try it again?

"Melanie? What are we really fighting about anyhow? It wasn't that I disliked you when you were Xander's assistant— my assistant. It's just, you were a bit of a little twit."

Sam walked slowly as she talked, listening for any tiny little movement each time she paused. The sirens just behind her now made it all the more difficult. If Melanie had another weapon, Sam was really putting herself in a bad situation.

"Look, I'm sure I wasn't the easiest person to get along with, but, my God, you were secretly working for a mafia boss. I must have been a walk in the park compared to that fatty."

The movement from Sam's left was fast, but she managed to get her arm up to shield her face before Melanie sank the knife deep into Sam's forearm. The piercing flame of pain was instant. Sam let Melanie's momentum push her to her back, but when she landed, Sam continued to roll and she kicked Melanie up and off of her. Sam rolled on over to her feet and immediately took a fight-ready stance. After skidding to a stop a few feet away, Melanie too went into a fight stance, holding the knife out in front of her.

Sam gave her arm a quick glance and found blood pouring

from the open wound.

"So she does bleed," Melanie mocked.

"Let's see you try that again." Sam welcomed the challenge. Melanie was in way over her head, whether she knew it or not. Sam Harrison lived for this shit.

Melanie began to move toward Sam, knife out in front. Then she lunged for Sam, shoving the knife forward. Sam easily parried the stab and slapped Melanie across the face.

"Now . . . you're going to have to do better than that," Sam taunted.

Melanie stabbed again and Sam again parried. This time she countered with a quick punch to the throat. Melanie gagged and doubled over. Sam Thai-kicked her square in the forehead. Melanie flew backward on her ass, groaning in pain whenever she could catch a breath. Sam felt invincible in that moment.

"You have no idea how long I've wanted to do that."

Melanie began to regain her breath as she scooted away from Sam on her ass. She glanced toward the street they had just come from.

Sam said, "Don't even think about running. It will only make things worse."

Melanie didn't listen. She jumped to her feet and sprinted for the street. Sam pounced, and just when Melanie reached the street, Sam yanked her back by the collar of her shirt. Without letting go of the fabric, Sam turned Melanie around and delivered a knee into her solar plexus. Sam maintained a grip on her collar, and just as she stood her up to deliver another blow, a police car skidded to a halt and a man's voice bellowed from the loudspeaker.

"Stop right there! Break it up. Let go of the shirt and back away!"

Sam didn't let go. Nor would she. Not until they made her.

Sam said to Melanie, "You are lucky. I would've killed you." She followed that with a devastating elbow to Melanie's forehead. Sam could see she had put the lights out even before Melanie hit the ground.

Sam then turned toward the two policemen running toward her and held up her hands.

"She started it."

King's Ransom

Under the thousands of sparkling little spotlights shining down on him from the iconic Eiffel Tower, Xander sidled his newly commandeered boat up to Khatib's dinner boat. At the exact moment he shut down the power, he leapt onto the rail of the dinner boat. He figured it best not to leave the boat running unmanned at full throttle. In the couple of minutes it took for him to catch up to the dinner boat, he had managed to cut the wire that Marv told him to cut, disabling the bomb, and he also managed to fit his Glock with the silencer from his go bag. Hanging on to the outside rail with his left hand, he quietly smoked two armed men who were walking around the corner to investigate who had boarded from another boat. Nine-millimeter bullets have a hell of a way of saying hello.

Xander hopped the rail and hugged the wall. Everything on this boat was similar to the one he had encountered Melanie on. The major difference was that the wheelhouse was situated more in the middle. And to his dismay, the dining room windows had been completely blacked out. He couldn't even tell if the lights were on inside. But he knew they were. What he didn't know was how many gunmen Khatib had waiting for him.

"Aaahhh!"

Xander heard a woman scream. It didn't sound like Natalie, but distress can have an effect on your vocal cords.

"Stop it! Please! You're hurting him!"

He heard the woman again. This time, he could tell she was shouting from above him and at the far end of the boat, closer to the stern. He remembered the large rooftop deck of the other dinner boat, so he knew that was where her shouts were coming from. Xander had a decision to make. The woman just screamed, "You're hurting him." He assumed that Kyle was the "him" she was referring to. He checked his watch, and he still had twelve minutes left to save Natalie. But what if the timing that Khatib gave wasn't exactly correct? He didn't have time to ponder the idea, but he couldn't make the wrong decision.

"No! You're going to kill him!"

That answered that question. Xander would have to trust that the timer was true. If it was Kyle being hurt, maybe killed, Xander had to do what he could for him. He couldn't leave his closest friend hanging. He jumped up and grabbed hold of the roof's edge and pulled himself up. In the bright cast shining down from the Eiffel, he could just make out a few people at the far end of the rooftop deck, at least a hundred feet away. He stayed low and sprinted along the roof past the wheelhouse. He didn't have time to worry around with whether or not the captain saw him. Fifty feet closer now, he could see that two men were holding a woman, while a man dressed in black tactical gear was beating on a man who had fallen to his knees.

Kyle.

240

The anger that fired inside of Xander at that moment was unmatched by anything he had ever felt. All the battles he had fought for the US, all the vigilante missions, and even more recently the personal wars he had endured, all of them paled in comparison to the fury he felt then. All he could see was red, and tactical maneuvering went right out the window.

"Khatib!" Xander shouted as he stepped over the rail at the perimeter of the deck. Khatib had his fist cocked, ready to drive it down into Kyle's mostly battered and semiconscious face. But when he heard Xander shout, he stopped and turned toward him, giving Xander his full attention. Xander took a long hard look at Kyle as he slumped over on his side. He let it fuel his rage.

Xander stalked toward Khatib, and without even realizing it, he dropped his gun on the ground. As he walked, his face was completely devoid of emotion. Khatib's men raised their guns, and Khatib made a motion for them to stand down.

Khatib let a sinister smile grow across his face. "Alexander King."

Xander continued his walk as he pulled his body armor vest off and tossed it to the ground. This left him in his black tank, his body now with total freedom of movement.

Xander growled, "Why don't you try to see if you can make that karate shit work on me?"

"I'm right here, big man." Khatib moved forward.

Xander swung at him with a haymaker overhand right. If it had connected, it would have wiped that smug smile right off Khatib's face. But Khatib moved quickly to the left, and before Xander could recover, Khatib hit him twice in the ribs, hard. Xander came back over the top with a left hook, but he was throwing his punches in anger, and it was pulling him off balance. Khatib ducked Xander's left and countered with a right hook to Xander's kidney, and a millisecond behind that came a left hook to the jaw. Xander staggered backward. He wiped his arm across his mouth, leaving behind a trail of blood across his forearm. Khatib was much faster than Xander had anticipated. Much more powerful as well.

Khatib mocked him. "Looks like my shit works pretty good on you too."

Rage again flooded Xander, and he lunged forward without regard for control or technique. Khatib stepped to his left and launched a Thai kick that landed directly in Xander's midsection. He turned away from Khatib and sucked for the air that had just been stolen from him. If he didn't get himself under control, if he didn't regain his focus, Xander was not only going to lose this fight, but he was going to lose the ability to save Kyle and Natalie. If he couldn't get it together for himself, he had to do it for them.

Khatib continued to mock Xander. "What's wrong, Captain America? Never met a man who was better than you? Never been bested in a fight?"

Khatib stepped forward and landed a quick one-two to Xander's forehead and chin. Khatib was moving swiftly on the balls of his feet. Very good technique. But Xander let him come in once more. This time when Khatib bounced in and landed another one-two, he left behind all the information Xander would need. Without knowing it, every time Khatib threw the straight right punch, he left his ribs wide open. This time when Khatib hit him, as Xander ate the punch, he shuffled his feet into a switch kick and brought his left leg around his body like a whip, striking Khatib at the bottom of his rib cage. When the top of Xander's foot connected, there was a pop, and Khatib reeled backward, grabbing at his newly-broken rib.

Xander began to bounce on the balls of his feet. Out of the corner of his eye he noticed Kyle raise his head. He could see that Xander's head was back in the game, and Kyle knew better than anyone what was coming next.

Violence.

Xander bounced forward, and when the injured Khatib threw a defensive right hand, Xander trapped it between his ribs and under his arm and whipped his head forward, shattering Khatib's nose with his forehead. Blood gushed from Khatib's face, but he ignored it and put his hands up, ready to defend himself.

It was Xander's turn to do the mocking. "Ouch, that one is gonna hurt your chances with the ladies," he said as he bounced around, hands up, ready to strike. Feeling like himself again.

Now it was Khatib who let anger get in the way of technique. He lunged wildly for Xander, leaving the left side of his face exposed. Xander capitalized by bludgeoning it with a powerful right hand. Xander could have sworn he heard the thudding sound his fist made echoing across the river. Khatib lost control of his legs, did the chicken dance, and dropped to the ground. Out of the corner of his eye, Xander noticed Kyle slithering across the deck toward the pistol Xander dropped earlier. The two men still holding Karol were so shocked that their leader was losing, they didn't even notice Kyle going for the gun. Khatib staggered as he got up, but he managed to make it to his feet. He may have been a son of a bitch, but he was a tough son of a bitch.

Xander moved forward and easily blocked the lazy three-punch combination Khatib threw at him. When Xander countered, he nearly drove his right hand straight through the back of Khatib's head. He had never hit a man so hard. Khatib collapsed again, this time on his back. Xander stalked over and straddled him, gaining full-mount position over him. Khatib was unconscious. Xander slapped him lightly across the face twice.

"Wake up, you son of a bitch. You are going to hear this." He slapped him twice more and Khatib opened his cold black eyes. "Look at me when I'm talking to you!"

Khatib's stare was blank, but Xander knew he was listening. Xander grabbed the dark hair on top of Khatib's head in his left hand and held him in place, not letting him look anywhere but straight into his eyes. Xander glanced over to Kyle, and Kyle gave him the knowing glare that Xander was hoping for. Xander then looked back at Khatib.

"You said it would take a King's Ransom to save Natalie . . . How's this for a ransom?"

Xander held out his right hand, and Kyle tossed him the Glock 19. Xander caught it, put it to Khatib's forehead, and just as Khatib's eyes widened in fear, Xander pulled the trigger and blew the brains out of the back of his head.

Without a moment's hesitation, Xander pivoted to his left and shot one of the men holding Karol in the neck and the other directly through his left eye. Xander turned back and rose to his feet. He stood over Akram Khatib and glared down at him. The vision he had seen in the murky river water earlier—Khatib with blood leaking out of his head—was now a reality lying there before his very eyes. Xander closed his eyes for a moment as he stood over Khatib's lifeless body. He let a vision of his beloved horse, alive and well, racing down the back stretch at the Kentucky Derby play like a movie in his head. This was the way he would remember his horse. The memory of finding him

244

dead in the stall would now be able to die with the man who was responsible for it. His terrorist blood would wash that horrible scene from Xander's mind forever.

Xander opened his eyes, and as he watched the blood leak from Akram Khatib, he tapped twice with his fist against his own chest, directly over his heart.

"For King's Ransom."

The Clock Is Ticking

The sound of a submachine gun firing from the other side of the boat and bullets hitting the deck and clanking against the rail around him broke Xander from his deadly trance. He dove to the floor and turned to shoot, but he couldn't find anyone in his sights.

Xander shouted to Karol, "Get down! Get down behind one of those bodies and don't move!"

Without hesitation, Karol dove back behind the bigger of the two men Xander had just gunned down. Xander could see that the shock of what she had just witnessed hadn't worn off, but at least she could still listen. It would be the difference between living and dying for her. He military crawled over to where she was, and Kyle followed behind him. Before he picked up the dead man's MP5 lying just beyond the man's hand, he checked his watch.

Four minutes.

Xander's internal clock started ticking in time with the

countdown on his watch.

A streak of panic flashed through Xander. He had to get to the dining room below.

Now.

"Kyle, is Natalie in the dining room below us?"

When Xander looked at his friend, his heart nearly broke. Kyle hardly resembled himself. He must have been taking that beating from Khatib for a while before Xander arrived. As Kyle propped himself up on his elbow, Xander could see that every movement caused him pain. Finally, Kyle nodded, confirming that Natalie was indeed in the dining room below them.

"I'm going to get us all out of here," Xander said to Kyle as he handed him the second gunman's MP5. "Just stay here and make sure no one gets close to you. It looks like the magazine has forty rounds in it. Don't be afraid to use them."

Xander checked his own MP5's magazine, and to his relief it was completely full. More bullets came flying from the direction of the wheelhouse. The dinner boat had slowed to a stop, right at the foot of the Eiffel Tower. This would help Xander see what was coming. And if Xander could see what was coming, everyone else was in trouble. He fired a couple of rounds back in the direction of the wheelhouse. The yellow lights from the tower were reflecting off its darkened windows. That was when he heard Natalie for the first time.

A muffled scream came up through the roof to their ears. It was so faint that Xander had to look to Kyle to confirm. He had heard it too. Emotion swelled inside Xander. He was so close to her, but still she stayed strapped to the wall in danger. He couldn't wait to hold her in his arms.

"I'll only be a minute, buddy," Xander assured Kyle.

Kyle managed a half smile through his bloody and battered

face as he looked from Xander to the Eiffel Tower. "Take your time, I'm enjoying the view."

Xander tousled Kyle's hair and rose to a crouch. He put the butt of the MP5 to his shoulder and began to move forward toward the incoming bullets. For the first time he saw a shadow move just beyond the wheelhouse. He squeezed the trigger, and a string of bullets shot toward the shadow. There was no way to tell if he had hit anything, so Xander used his bullets as a moment of cover and sprinted forward, closing the distance between himself and the end of the deck in just two seconds.

Three minutes.

This time, Xander was close enough to see the man leaning out from behind the wheelhouse. When Xander fired from behind the deck rail, the man jerked and fell to the ground. In the next moment, it was dumb luck that Xander glanced back over his shoulder at Kyle. If he hadn't, all three of them might have been dead. Instead, the man who had climbed the stairs to reach the rooftop deck behind Kyle was met with a burst of three nine-millimeter bullets in the chest. He collapsed backward and fell back down to the lower level. Kyle jerked his head from Xander to the man falling, then back again to Xander.

Xander shrugged. "Maybe don't spend so much time enjoying the view?"

He didn't wait for a response; he had to move. He jumped over the rail and sprinted across the roof, past the wheelhouse, but had to dive to the roofing when he saw another man hidden behind its wall. The man shot at Xander, but Xander managed to roll out of the way of the three bullets that clanged against the metal roofing right beside him. He quickly returned fire, and the man dropped when Xander's bullets hit him. Xander rose to his feet and trained his gun toward the wheelhouse. There was an itch that he would never be able to explain—an itch at the top of his spine that told him someone was aiming at him from behind the tinted windows of the wheelhouse.

Instinct.

A veteran soldier's sixth sense.

Xander shot out all three of the large windows that made up the front of the wheelhouse, and as soon as the glass crashed to the rooftop below, a man holding an assault rifle was revealed. Xander again dove to the flat rooftop below him, and because the man had been so startled by the crashing glass, he was an easy target for Xander, who fired four shots but unfortunately missed the man completely. The man in the wheelhouse recovered and returned fire. Xander shot back as he rolled to his left. The bullets clanged away beside him, and luckily one of his bullets landed, and the man dropped out of sight.

Two minutes.

Xander jumped to his feet and ran for the back of the boat. Without taking the time to look, because he had no time to spare, he dropped down to the walkway below him. As soon as he landed, a man fired a shotgun and Xander felt the MP5 go flying from his hand and out over the rail into the river. A quick flashback of taking a bullet to the stomach on his yacht in the Virgin Islands sprang to his mind. But there would be no rescue from Sam and Sarah this time. This recue was up to him.

When the man in black racked the slide on his shotgun, Xander did the only thing he could and dove at the man. The shotgun went off, and the hearing in Xander's right ear went dead. He didn't feel anything on his body burning as he landed on the man, crashing to the deck, so he pushed through. He forced the shotgun back over the man's head and slammed an elbow down on his nose. When the man continued to struggle, Xander felt someone jerk him backward by the back of his tank top. All of a sudden, Xander was on his back, looking down the barrel of another man's shotgun. Xander kicked at the gun's barrel and threw it off aim just enough that the slug bore a hole in the teakwood walkway right beside him.

Now the hearing in his left ear went dead.

Xander whirled around, moved his left leg to the back of the man's knees, and scissor-kicked backward on the man's stomach at the same time, forcing the man onto his back. He was also simultaneously reaching in his pocket and pulling out his knife. He pressed the action button and the blade shot from the handle; Xander drove it down into the man's Adam's apple. With his right hand he grabbed the man's shotgun, and as the other gunman sat up and aimed at Xander, Xander pulled the trigger and the man's head disappeared in a bloody mist. The other man made a gurgling sound as Xander removed the knife from his neck, and as Xander stood up, he saw another gunman coming down the walkway toward him.

One minute.

Xander dropped his knife to put two hands on the shotgun, but it was too late. The gunman fired at Xander, and with a wall on his left the only move Xander had was to hop the rail separating the walkway from the water below. It was a massive gamble. If he lost his grip on the shotgun as he hit the water, the gunman would easily shoot him, and then Natalie would be dead. Xander's feet hit the water, and he squeezed the gun in his hand as hard as he could as the cold wetness enveloped him completely. He kicked with his legs as hard as he could, and as his torso came up out of the water, he located the gunman looking for him over the rail, squeezed the trigger, and the man blew backward onto the walkway.

30 seconds.

Xander dropped the shotgun into the water, reached up, grabbed the railing, and pulled himself out of the water. He immediately jumped the rail and bent down to pick up his knife. As he retracted the blade and pocketed the knife, he realized his hearing was finally returning to normal.

25 seconds.

Xander rushed to the back of the dining room and pulled on the door. Locked.

20 seconds.

When he kicked the door, it buckled inward but didn't open.

"Natalie!" he shouted. He wanted her to know he was right there. He kicked again, this time with everything he had. But it yielded the same result.

The door wouldn't open.

15 seconds.

Even though Xander was entirely enthralled in the current struggle to get to Natalie before time ran out, he still managed to picture her terrified on that wall. He had time to picture the millions of terrified viewers that he was sure would be watching all around the world. He couldn't let this happen. Though Khatib was dead, he couldn't let him win.

Xander picked up the dead man's shotgun that lay at his feet, turned, and shot out the blacked-out window beside him. Glass blasted inward, shattering over the dining room floor. He immediately heard Natalie screaming madly through her gag.

10 seconds.

Xander hurdled the short seal of the window, and when his right eye found Natalie strapped to the wall with the long sharp spears just millimeters from her ears, the periphery of his left eye caught movement in the back corner. He squeezed the trigger of the shotgun without hesitation and blew the waiting gunman back against the side wall of the dining room. He dropped the shotgun and pulled out his knife as he sprinted toward Natalie.

5 seconds.

Though there was only a second between Xander and Natalie, he had time to see one of the worst sites his eyes had ever realized. The fear in her eyes was nearly debilitating. Her face was glistening from her tears, her voice strained as she screamed into the cloth gag.

3 seconds.

Xander pulled his knife with the steadiness of a surgeon. As he ejected the blade, he moved his hand toward the leather strap that held her head back against the wall. He sliced through the leather and when he pulled her head forward, the sharp tips of the rotating spear had already moved inside her ears, and the forward motion, though it saved her life, had ripped through the outside edges of her earlobes. As he held her head forward, he sliced through the leather strap holding her left hand in place and she fell forward into his arms. He reached behind her back as he held her and cut the strap holding her right hand. Most of her weight fell onto him. He quickly freed her feet, and when he took all of her weight, he cradled her in his arms.

He had made it.

Natalie was safe.

For the first time, he and Natalie locked eyes. Her body jerked in his arms from her uncontrollable sobbing. Xander let her feet down to the floor and pulled the cloth gag from her mouth, then scooped her back up into his arms. Blood poured from the outsides of her ears, but she would be okay.

"I'm so sorry, Natalie."

It was all he could think to say. Though he had saved her, he was still the only reason she had been in that position to begin with. For a moment he just let her cry.

"I'm sorry."

She wiped the tears from her face, then looked him in the eye once again. She looked entirely exhausted. But without saying a word, she managed to throw her arms around his neck. She squeezed him. That hug around his neck would be a feeling that Xander would never forget. It meant far more than words. He squeezed her in return and continued to let her cry.

"You're safe now."

For a long moment, Xander didn't move a muscle. He couldn't move a muscle. The weight of the reality of what was only a second from happening washed over him, it nearly overcame him. He let his head fall against hers as she wept on his shoulder. He closed his eyes and took in the scent of her hair. His heart pounded in rhythm with Natalie's. He never wanted that moment to end.

However, the buzzing of a motor in the distance forced the protector to push out the nurturer in him. Natalie heard it too, and once again fear masked her face. Xander remembered the cameras. He knew they hadn't seen his face, and he knew it needed to stay that way. He put Natalie back on her feet.

"It's okay. I promise you are safe," Xander told her as he backed away.

For the first time, she spoke, and her voice was near panic as she reached for him. "NO! No, don't leave me!"

Xander took her hand from his arm, kissed her knuckles, and let go. "It's okay. I'm just going to take out these cameras."

He pointed back over his head without turning toward them. "Then I am going to pick up the shotgun and make sure whoever is coming down the river in that boat isn't going to hurt us."

Natalie nodded. Xander stepped back several more feet until he was under the chandelier. He reached up, took all three cameras down, and smashed them under his feet. The motor was close to them now. The boat would be there in seconds. Xander picked up the shotgun and blew out both cameras that were fixed to the walls above both rows of windows. Natalie jerked at each blast. Xander walked over to the dead man in the corner and traded shotguns so he could have full ammo. Then he turned back to Natalie.

"I promise this will be over soon. Just stay right here and—"

"Xander, no! I can't be alone in here. What if that man wakes up?"

"He's dead. And it will only take me a minute. Kyle is hurt up on the rooftop deck. I have to make sure whoever is coming can't get to him. I'm here now. I promise, I'll keep you safe."

No One Knows

Sam nearly dropped the phone on which she'd been watching the live camera feed. The moment she saw Xander walk toward Natalie on the small screen, pride swelled inside her like nothing she had ever felt.

Xander had saved her.

And somehow she knew he had already avenged the death of his horse, King's Ransom.

"It will take a King's Ransom to save her, my ass! Ransom that!" Sam shouted and pointed to the screen for Sarah, Jack, and Viktor to see.

The four of them erupted in cheers as a local fisherman steered their boat down the river toward Xander and Natalie.

"That is my boss right there!" Viktor shouted and pumped his fist.

Jack grinned as wide as his mouth would spread, and he put his arm around Sarah's shoulder and gave it a squeeze. Sarah let out a sigh of relief but quickly looked away from the screen once she saw Xander take Natalie into his arms. Sam knew it was painful for Sarah to watch, so she clicked off the feed and put the phone away.

Sam said to the group, "Okay, we know Xander and Natalie are all right, but we still don't know about Kyle and the President's daughter's friend. When we pull up, we need to be prepared for the worst. There still may be men on the boat with them. We need to secure the four of them as quickly as we can."

The others dampened their celebrations as Sam turned her attention back to the water ahead of them. The Eiffel Tower was close, so she knew they were nearing the dinner boat. Her stomach turned at the thought of Kyle being injured, or worse. She knew Xander would have done everything he could to save him, but that didn't mean he made it in time. As they rounded a bend in the river, Sam readied her pistol and steadied her nerves. She was going to do her best to listen to her own advice, but every ounce of her was hoping that they wouldn't find the worst.

Marv too was elated to see that Xander had made it to Natalie in time. Not only for the obvious reason that he saved her life, but also because Xander had thwarted the efforts of Khatib to have the entire world witness a horrible terrorist murder a beloved American live on camera. He knew the world had been watching live, so he switched over to the first news channel he could find: BBC news. A short-haired blonde woman was narrating the replay of Xander pulling Natalie down from the wall.

Ladies and gentlemen watching all around the world, it seems as though Natalie Rockwell, in true movie fashion, has been saved. You are watching video of a man pulling her from the wall, saving her from the awful horror of those approaching spinning spears. The question now, and the Internet is already abuzz about it, is just who is that man who pulled her down from certain death? We have been in contact with our sources in the US, and no one seems to know. We are to assume that he is either part of US military or maybe a CIA operative, but for now we have no further information about Natalie Rockwell's hero.

Marv turned the television off and pushed his glasses back up to his eyes. He wasn't sure it was over on that boat. He didn't know whether or not Xander had been able to fully clear the threat. As soon as he had seen Xander pull Natalie free from the wall, he sent a car to pick them up and dispatched the French police to the location of the dinner boat. The only person he hadn't heard from yet was—

"Sir?" Marv's second-in-command broke his train of thought and stole his attention.

"Yes, Dana, what is it?"

"It's the President's daughter."

Marv whirled around from his computer screen and gave the short, round, cropped-haired woman his full attention.

"Yes?"

"Well, um, no one knows where she is."

Marv stood up; he would have answered immediately, but all the air in his lungs escaped him before he could. He inhaled sharply and tried to keep his cool.

"You mean, Zhanna hasn't brought her in?"

"No sir. I know you said that Sam told you Adeline was safe with this . . . Zhanna, but we haven't heard anything. I told the police her last known location, but they haven't found anyone alive there at the warehouse. They searched the place thoroughly after Sam handed Melanie over to them. But they only found a couple of dead bodies on the premises. No sign of Adeline Williams or—"

Marv's phone began to ring. He pulled it from his pocket, and when he saw the Langley, Virginia, number on the screen, his heart jumped into his throat.

As the phone continued ringing, Marv said to Dana, "Get Sam on the phone, ASAP." Then he answered the call. "This is Marvin."

"Marvin, what the hell is going on over there? Tell me good news, and I don't mean what I just watched on the Internet."

Marv swallowed hard. This was the first time the newly appointed director of the CIA had called him, and he didn't have good news. "Director Hartsfield, I am getting Samantha Harrison on the phone right now. She will be able to tell me where the President's daughter is."

"She'd better. I don't need to tell you what a shitstorm it is over here right now, do I?"

Marv cleared his throat. "No ma'am. And you will be my first call after I reach Sam."

Dana walked back over to Marv. He looked at her, hoping for good news, but Dana just shook her head.

"I want good news in sixty seconds, Marvin. Call me back."

"Yes ma'am."

Marv ended the call and immediately dialed Sam's SAT

phone.

Dana spoke while he dialed. "Sorry sir, Ms. Harrison didn't answer."

Marv heard her but gave no response. He was focused on the ringing he heard through the receiver. He was sending up silent prayers for Sam to answer.

But the phone just kept ringing.

Hide and Seek

Zhanna cupped her hand over Adeline's mouth. She could feel her shaking and doing her best not to make a sound. But there were still muffled sobs leaking and frightened tears running down her face. It was dark in the alley, but there was just enough light for Zhanna to hold Adeline's eyes. She held the barrel of her pistol vertically to her mouth and pouted out her lips in a shushing motion, begging with her eyes for Adeline to calm down. She then motioned by patting her gun to her chest; Adeline understood and took a nice deep breath with her. That seemed to help.

A man's voice echoed down the dark alley. "There's no way out of here, red! Hand the girl over and I'll let you go. But if you keep hiding from me, I am going to kill you both when I find you. I never did like playing hide-and-seek!"

The man had been tailing them for over half a mile now, ever since Zhanna and Adeline bolted out of the elevator and made a run for it through the underground parking garage. The sniper in the building behind the warehouse gave them away.

They were just lucky he missed. The sniper had been able to trap them long enough for the other man with Melanie in the warehouse to come out after them. The last half hour had been nothing but dodging the men following them. Zhanna would have already taken out the three men, but having to protect Adeline meant she had to change her tactics. But now they were trapped. She didn't know Paris very well, and in a last-ditch escape effort, Zhanna had accidentally run them into a dead end.

There was a cluster of trash cans in the darkest corner of the alley. Zhanna pointed to them and whispered as softly as she could in Adeline's ear.

"Get behind trash containers. No matter what you are hearing, you do not move. It is only way I can keep you safe. You understand?"

Adeline closed her eyes and nodded, and on all fours she slowly slinked away and tucked herself behind the trash cans. Zhanna unlatched the safety on her pistol and took a deep breath as she peeked up and over the dumpster between her and the man who earlier had introduced himself as Sebastian. She immediately saw three men at the edge of the street. She raised her pistol and fired at the man on the left. It was dark and the men were some fifty feet away, so she couldn't tell if her bullet found its mark. However, the sound of her gun erupted through the quiet streets and seemed to reverberate a never-ending echo. Whether it was the sound or her hitting one of them, the three men dove for cover on either side of the alley.

Zhanna bolted around the dumpster and sidled up behind a car parked about twenty feet in front of her. This changed everything. The lighting greatly improved, and now she was close enough to know whether she hit her mark or not. She

261

raised up, and as soon as her head crested the roof of the car, a gun went off and a bullet grazed the top of the car and nearly caved in the right side of her face. So close she could feel the wind from the bullet. She dropped to her stomach as quickly as she could. Under the car she saw a man come out of the shadows on the left side of the alley.

"I think I got her, Sebastian!"

Zhanna didn't hesitate and fired her gun. She aimed as high as the undercarriage of the car would allow, and she could see the man reach for his knee in pain. Immediately she rolled out from behind the car and took cover behind another nearby dumpster to her right. And it was a good thing she did. The other two men began firing on the car. One man blasted away with a semiautomatic rifle, and another was shooting a pistol. Glass blew out of every window in the car, and a couple of tires blew as well. Lights in nearby windows of the surrounding buildings began to dot the skyline like stars coming out at night. She knew the police would be on their way soon, but she didn't think they would arrive before she had to handle this herself.

Finally the blasting of the car stopped, and Zhanna wheeled out from behind the dumpster with her pistol raised. The tip of her gun found a man still holding his rifle on the car. She squeezed the trigger as her gun hovered over his chest, and after the recoil of her pistol bucked, the man dropped to the ground. She moved her gun to the man on the ground beside him. He was still holding his knee. He looked up just in time to watch Zhanna fire again, and she was the last thing he ever saw.

Zhanna once again took cover behind the dumpster. "Now it is just one on one. I like these odds, Sebastian."

"Just hand over the girl. What do you care anyway? You clearly aren't American. Hand her over and I'll let you live."

Zhanna stepped out from behind the dumpster and began to move quietly toward Sebastian's voice. "You are right, I am not American. But I am human. And I am human who does not like bullies. And these bullies don't last very long when I am around."

After her last word she sprinted toward where she thought Sebastian was hiding, behind a car of his own. To her surprise, he had moved closer as well, and when he sprang out from behind a dumpster, they collided and crashed to the ground. Zhanna lost her pistol and immediately wrapped both hands around the wrist of Sebastian's gun hand. One bullet went off as she wrapped her legs around his waist. She was in full-guard position now, with Sebastian on top of her. He was trying desperately to free his gun hand. The problem for Zhanna, and she knew it, was that she was completely exposed. She had to use both of her hands to keep from getting shot, and this left Sebastian with a free arm. She knew it was coming, she just hoped it wouldn't be enough to knock her out when it came. That was when she felt a sharp pain against her right temple. She had the wherewithal to figure it must have been his fist, because if he had used his elbow, she wouldn't have been awake to contemplate it.

For a moment she saw darkness, but she was sure she maintained her grip on his wrist. When the darkness faded, it became clear that she had indeed lost her grip. And instead of staring into Sebastian's eyes, she was staring down the barrel of his pistol. The last thing she heard was the blast of a gun.

Yahtzee!

Kyle heard what Xander said; he wanted him to stay put. But after hearing a few gunshots and a lot of commotion, it had been a while since he had heard anything. Except for the motor of an approaching boat.

"Karol, stay here. I'll be right back."

"Kyle, no! Please don't leave me here with . . . them!" Karol looked in fear over the two dead men lying beside her.

Kyle knew what it was like to see dead people for the first time. It was one of the many messed-up pleasures you get to enjoy being the best friend of Alexander King. His heart felt for Karol, but he didn't have time for it. If something was wrong, the oncoming boat could be trouble for Xander and him.

Kyle tried to look sympathetic, but even that hurt his battered face. "I know, it's awful. But Karol, this will all be over in a minute. Then we'll get you out of here, back to Adeline, and back to the States."

"What if she's not okay?" Karol's voice caught, and the quiver in it was hard for Kyle to bear. She was so young and innocent. Well, she used to be innocent.

"Adeline is fine. I promise. Now hold tight, I'll be right back."

Karol nodded and Kyle managed to get to his feet, which was somewhat of a miracle in and of itself. Khatib had really worn him out. Kicks to the legs, the liver, and the head. Every fiber of Kyle's body ached. But hearing the motor of the approaching boat shutting off shot enough adrenaline into his veins that the pain became an afterthought. The boat had pulled up, and he needed to help if he could.

He shuffled over to the rail of the rooftop deck. His right leg was dead, almost surely broken. But his left leg had enough strength left to move him. The shimmering lights of the Eiffel Tower continued to sparkle behind him, and when he peeked over the rail, it was just in time to watch Xander emerge from the interior of the boat and blow the man boarding the dinner boat back into the river with his shotgun. The blast echoed over the water, and he watched Xander rack the shotgun's slide and fire another slug into the boat. What Xander couldn't see, however, was what Kyle was able to watch from his vantage point on the roof. Another gunman on the opposite side of the boat was rounding the corner just as Xander stepped onto the boat. Kyle, as quickly as his beaten body would let him, began to raise the MP5 to his shoulder.

He wasn't going to make it in time. So he did the only thing he could think to do. Just as the man rounded the corner and raised his gun on Xander, Kyle shouted, "YAHTZEE!"

Both Xander and the gunman whirled their guns toward Kyle, and Kyle fired a six-round burst at the man. The gunman took several of the bullets and stayed on his feet until Xander turned and blasted him with the shotgun. He fell to the ground in a thud, blood leaking from several places on his body.

Xander tossed his empty shotgun to the floor of the boat and looked up at Kyle.

"Yahtzee?"

Kyle knew Xander was going to have a smart-ass remark. Even in this intense moment. It's just who he was.

Kyle laughed. "You're alive, aren't you?"

"Yes. Yes I am. But I'm still telling Sam."

"Asshole . . . Is Natalie okay?"

Xander stepped back onto the dinner boat. "She's alive. I'm not sure she'll ever be okay."

Kyle nodded.

"You okay?" Xander asked.

"I'm alive."

Suddenly they heard another boat approaching, and it was coming fast. Both Kyle and Xander looked in the direction of the boat, then back to each other. Xander held up his hands and Kyle tossed him the MP5.

"Just stay put. I'll come get you when it's over," Xander said.

Kyle looked up and out over the dark river. The boat had already rounded the bend. But before he could be filled with concern, the light on the front of the boat began to flash. He looked down at Xander, who had noticed it too. Xander still stood at the ready, gun pointed in the boat's direction.

Kyle asked him, "What do you think it means?"

Before Xander could answer, a sound carried over the water to them as the boat approached. A sound they both knew all too well.

"WHOOP WHOOP!"

Sam.

Xander immediately lowered his weapon, and Kyle could see his shoulders relax. Then he looked up at Kyle.

"Sam's gonna want to see you as soon as she boards. Can Karol help you down? I'm gonna get Natalie."

Kyle felt himself relax as well.

It was over.

"I can make it. See you in a second."

Xander scooped Natalie up into his arms. She wasn't unconscious, but she was exhausted. Her face was still wet with tears, and he gave her forehead a soft kiss. Natalie opened her eyes, and her bottom lip quivered when she saw it was Xander.

"It's okay, sweetheart. I'm getting you out of here."

Natalie could only manage a whisper. "Are they all dead?"

Xander nodded. "They're all gone. Don't worry anymore, I'm not letting you out of my sight ever again."

As Xander said it, he meant it with all his heart. His only hope was that she would let him keep that promise. Natalie didn't respond; she just let out a long exhale and closed her eyes. Xander heard the boat's motor shut off at the back of the dinner boat.

"Xander? Xander, are you all right?" Sam called to him.

"I'm fine! We're in here!"

Xander turned toward the back of the dining room just as Sam appeared in the doorway. Sam practically ran to him. She threw her arms around him and gave him a solid squeeze.

Sam looked down at Natalie. "Is she all right?"

Xander gave a half smile. "She's going to be."

Sam put her forehead to Xander's for a moment, but when she pulled away, he could see the worried question hanging in her mind. He knew she wanted to know about Kyle. Right on cue, Kyle appeared in the doorway over Sam's shoulder. Karol was holding him up as best she could.

"You miss me?" Kyle said to the room.

Sam's eyes lit up, and she turned to him. Xander couldn't help but laugh, because Sam was clearly trying to hide her true feelings, as she normally did.

Sam looked at Kyle, then at Karol. "Mr. Hamilton, no matter the circumstance, you've always got time for a younger woman, don't you?"

Kyle let his head slump. "I love you too, Sam."

Xander lifted his foot and gave Sam a nudge on her bottom in Kyle's direction.

"Oh, all right," she said. Then she went to him, and when she hugged him, Kyle held on for as long as he could.

Xander carried Natalie over past the two of them hugging and out the door into the cool Paris night. And he just couldn't help himself. "Would you two get a room already?"

Sam backed away almost fast enough for Kyle to drop straight to the floor. Jack and Viktor shared a laugh with Xander as they watched Sam stiffen. But Xander's smile quickly faltered when Sarah stepped out from behind Viktor. He could see the hurt in her eyes as she watched him carry Natalie in his arms. He wanted to comfort her, but he couldn't. And she didn't let him see her hurt for long.

"Thank God you made it to her in time, Xander."

Xander started, "Sarah, I—"

"Don't," Sarah interrupted. "You don't have to say anything. I'm just happy everyone is okay."

She had made it easy on him, no surprise there. But he knew he needed to talk to her soon. He had no idea what he would say, but after everything they had been through, Sarah deserved a full and completely honest download from Xander. Whatever that ended up being, good or bad. Even if it was him telling her that his heart belonged to Natalie.

Xander turned back to Sam. "Where's Zhanna and Adeline?"

Karol perked up and walked around to make sure she could hear the news about her friend.

Sam tugged at her pocket for the SAT phone. "Oh bugger, Marv was calling me as I pulled up, but I couldn't answer until I knew you lot were all right. I'm sure it was about Zhanna."

Xander looked concerned. "You mean you don't know where she is? Where the President's daughter is?"

"We got separated when I went after Melanie. Zhanna pulled her out of the fray into the elevator at the warehouse. I just assumed she went straight to the police." Sam dialed a number on her phone.

Xander had a terrible feeling that something had gone horribly wrong.

Sometimes It's Safe to Smoke

Zhanna knew she heard the gun go off. She was positive of that. She could still think and she didn't feel any pain, but the weight of Sebastian on top of her was different. Was this what it was like to be dead? She was afraid to open her eyes to find out. As her hearing returned to normal and the buzz of the gunshot subsided, she heard . . . sirens?

"Zhanna?"

That didn't sound like God. Was it an angel?

"Zhanna, are you okay?"

The voice was closer, a female voice. Then she felt someone touching her shoulders, and the sirens sounded as if they were right beside her.

"Zhanna, wake up!" This time the voice sounded more urgent.

Zhanna opened her left eye only, as if that would somehow soften what she was about to see. To her relief, Adeline Williams's young and beautifully concerned face was staring back at her as she continued to try to wake her up.

"Adeline? What—what happened?"

Adeline picked something up off the ground beside Zhanna. "When you dropped your gun, it slid out into the middle of the alley. I didn't really know what to do, but I have seen a lot of movies, and I just did what I always saw people do on there, and I aimed the gun at the bad guy on top of you and squeezed the little thingy like they do on NYPD Blue, you know, and I wasn't sure if I hit him, but then he fell over and I ran over here to see if you were okay! Are you okay?" Adeline's nerves were shot.

Zhanna took a breath for Adeline, then smiled. "I am. You saved my life."

"You saved mine." Adeline smiled back.

The sound of the police siren sounded to Zhanna like they were right around the corner, and she jumped quickly to her feet.

Adeline stepped back. "What's wrong? It's just the police, right?"

"Yes. But we don't know if we can trust them. They may be on payroll. Follow me!"

Zhanna grabbed Adeline by the hand. Adeline's face showed that she couldn't handle much more. Zhanna understood completely. Before Zhanna started her new life with what used to be the KGB in Russia, she had to bear witness to far too many things like this herself as a girl. When your father is the most notorious gangster in the world, you see a lot of things you shouldn't as a child. Being moved quickly from a home or an office to dodge imminent danger was as regular an occasion for her as it was for most kids to go and get an ice cream cone. It hardened Zhanna. It also made her a fantastic agent. But it left her personal relationships in a less than

271

desirable situation. It was what she admired most about Xander in the short time she had known him—his ability to maintain a warm heart when being perpetually surrounded by the coldness of the world. She knew how difficult that was to do. But he did it with grace, and Zhanna wanted to be more like that. Getting Adeline to safety without being a complete bitch would be a good start.

"Come on, you can do it, Adeline. I will get you to safety!" Zhanna told her as they rounded their way out of the dead-end alley and onto the street. Was that a comforting thing to say? She had been told before that her Russian accent made her seem all the more cold. Nothing she could do about that.

The two of them sprinted down the road. Zhanna looked back over her shoulder, and a couple of blocks back, two police cars swerved out onto the street behind them. They would see whichever direction Zhanna chose to take in an attempt to get away. She remembered grabbing the smoke grenade that Sarah dropped when Sebastian tackled her back at the warehouse. She snatched it from her waistband and pulled the pin.

"This is going to create a lot of smoke when I drop it!" Zhanna shouted to Adeline. "When I say, we are going to move to a street on our left. Just stay with me and we will be fine!"

Zhanna and Adeline nodded to each other. Zhanna dropped the smoke grenade, and after a loud pop, white smoke contrasted against the dark night as it billowed into the air. Zhanna gave it a couple of seconds and two side streets before she shouted, "Now!" The two of them darted to the left down another side street. This one was not a dead end. To Zhanna's surprise, Adeline was fast. She was staying with her, stride for stride. She was proud of Adeline's bravery.

"To the right!" Zhanna shouted, and they moved down

another street, passing a group of teenagers drinking on the corner. But then Zhanna was forced to stop dead in her tracks as a black SUV skidded sideways in the street in front of her. Just as Zhanna was about to pull Adeline into another side street, a voice shouted for Adeline from the window of the vehicle.

"Adeline! Wait!"

Zhanna could tell by the look on Adeline's face that it was a voice she knew. The door opened and Zhanna put herself between the SUV and Adeline.

"Addie! It's okay, it's me, Jeremy!"

The man shut the SUV's door behind him. In the casted light of a streetlamp, Zhanna could see that he was wearing a black suit.

Zhanna held Adeline protectively behind her as she spoke. "Adeline, do you know this man?"

"Yes! Yes! It's my Secret Service agent! Jeremy!"

Adeline wiggled out from behind Zhanna and ran to Jeremy. Zhanna let out a long breath of relief as Adeline jumped into his arms. Two police cars squealed to a stop behind her, and two more swerved in behind the SUV. The doors opened, and the policemen drew their guns, pointing them at Zhanna. They shouted something in French. Zhanna assumed it was something to the effect of "Get down on the ground!" She reached her hands above her head, but she did not go to the ground. Not until two police officers put her there. And the force by which they did it was far too much for Zhanna to take. She rolled to her back, and as she started to fight them, another man stepped out of the SUV.

"Hey, wait! Let her go! Laissez-la partier!"

The two police officers stopped fighting Zhanna, and the three of them looked up at the man walking toward them.

Zhanna thought she recognized the voice, but the short, salt-and-pepper-haired, glasses-wearing skinny guy in front of her wasn't anyone she had ever seen before. He said a couple more things to the police officers in French and then showed them a badge. The only thing Zhanna understood in the exchange was when the man with the glasses said, "American CIA." The two officers backed away, and the man reached down and helped Zhanna to her feet.

"Sorry about that. Are you all right?"

Zhanna smiled, but he must have noticed that she was confused.

He extended his hand and said, "Oh, sorry, Zhanna. It's Marvin. Marvin Cameron."

Zhanna took his hand, and the confusion on her face turned to elation. "Marv?"

"Yep, that's me. Thank you so much for taking care of Adeline. You have no idea what it means, to me and my superiors."

"How are the others? Did Xander reach Natalie in time?"

Marv pushed his glasses back up on his nose. "He sure did. But he couldn't have done it without all of you."

"And Sam?"

"Sam apparently beat the hell out of Melanie before the cops made her quit."

Zhanna couldn't help but laugh. She didn't really understand why she was so happy about the outcome. She barely knew the group. But there was just something about the way they made her feel like they had known her forever. Like they were this exclusive club and they just brought her right in. She had always been a loner, so the feeling of being part of a group meant more to her than she could ever have imagined.

274

Marv continued, "I know Xander is going to be so grateful for all you've done."

"It's the least I could do for what he did for me in Moscow."

Marv nodded. Then his phone began to ring.

"Oh God, I forgot to call Director Hartsfield back! Do you mind?"

"Sounds important," Zhanna said.

As he answered the phone, he took her by the hand and led her back to the SUV. Zhanna listened in.

"Mrs. Hartsfield, yes. No, I know. I know you've called several times. I know. I'm sorry. I know, but you can tell the President his daughter is safe. Zhanna pulled her from the warehouse and kept her safe. We have Adeline in our truck now. It's all over. They did it."

Saving the World Is Hard, But *Love* Is Harder

Xander put away his phone, sat back in his chair, and closed his eyes. He was exhausted, but he couldn't sleep. He couldn't believe the nonstop coverage of Natalie's kidnapping and her subsequent rescue. He knew she was famous, he knew she was widely loved, but every single media outlet on the planet was only reporting on one thing.

Natalie Rockwell.

Of course, they had no idea about Adeline. If they had discovered how the President's daughter had gone missing, coverage certainly would have been more split. The President himself had called Xander a little over an hour ago. Xander was honored to speak with him, but it was a short conversation. He told President Williams that it was his team that had found and kept Adeline safe. He was proud to say so. Kyle showed unbelievable courage by putting Adeline's safety ahead of his own. In Xander's mind, that was the very definition of hero.

Sam of course had been her normal self, as had Sarah, but Zhanna really showed what she was all about. Adeline herself said that she would be dead if not for Zhanna's quick thinking and all-around badassery. Xander told the President that it was his team that deserved the praise, and he happily passed their information along so that the President could call them as well.

It would be a bit before Kyle would be able to take that important call. Xander left Natalie's hospital bed only long enough to check on his friend. The battered and beaten Kyle was sound asleep. Completely exhausted. Xander tried to get Sam, Zhanna, and Sarah to go with Jack and Viktor to a hotel, but every last one of them insisted that they stay until Kyle came around. The doctor said it would take him a while to heal, but he would make a full recovery. Several broken bones and a nasty concussion were an odd way to get lucky, but Xander knew that his friend was just that. Lucky. He very well could have been dead.

As Xander looked over at Natalie sleeping peacefully in her hospital bed, his heart was heavy. It seemed to him like a broken record now, but he couldn't believe the danger that he had thrown his friends into once again. And even more amazing was how they responded. Throwing themselves into the danger when most would run away from it. Giving everything they had to see to it that Natalie and Adeline were safe. Xander knew it was a big deal that they stopped Akram Khatib from killing Natalie on the live feed, that they stopped the bombing at the nightclub, and that they saved the President's daughter. But the biggest deal to him was the fact that they would do it all again tomorrow if something else came up. That was why he had to make certain that it didn't. This life of violence was where Xander thrived. But it was also where his friends would die if he let it continue. He knew what he had to do; he would distance—

"Xander?" Natalie called to him softly from her bed.

Xander jumped up and ran to her side. He took her hand in his and brushed the hair away from her forehead.

She asked, "Is everyone okay? No one got hurt trying to help me, did they?"

Xander smiled. Even after all that she had been through, Natalie was more worried about everyone else than herself.

"Kyle got a little banged up, but he's going to be okay. He'd do it all over again a hundred times to make sure you were all right."

Natalie looked sad. She scooted over in her bed, then patted the empty space for him to lie beside her. He quickly obliged, and once he laid down, Natalie nestled her head on Xander's chest as he held her in his arms.

"Why did they come after me? Just to hurt you?"

"Yes. Sam and I took down his brother's terrorist faction, and he wanted revenge. I suppose he found coverage of us at the Kentucky Derby together. I'm sorry I brought you into my mess. I should have just steered clear of you that night in San Diego."

Natalie looked up at him and smiled. "Like you even had a choice."

Xander returned the smile and gave her a squeeze. He knew there was absolutely no disputing that fact. Then he felt Natalie shaking. When he looked back down at her, she was crying.

He gave her another squeeze. "It's okay now, Natalie. You're safe."

She sniffled twice, wiped her tears away, and propped herself up on her elbow. Xander could see in her eyes that she wasn't scared, she was heartbroken.

"It's not that, Xander." Her voice faltered. She looked away toward the back of the room, stifling more tears.

Xander knew what was coming, but he didn't see what came first.

Natalie looked back at him, holding his eyes. "I love you."

Xander sat up. "I—"

"Wait," Natalie interrupted. "Please, just let me get this out."

He nodded.

She continued. "I love you, Alexander King. I have never felt this way about anyone in my entire life. Every second of every day I think of you. Whenever anything happens to me, whether it be getting that new role in a movie I wanted, or if it is just something stupid like the lady at the grocery store who looks like Carol Burnett, all I want to do is share it with you. I've never met a man like you. A man who cares more about the people close to him than he cares about himself—"

Xander interrupted, "That's not exactly true—"

"Please. Please let me finish."

Xander nodded.

"And there are a thousand more things I could mention. Your sense of humor, how sexy you are, but it's your heart that makes you irresistible. And in your case, the very thing that makes you is also the very thing that breaks you. You want to fight everyone's battles for them. Because you know you can. But as selfless as you are in doing that, it would be the thing that will always keep us apart. Because I can't fight those battles with you. I'm not like Sam or Sarah. They were made for your world."

"I can change my world."

Natalie hung her head. Then she began to shake it. "No, you can't." She looked back up at him. "It's who you are. There is something in you that is special. It's what makes you the guy that people can call to come and save them. But I need someone that I know won't go off and die for a righteous cause when he has a family at home that he needs to be around to protect."

Xander was the one to hang his head this time. She saw enough in him to see herself having a family with him. Xander's heart twisted inside his chest. He knew she was right. He knew it because his sister had been giving him this same speech for years. "You can't save the whole world, Xander, and it isn't your job to do so," she would always say. And whenever Xander told her that he wasn't trying to save the whole world, he always went running the next time he was called upon. And that is exactly what Natalie was saying to him now. But he would do anything to be with her. Whatever it took. She needed to know that.

Natalie spoke before he could. "And I know what you're thinking. You could give it up if you wanted to. And I know you believe that, Xander. But one day, and it could be a month from now or it could be ten years from now, but one day your phone will ring and someone on the other end of that line will convince you that going and saving the country from another madman will actually be saving your family. And they may be right. But one of those times you take that call, I will get one from someone else telling me that this time, you didn't make it. And that would destroy me."

Xander shook his head, then made an attempt at lightening the mood. "So I take it you don't believe in the old saying that it is better to have loved once than to never have loved at all?"

It fell flat.

"My heart wouldn't be able to take it."

"So that's it?" Xander paused. He was trying not to get angry, because he knew she was right. But . . . "You're just going to give up on someone you say you love?"

"You don't understand—"

"No, you don't understand, Natalie. You are right. I am a fighter. I will fight for those closest to me and those who need me. But I would never fight for anyone like I would fight for you. For us. And you're right, maybe one day there would be a call I couldn't refuse. And then I may not make it back home. But until that day, no one will ever love you like I will. No one will ever give more of themselves to you than I will. And if you think denying what we have forever is better than giving it all we've got until it's over is the best way forward, then we see things very, very differently."

Natalie just stared back at him. He hoped she would understand and see things his way. But if she didn't, she didn't. And he would spend as long as it took to try to change her mind.

"I'm sorry, Xander. It's not that I disagree with you, I just can't put myself through that. If I give myself to you fully and then lose you, I would never recover."

Xander settled back down into the hospital bed and pulled Natalie into him. Neither one of them said another word, and he held her until they both drifted off to sleep.

First Kisses Beat the Hell Out of Last Kisses

When Xander woke up a couple of hours later, his head was pounding. He hoped that his conversation with Natalie was just a bad dream, but he knew that it wasn't. He managed to free his arm from under her neck, shimmy out of the hospital bed, and make his way out of the room without waking her. Since that went so terribly with Natalie, he decided he may as well make it 0 for 2 and go ahead and have a conversation with Sarah. He knew better than anyone how Sarah was going to feel, having just been rejected himself.

He walked around the corner of the hallway into the waiting room, and Sam and Sarah both stood when he entered.

Sam said, "You look like hell. You need to get some sleep, Xander."

"Thanks, Sam. I can always count on you for a nurturing hand."

Sam put her hand to her hip. "I didn't mean it like that. But bloody hell, at least let the nurse get you an Advil or ten."

"I'm fine. Sarah, will you walk me down to get some coffee?"

Sarah gave a half smile. "Of course."

"We'll be right back, Sam."

Xander started down the hall, and Sarah quickly caught up to him.

"Are you all right? You've been through a lot," she said.

"I'm okay. Listen—"

"Xander, you don't have to have this conversation with me. I'm not like a lot of girls. I don't need you to coddle me. And I'm not blind. I can see how you feel about Natalie."

"I'm sorry I took advantage of the situation and took it too far with you. I should never have let it happen feeling the way I do about Natalie."

"It's fine, Xander. You were confused. And it takes two. I wouldn't change a minute of it. Don't you remember how much fun the other night was?"

There Sarah was, letting him off the hook again. Unbelievable. Two amazing women and he couldn't be with either one of them.

Karma.

He gave Sarah a wink. "It was an electrifying night, wasn't it?"

Sarah smiled. "It really was. I'll never forget it."

Xander stopped walking and wrapped his arms around her. She hugged him back, then leaned away to look him in the eye. "Just promise me one thing?"

Xander nodded. "Of course."

"Marry that girl. Make her the happiest woman in the world?"

Xander really didn't know what to say, so he just went with what he felt. "I will do everything I can do. I promise."

Sarah gave him a genuine smile. Then she leaned in and kissed him softly on the lips. Xander thought she was trying to let him off the hook, but instead it was clear that she wanted him to remember what he was missing. And miss it he would.

Sarah ended the kiss and gave his jaw one last caress. "I really have to go now and file all of this back in Langley. It's going to be a mile of paperwork, so I'd better go so I can get started. Do me one last favor?"

"Of course."

"When Kyle wakes up, tell him to call me," Sarah said with a wry smile. "Tell him I still don't believe he's the ladies' man everyone says he is."

Xander raised his eyebrow, nodded, and smiled from somewhere deep inside himself. "I will absolutely extend that challenge."

"Goodbye, Xander."

Xander watched as Sarah walked away, disappearing through the door to the stairs. He turned and walked back to the waiting room where Sam was waiting. She walked over to him, shaking her head in total disbelief.

"What?" Xander asked.

Sam continued shaking her head. "Have you got *actual* silver on that tongue of yours, or what?"

"Me?" Xander played coy. "Nah, it's platinum."

"I believe it after seeing that."

"What do you mean?"

Sam stood with her hands on her hips. "Please. You break it off with a woman and she kisses you on the lips. What have you got hiding in those underpants of yours anyway?"

284

Xander just raised both arms, palms up, and made a "what can I say?" face. But it was clear that he didn't pull it off. Sam saw right through it. Just as she always does.

"I take it, it didn't go so well in there with Natalie."

He shook his head.

"I'm sorry, Xander. I know what she means to you." Sam leaned in and gave him hug.

"Thanks. Don't get too mushy, though, you'll ruin your reputation."

Sam smacked him on the arm, and they walked over and sat down in the waiting room chairs.

Xander cleared his throat. "So, Viktor told me that he overheard Marv telling Director Hartsfield that one of the police officers told him you put quite the beating on poor ol' Melanie."

Sam let out a satisfied sigh. "Ah, you should have seen it, Xander. She wilted like a flower in a drought. It was embarrassing really."

"I wish I could have seen it." Xander laughed.

"Speaking of beatings, Kyle managed to tell me Khatib beat your ass out there on that boat." Sam laughed.

Xander laughed and nodded. "Oh, is that what Kyle told you? Who's the dead man? Answer me that."

"Tough terrorist bloke, huh?"

"Right up until I put a bullet in his forehead."

The two of them sat back and let a wave of exhaustion flow over them.

"Sam, what the hell is wrong with us?"

"What do you mean?"

Xander clasped his hands behind the back of his head. "What kind of people constantly run *toward* danger instead of

285

away from it?"

"Real morons, I assure you."

"Yeah?"

"Yeah," Sam confirmed.

"Yeah," Xander agreed.

"But—" Sam stood as Kyle's nurse entered the waiting room. Xander stood with her. "We may be complete morons, but at least we don't run from who we really are."

Xander nodded, but as the nurse told them that Kyle was awake and they could go in and see him, Xander realized that the conversation he was about to have with all of them couldn't contradict that sentiment more.

It's All Over but the Crying

Xander and the team walked into Kyle's hospital room to find him sitting up with a smile on his battered face. Xander would never be able to express how much he loved that crazy son of a bitch. You just couldn't keep his spirits down. But Xander thought he'd give it a shot.

"You wouldn't be smiling like that if you knew what your face looked like." Xander and everyone else, including Kyle, had a laugh at his expense.

"Ha, ha. I still saved your ass by nailing that guy coming up behind you on that boat."

Xander walked over and gave Kyle a hug. "That you did." He decided to let Kyle have the moment. He would of course tell Sam as soon as he could about the whole "Yahtzee" thing. It was too good not to share.

Kyle said, "Thanks you guys, for hanging around. You didn't have to do that."

Zhanna spoke up as she pointed to the casts on Kyle's arm and leg. "This might cramp playboy style for a little bit, no?"

Kyle smiled. "Oh, I see how it is. Zhanna does have a sense of humor. And you mean these?" Kyle furrowed his brow and scoffed as he looked down at the casts. "These, I assure you, will only help."

They all laughed. Jack tipped his cowboy hat. "Kyle, you got more lead in that pencil than a Number 2 factory. I swear, I ain't seen nothin' like it."

Viktor laughed. "Maybe Kyle and Viktor look for women together in Kentucky. I heard it is land of beautiful women and fast horses."

Xander laughed. "I agree, Viktor, the two of you should definitely look for women together, but you've got the saying backward. Kentucky is the land of fast women and beautiful horses."

Viktor really liked that one. After the laughter died off, Sam spoke up before Xander had the chance to say what was on his mind.

"I've got a bit of news."

Kyle jumped in, "Let me guess, it's about work."

"Are you certain they don't need to wire your jaw shut?" Sam quipped back. "Anyway, okay, it is about work. But it's phenomenal news if you ask me."

"All right, well spill it," Jack said.

Sam explained, "I had a talk with Mary Hartsfield, whom you are all aware is the director of the CIA."

Marvin walked in at that moment, and everyone gave him a happy hello.

After everyone finished their hellos and thank-yous, Sam said, "Good timing actually, Marv, this concerns you as well. Director Hartsfield was so impressed with how we all have worked together over the last couple of weeks that she wants to continue on with a good thing."

"Okay," Kyle said. "What exactly does that mean?"

"Well, if everyone wants to remain involved, she has discussed it with the higher-ups, including the President of the United States, and she wants to make an unprecedented move and give us a special unit of our own within the CIA. To operate however we see fit when we are tasked with a mission. It's the first time something like this has happened in the program's history. Free reign."

Everyone was shocked to hear the news, and it was something everyone was excited to hear, because none of the ragtag group had any allegiance outside of the group. Staying together was the best-case scenario for them. Everyone was happy to hear the news except Xander, that is. And Sam could see it all over his face.

"Xander, I know you don't want to be encumbered by the government. But this is the only way they will let us work together in this capacity going forward. Mary said we get to choose the name and all. And the way she explained it, you and I will truly work independently to set the rules of engagement. We'll answer to no one."

Xander nodded, but his mood didn't change. "That's great, Sam. It really is."

"But?" Kyle asked.

Xander nodded to his friend. "But . . . I'm just going to come right out and say it. I'm done."

Everyone was silent for a moment; then Viktor let out a laugh. "Boss, that is good one. You almost had Viktor. You really are funny guy. That is like fat man saying he is done eating forever. Ha-ha. Boss could never quit taking out bad guy. That is good one!"

Everyone else remained silent, including Xander.

Sam broke the silence. "I don't think he is joking, Viktor."

Xander crossed his arms. "I'm not. I'm finished. This entire thing, the last few weeks, I am so proud to have fought beside you all. But none of it should ever have happened. All of this has been because of my inability to just let things go. And I have put every single one of you in danger, which you should never have been in."

"You know we wouldn't have wanted to be anywhere else," Jack said.

"I know, Jack," Xander said. "But that doesn't change anything. This last twenty-four hours just happened to end up that no one died. But there sits my best friend . . ." Xander had to stop; emotion overwhelmed him. Sam stepped over and put her hand on his shoulder. Xander took a moment, then pointed to Kyle. "There sits my best friend in the world, broken, and he is lucky that it wasn't worse."

"Xander, I'll be fine, brother. This shit will heal." Kyle tried to soften the mood.

"I know it will. This time. But Natalie is right. One of these times when I go playing hero, someone else, if not me, is going to end up like Sean back in Syria, dead. And I can't go through that again."

Everyone was silent. That was a point that was hard to argue.

"But that doesn't mean you all can't go on and be a part of this special unit. It just won't involve me."

Zhanna said, "Well, then, unit would not be so special."

"Thank you, Zhanna. You're sweet. But this is the way it is. I have too many wonderful things to live for. I have you guys, my sister and my niece, and hopefully a shot at that woman in the other room. Time will tell. But I need to get back to the other things I love in life. My budding bourbon company, my horses that are training hard every day. I want to be a part of those things. If I throw myself into that, it will be easier not to answer that call when it comes."

Jack cleared his throat. "If I may?"

Xander nodded.

"Son, that all sounds real good. And I believe you really mean it when you say it. But a shark kills his prey to live. It's just his nature. Same as you and going after the enemy. It's just the man you've become. I support you no matter what you decide, but just don't lie to yourself."

Marv said, "I agree with Jack. I've known you for a long time, can't see you hanging it up so young, X. The country needs you."

"Understood, Jack, Marv. But I'm sorry, guys, I can't do it anymore. But I am certain if it's the life you all still want, the CIA will absolutely find a place for you."

"Well, that was a buzz kill." Kyle winked. "But I hear you. I'm glad you said it. I want you around for a long time. Let's get back home and sell some bourbon! Sam, you can scare off the drunks at the parties."

Sam went more literal. "More like actually put some decent security in place. No more villains sneaking into the stables."

Xander gave Sam a squeeze. The six of them hung around for a while, filling each other in on just how crazy the last twenty-four hours had been. All the while sharing some laughs and signing Kyle's casts.

Time Will Tell

After a couple more days in Paris waiting for doctors to okay
the flight home for Kyle, Xander was chomping at the bit to get
out of that city. Natalie had already gone back to work. Xander
was stunned by her bravery. However, he did make sure Marv
pulled a few of the best bodyguards in town and wouldn't take
no from Natalie about them being around. He and Natalie saw
each other a couple more times before he and the team boarded
Xander's plane, but they never really spoke about their
conversation in the hospital bed. All Natalie said was that she
would see him back in the States once she wrapped the filming
of her movie in Paris. He didn't know exactly what that meant
for them as a couple, but at least it meant he would see her
again. And Xander had decided that a little bit of Natalie was
better than none at all.

   As he sat on his G6, thirty-five thousand feet in the air,
sipping on some King's Ransom bourbon, he was content with
what he had told the people who were sitting all around him
now. He wanted to see if he really could live life without the

fight. The thought of slowing down and playing a bigger role in his businesses sounded like a breath of fresh air. And some fun times with his friends, old and new, sounded even better.

He already spoke with Director Hartsfield. And while she was disappointed to hear Xander say he was hanging it up, including the vigilante stuff, she was happy to take in the rest of the team, who all wanted a role in helping the United States. She said Zhanna and Jack would fit in nicely. However, she told Xander that Viktor would be best suited for a straitjacket. Xander couldn't disagree, but he had grown to love that crazy son of a bitch. In small doses, at least. And he told Viktor he could find a place for him if he wanted. Viktor actually did a cartwheel at the prospect. Director Hartsfield ended the call with an open invitation for Xander to return if he ever so desired.

As he took another sip of bourbon, he tried to have an honest moment with himself. He realized that the last twelve years of his life had been dedicated to one mission: become the greatest killer he could and use what he learned to avenge his parents' death. Now that all of that was behind him, he didn't know how he would feel in the weeks and months to come. Could he find satisfaction in civilian life after all the years of adrenaline-pumping battle? He couldn't say for sure. Couldn't say for certain if that itch would ever creep back under his skin or not. He just knew he hoped it wouldn't.

As he looked around at his friends, especially Sam and Kyle, he truly wanted to be done with that side of himself. He prayed he could stay away so he could prove to Natalie he was really finished. But Xander had always been a realistic man, and he knew that sooner or later that phone was going to ring. All he could hope for was that when that time came, he could call on that inner strength, tap into that mental toughness that made him the legendary soldier that he was, and *not* scratch that itch.

As cliché as it sounded, he knew that only time would tell.

Acknowledgements

To my friends and family, for not only being my life, but for always making it fun.

To Deb Hall, for giving my sentences structure, and making me seem more clever than I really am.

To Gary Guilmette, for taking my complete lack of weapons knowledge and guiding me toward something that resembles functional. If any errors were made in describing the tools of the trade, fault the author, not the expert.

To Xander King fans, for always being there to boost my fragile ego. Interacting with you on Facebook and via email has been the most surprising aspect of this journey. I always thought the work would bring me satisfaction, but it has been sharing with you that has truly made writing special. Thanks for that.

Bradley Wright is the author of the Xander King series. He and his wife spend time in both sunny California and the great state of Kentucky, where he does his very best to be charming, witty, and clever. When those attempts inevitably fail, he locks himself in a room and makes up characters who seem to always find him far more interesting than real people do. Funny how that works.

Bradley has been writing since he was a child. He started with songs and poems, but finally gave in to writing stories when the voices in his head resorted to shouting. He is inspired by every author he reads, most notably, Stephen King, and Carsten Stroud.

For more information visit: www.bradleywrightauthor.com

Cheers!

44807820R00183

Made in the USA
Middletown, DE
17 June 2017